Honey Walls

by Bones McKay
illustrated by Alex Dingley

ISBN 978-1-9994044-7-5

McKay & Gray Publications
www.etsy.com/ca/shop/McKayAndGray

For Treasury, a lovely and
very real cat.

Stars Like Confetti

by Rose Gareau

A long time ago, there was a house of sticks and stones, and in that humble house, there lived a Princess, her father, and mother. To their Kingdom, each was more beloved than the last. The Princess for her smile. The King for his kindness. And the Queen, for she loved every one of her subjects.

Many times the Queen was offered gifts from her people, and she took no more than she needed. In her youth she'd been offered an abundance of riches in exchange for betrothal. From gold to cattle. From flowers to the sun itself. But the Queen accepted none but her King. He had little to show beyond love for her and her land. All that mattered to the Queen was love, weightless to all but the heart.

They lived together happily, growing flowers, keeping peace. In the night they'd rest together staring up into the sky. When the spring came, they had a daughter with eyes of sunlight.

Said the Queen to her daughter, "There is nothing more magical than light. Be watchful of the stars, and reach for them when they fall. If you can, catch them. Keep them in your heart."

The Princess looked up, bathed in light. She spent her nights like this, in her mother's arms.

However, for all the happiness in their family, shadows still formed in their lands. One day, the Queen and company took a ride through the trails of her Kingdom. The young Princess rested on the saddle, dozing off to the rhythmic steps.

"Come no closer," said a voice in the dark. "You aren't welcome here."

The Queen pulled back on her reins and the sudden jerk roused the Princess. "I've travelled this path many times, the village beyond knows me well."

The voice hissed, pained by hearing the Queen. "Step closer and I'll lay a curse on you!"

Beyond the darkness and the voice, the Queen's heart ached for the village. "Please, our family's promised to see the village. There's a wedding to be had, and I must give my blessing."

There was no response from the shadow.

"Could we barter perhaps? I'm sure there's a trinket I could part with." The Queen slid from the saddle. Her foot touched the ground.

Crack!

The Queen turned to stone, a statue lined by fractures. The King ran to her side as she crumbled into sand. He went no further than where his wife stepped, tearfully gathering the pile.

The Kingdom remained fractured by the voice in the dark. Her majesty was gathered into an hour glass; the King built it above the throne, calling all able to help build her a tomb, a monument of her love.

Day by day they built upon the house of sticks and stones, cutting into the green hill. At night the King looked at the stars, and the Princess alone mourned the grass.

"My Love," said the King to the hourglass one night, "what do I do to make you safe?"

The glass replied, reflecting the light of falling stars.

When the morning came, the King announced his latest plan. All in the Kingdom, big or small, old or young, would work to build a castle. The castle would reach up, and up, and up, until they could take a star. They would do it to save their Queen.

For years, they built the tower. And as planned, it grew and grew. The King remained at its top, stretching for the stars. Forgetting love. Forgetting his land. He was no longer a person, but a task.

The Princess watched the faces of the Kingdom change from friendly to mean. Each weighted down by their resentment, their hunger pains and tired joints. The gardens of the lands turned barren and dusty. The forests became bare.

Night fell over the land and a new shift of workers climbed the endless steps. Above the throne the black sands were emptied, neglected for years. As the Princess stared at the sand, she felt panic in her heart. Her mother had left the tower long ago. And so the Princess ran.

Outside of the castle, she breathed the sour air. Her eyes spilled over with tears.

"Momma, please make it better," she pleaded with the stars.

She stretched up, fingers nearly knocking one loose.

"Please, stars, bring Momma back. It's not the same without her, the Kingdom's forgotten about love. I need your help, I—"

The stars swirled at her fingertips, falling like comets into her hair. They burned. Falling faster as they caught in her eyes, getting hotter and hotter still. The Princess radiated, breaking apart into golden sand as the stars burned into her heart.

In the dark of space, she heard her mother's voice.

Chapter One

A Completely Non-Magical Day Without Any Ghosts, Spirits, or Talking Animals

There was no stopping it. Once someone became entrenched in fiction they rarely found their way out. Elves, aliens, talking teddy bears, Row rarely met a person that had gotten over every childhood story. Even his no-nonsense old boss still walked around in his completely nonsensical lucky socks. Row's accountant liked sevens a bit too much. The barista downstairs read tea leaves. No one but Row got over the childish belief that there was something special about anything. He'd left all that nonsense back home, a place he would never return to. Ever.

His mother's stories had been particularly sticky things to get away from, and he never wanted to tempt fate and near them again. He didn't want to suffer the fiction affliction with the rest of the nonsense world.

Row didn't think fiction needed to be banned or anything like that, it just made him personally uncomfortable. That wasn't to say nonfiction was always warranted in his mind either. He certainly didn't care much for Chrys's collection of "Totally Real Hauntings and Other Nonsense about Faeries" books. It was the general principle of the thing. If something wasn't real (or even sounded the least bit fake) there was no point in putting it to words. As for fantasy? Well, for adults it seemed like reasonable escapism, but maybe something a little too corrupting for the fragile minds of children.

Take Chrysocolla for example. There was nothing wrong with his girlfriend, she was sweet and caring, and optimistic to a point of uncanniness. While she never wore shoes, there was nothing about her fashion sense that was wrong. She could have easily turned out to be a normal woman. That is, she could have if she'd never heard a ghost story. From the early days of her childhood she'd been told about "her gift". According to her mother, Zelda, Chrys was in tune with the spirit world. In actuality, Chrys had a good ear for houses creaking, a gullible personality, and a talent for cold readings.

Row took a seat at Zelda's coffee table. Chrys's mother lived above a coffee shop uptown. The apartment was always musty, stuffed tightly with old dark blankets and quilts. Incense lingered in the air. And while Zelda believed in ghosts, she didn't believe in chairs. Row fell backwards as he tried to balance on one of the throw pillows covering the floor.

Zelda sneered in his direction before focusing in on her daughter. "Do you feel that in the air, Chrys?"

Chrys nodded, closing her eyes in an all-knowing stoicism. "I sense a shadow nearing town."

"Spooky." Row looked back to the window. The sky was looking a little on the grey side. "Here, I think I have a prediction on this." He reached into his pocket, pulling out his rare and all-knowing prediction brick, then consulted the weather app. "Oh, never mind it's saying there's a thunderstorm watch. Too bad, no demons or ghosts tonight."

"Row…" Chrys opened one eye slightly. "You know that thunderstorms are catalysts for spiritual activity. With that sort of raw energy. Honestly."

"Oh right, how silly of me." Row sighed louder than expected, burying his face in his phone. Maybe there was work he could escape to? Nothing.

He forced his attention back to the spectacle unfolding in front of him. Zelda and Chrys had met hands across the table and were now chanting. It was all gibberish, of course, but impressive gibberish. With the ambiance of the room and a little lead in, Row could easily see the two swindling some poor widow or lovesick teen. Not that they'd do that, since they were equally hoodwinked by their theatrics. They gave away predictions for free, sharing the gifts as was "the right thing to do".

As their chanting continued, the room became eerily dark. The storm quickened its pace, blacking out the dismal grey. The women synchronized into a hum, a buzz like static before a lightning strike blinded the room.

"Death approaches," Chrys whispered, flinching back at the thought. "It's in a garden. There's roses. Do you see them?"

Row crinkled his brow and spoke dryly, "Oh no, did I kill the rosebush?"

"Ignore him." Zelda squeezed Chrys's hands. "I see it too."

"It's not our garden, this is somewhere else. It's far away." As Chrys worked herself up, tears built in her eyes. They welled up, then poured down her cheeks while Zelda, too lost in the game, failed to notice. "There's a sickness." Chrys trembled, wincing back in an imagined pain. Their seances were usually a lot more lighthearted than this, involving giggly messages from happy spirits. The tears quickened down her cheek, her body beginning to look frail and sick. Even if it was fake, Chrys thought it was true. She thought she was sharing somebody's pain.

Row jumped forward, grabbing Chrys's hand as a boom of thunder shook the house.

"Row!" she cried out, eyes open and staring at him. "You're not supposed to interrupt."

He scowled at her, grabbing one of Zelda's many scarves from a nearby stack of clutter. He used the silk to dab her eyes, wiping every last tear away. "It looked like you needed help," he said as he finished his work.

While Zelda glared at him, Chrys softened. Her blue eyes glistened like a vast but stormy sea. Her hands relaxed from their trembling, finding their way back to the safe and mundane reality.

"He's right, Mama." She nodded back at Zelda. "We need to be careful, we could be letting evil spirits into this house."

Zelda's mouth became a flat line as she looked up at Row. Even after six years, she couldn't puzzle out what her daughter was doing with someone like Row. Zelda once approached him about whether or not he was possessed, or just a monster. Row hadn't given her a response, and after that he stopped leaving himself alone with her.

"You're right. He should leave," Zelda said.

Row flinched. "Me?"

"Yes, you." Zelda folded her arms over her chest. "You're always bringing evil spirits in here. With your heart the way it is? It's really no wonder."

"You mean my hypotension?" Row raised his brow. It wasn't exactly the right word, but it was the best descriptor he had. After a blood test gone wrong, Row came to the realization that something was wrong with his heart. After numerous poking and prodding doctors, he still wasn't closer to the answer on what exactly was wrong with it. In fact, he didn't really care to find out.

"You know exactly what I mean," Zelda scolded, glaring right over the top of her glasses.

"Actually, I really don't." He huffed, but got off of his seat all the same. "But if you really don't want me here, I guess I'll be off."

"Row." Chrys gripped his hand before he could make it any further. "I don't want you leaving mad. Mama, it's not Row's fault that his heart is a vector for evil spirits."

"A vector for evil spirits?" Row furrowed his brow. That was a new one.

"Oh, we didn't tell you?" She glanced back at Zelda. "It's just a guess, but no matter what, it isn't your fault. I wouldn't want you walking home in this weather anyways, right Mama?" She gave Zelda a stern look.

"I guess it wouldn't be wise," Zelda admitted. "If death is looming — fine. But at least leave the room. Maybe we'll get a clearer picture of whatever is trying to reach us."

"Fine." Row rolled his eyes, giving the ladies their space. He turned his back to Chrys's concerned face and made his way for the kitchen.

It was a little while longer before their silly chanting resumed, when Row was gone from sight. The kitchen was no different than the rest of Zelda's house. The woman was a packrat who made optimum use of every inch of space available. This was, of course, a complete opposite to Row's minimalistic approach to life. He only owned what was needed and didn't care much for knickknacks. Her crystal collections rattled as thunder rumbled the house, the storm awakening as they resumed their chants.

Through the window at the end of the junk tunnel, Row watched the flurry of rain. It pelted down onto the glass, turning it into a warbled reflection of himself — a face staring back at him from beneath the water. He stared for a moment, transfixed by the image and the electricity created by the voices down the hall. A stinging started in his chest the longer he stared. As he winced, the reflection glared at him. It raised its hand, pressing its fingers to the glass as Row remained still. The picture became clearer when the lightning flashed. It illuminated the reflection. Then it became a woman, a completely different person in a completely distant world. She looked a lot like Row, same eyes, same chubby cheeks. But her hair was longer than Rapunzel's and anger burned in her eyes.

"No." Row shook his head. "We're not doing this."

The woman said nothing, though her brow raised like a villain whose patience was being tested.

He stomped across the floor, pushing past the tight corridor of junk. They met eyes at the end, both an inch from the glass. In either hand he grabbed folds of burgundy curtain. "You stay out of my life, Sundew." He threw the curtains shut.

After his run in with the window, things returned to normal. In fact, Row decided that it hadn't happened at all. Sundew? What Sundew? He rolled his eyes at the thought. He hadn't seen his… um… eccentric sister in years, and it was doubtful he'd see her again. He took Chrys by the hand and walked home with her.

They hadn't needed to wait out the storm. It ended as quickly as it had appeared. Chrys and Zelda's second attempt at contacting the spirit world failed because of this. Zelda blamed Row for knocking them off course of the energy. They couldn't catch up their power to match the storm before it ended. Or something like that. Row dozed off somewhere in the middle of the explanation.

Chrys held his hand tight in her own. She pulled and jerked his arm as she danced across the street, splashing through the puddles. She'd certainly pepped up after the seance. Puddles did that to her. She couldn't resist running barefoot through a puddle, ocean, lake, you name it. If she came across a bog it was likely that Chrys would dive in and live with the turtles. Row had many reasons why he didn't join her, not the least of which being a slight fear of drowning. Even puddles were too close for comfort — but he walked through them because he wasn't silly. He tried his best to fear only reasonable things.

"It's a pity that we didn't get back on track." She sighed, bouncing into him. She wrapped her arms around the closest of his, then rested her head on top of him. "The image that I saw was so clear, you know? I want to know who it was, maybe warn someone before she died."

"She?" He scrunched his brow.

"There was a woman in my vision, older — but not too old. She had these beautiful green eyes, and I could tell that everyone around her loved her."

Chrys drooped, saddened by her story. "She was in this beautiful garden and was tending to her roses, and then I could see death shroud over her. She started getting sicker and sicker."

Row squeezed her hand. "People die every day."

"I know that." Chrys's shoulders slumped. "But that doesn't mean I don't want to help. You'd be surprised how many souls don't make it to their resting place. People hold onto them, and they hold onto people, things, their homes. Sometimes, they need the permission to move on."

"I'm sure she'll contact you if she needs the help."

Chrys leaned into him more with a wistful breath. "I guess so."

"There's no use worrying about it. You're plenty helpful, so don't get down about yourself."

She met him with a smile. "Thanks, Row."

He shrugged. Even if she was playing pretend, her heart was in the right place. He couldn't knock that.

"You know, I'm sorry that Mama's always on your case," she said. "I've tried talking to her, but honestly it does get a little uncalled for."

"It's fine, I'm used to it."

As much as Zelda chased him down about his tainted soul and demonic possession, it didn't seem to come from a bad place. There was plenty that a mother could hate about Row for no good reason. This included his heart issue, so maybe some points had to be taken from Zelda, but it mostly involved a part of his life that Row didn't like to put to words. Row used to be a girl. No, Row was assigned female at birth. No, Row was transgender. No, he didn't like any of the phrasings. If phrases had flavours, all them tasted like vomit.

But returning points to Zelda, no matter how it was phrased, she didn't care. In fact, Zelda cared so little that the second she knew about it, she invited the self-described "non-binary goddess" Fox Mackenzie into her life. She did this to drive home how much she didn't care about that particular aspect of his person. She assured him that she hated him because he was him. She did this by insisting Chrys was available and definitely not dating that man in the corner — just ignore the grumpy man in the corner, Fox.

Fox certainly got along with Chrys. Ze was a confident and self-assured barista, with those ear hole things that were all the rage. Ze drank almond milk, had a quaff of red fire for hair, and was the only person on earth that was taller than Chrys. Any time ze asked the question, "And what can I get for you today, Hon?" zir customers fell in a hopeless and heartfelt love. Well, except for the grumpy man in the corner.

But for however much Zelda pressured the two to fall in love, they only ended up as friends. Good friends, church-going pals but nothing more.

A flutter from above caught Row's eye. The heavy thump of a crow landing on a branch above startled him from his thoughts. He jumped back, stumbling into Chrys.

"Hm?" Chrys trailed his gaze up to the bird.

It stared directly at Row with its button eyes. Actual buttons, not a metaphor. The bird was completely made of craft supplies. It stretched its wings and amongst the shadow was a rainbow of mismatched craft feathers; pink, blue, green, even swirls of glitter glue. It gripped the tree above with pipe cleaner feet.

"Oh, what a pretty bird." Chrys squinted up at it. "Aw, poor thing's got its foot tangled."

Row swallowed a lump in his throat. A perfect pink bow was secured to its purple pipe cleaner feet. At the end of the ribbon's tail there hung a pink envelope, the colour of magnolias.

"Come here, bird," Chrys cooed. "I'll untie you, sweetheart."

"Chrys." Row grabbed her arm before she got closer. "This is dangerous."

"Dangerous?" She turned back to scowl at him.

"It could peck you. Or maybe it's diseased."

"I am not diseased," the crow said.

Row froze.

The crow fluffed her feathers, leaning down to get a good look at Row. "Very rude to say about a lady. But that's what we've come to expect from the likes of you."

Row tightened his hand around Chrys's. As he looked to her, he expected some sort of excitement or shock, but she didn't appear to notice that the crow had spoken at all. She was still stretching forward, cooing at the bird like a mad woman. He jerked her back. "We're not going to get it out, let's just go."

"Oh." The bird scoffed. "Ignoring me?"

"But what if it's hurt? It could lose its foot in the twine," Chrys said.

Row turned his back on the crow, dragging Chrys along with him. "There's nothing we can do. It's up too high."

"What are you talking about? If I stretched only a little bit—"

"No." Row stomped on ahead.

"What's gotten into you, Row?" Chrys struggled to keep up, scraping her heels on the sidewalk as she tried to slow them down. "You're so moody today."

"Moody?" He scowled as he checked back to see the bird. It remained in the tree, watching them as they disappeared down the sidewalk.

"Yes, since the seance. Oh no! Did a spirit find its way into your heart?" She gasped.

"You two are more obsessed about my heart than the doctors." He rolled his eyes, keeping watch for the bird until it was gone from view entirely.

"There's something bad in town, Row. You're highly susceptible to things like this, and honestly, you're not careful about it at all. At the very least you could drink some clover tea, wear a luck charm or two."

Row frowned. "Wouldn't avoiding bad luck be good too then? Avoiding death omens like — and this is just an example — crows?"

Chrys rolled her eyes. "Fine."

When Row returned to his house, things seemed normal. The normal squirrels chased one another in a normal way around the oak tree in Row's normal front yard. As much as Row couldn't stand the thieving squirrels, it was nice to be away from the strange encounters. The squirrels bounced after one another down his driveway, weaving through the sunflower stalks in the flower bed.

Row's house was small, a teal thing that Chrys demanded they rent because of its colour. She would have preferred a sea foam house, but there weren't any around town. To make up for its faults, she enlisted Row to tend to a garden, filling the front and backyard with flowers and her whims. The front lot was packed with sunflowers which grew above the living room windows. In the winter she bemoaned their absence daily. The backyard was more complex, a sprawl which centred around Chrys's absolute favourite flowers, the roses.

As the two went inside, they split apart at the kitchen. It was Chrys's turn to make dinner — or she said it was at least. She preferred to make the meals so she could hide broccoli in the soups and kale in the sandwiches.

Today's health food endeavour was pasta and flax with a medley of vegetables. Row grimaced at a zucchini as he passed Chrys. To avoid any meddling, he went outside to tend to the roses, scoffing as he remembered Chrys's silly prediction.

An audience of squirrels gathered in the branches of the willow and spruce trees, staring at Row as he began to garden. Five or six of them were already fat for winter, stuffed with tulip bulbs they'd stolen the day before. They made great work of tearing up the garden after he'd worked for hours. It wasn't enough to make him give up (unfortunately for him). As much as he disliked gardening, it was something that made Chrys happy.

He trailed his focus back up. The squirrels twitched and shifted, squabbling to get a better view of potential snacks. But too bad for them, because today Row only planned to tend to the roses. He scraped the dead leaves from the roots, thorns catching his sweater as tails twitched incredulously above him.

As he dug out the dampened leaves into a pile of sludge, one of the squirrels grew bored. This particular squirrel reminded him more of a chinchilla, a circular grey puff. The branches wobbled as another rotund squirrel climbed off the trunk. Then another. Row rolled his eyes. The boughs above shook as a final squirrel made her way down, a leaner one, not grey. Not red either. She was made of paper, her tail a smudge of black charcoal.

The colour drained from Row's cheeks.

She stared at him like she was a normal squirrel.

"Shoo!" He waved his hands in front of her. "I don't want anything to do with you guys."

The squirrel said nothing, sniffing him quietly.

A haze of clouds passed over the sun, and the squirrels looked up before breaking away like dandelion fluff. Row stood, continuing to look around him for where the craft squirrel had come from. *There's no way they found me,* he thought. *We're too far from Honey Walls. They'd never...*

The big black crow thumped onto one of the low branches. Her two button eyes transfixed on Row, envelope still shackled to her foot. As she leaned forward her beak nearly touched the rosebush.

"Why are you making things difficult, Rosie?" The crow cawed, clearing her throat.

He stumbled, the name enough to knock him back. It'd been so long since he'd heard it. Since he'd heard an animal talk. He eyed the window of his house. Inside Chrys was dancing, making spaghetti and lost in a trance.

"Don't mind the squirrel, she came with me." The crow flapped her wings, tucking them at her sides. "Paper Squirrel only came for the tulips. If you're thinking of planting more, it's a fight you're guaranteed to lose." The crow preened as she spoke. "Free wisdom from me to you."

"What are you doing here?" He stood, shielding the crow from the window, so Chrys wouldn't see the absurdity.

The crow tilted her head, examining every inch of Row. "I don't usually part with information like that."

"You're a lousy messenger to send if that's the case," he said.

She hung on his last word, staring at him intently with her button eyes.

Row fidgeted, monitoring the window as he searched his pockets for something to trade with her. If he had something shiny, he could maybe get her to leave. But there was nothing a crow would like. *Just my keys.* "Sorry, I've got nothing."

She froze. "So the rumours are true, the city's made you greedy?" She tilted her head, inspecting his rose bush with one eye. "I'd make a deal with you for your roses."

His expression soured. "One rose."

"Greedy," crowed the crow. "I'll take one of your wilted roses if you really must be stingy."

Row glared at the crow. The flowers were meant for Chrys. Tending to them was always the trickiest, always leaving him scarred by thorns. But he couldn't risk having the bird around either. He searched the bush for the bloom with the least potential and cut its stalk. With obvious disgust, the crow snatched the rose with her beak. However, despite her distaste for the flower, she loosened the ribbons from her legs. The envelope fell free onto the rose bush.

"I don't want that." Row kept back.

"Too bad."

Row felt a burning begin in his chest. The letter was the same magenta as the ribbon, subdued like magnolias and resting on a bed of thorns. The lip of the fold was embossed with swirling flowers. "Is it... it's not from Mom, is it?"

The crow leaned forward, beak outstretched for another rose.

"You can't answer a question without a present?" He rolled his eyes. "And you call *me* greedy."

She ruffled her feathers in opposition.

Row ignored her, bracing himself as he took the letter from the bush. Written across the front was his old name, Rose Gareau Jr. "Right, I guess—" He shook his head. "No. This is ridiculous. What am I doing?" He shoved the envelope into the crow's face. "Take it back where it came from. I'm not getting involved in this again."

The crow turned her head away, beating her wings wildly. Within seconds she took off, snapping the branch with her weight. She left the envelope in Row's hands, a definitely real envelope. He pressed his fingers down hard on the paper, watching the bird swirl into the grey sky.

His fingers trembled. He checked back to the window, making sure Chrys wasn't watching. When all was clear he tore the envelope's side. The inner paper had a weighty tooth and ridged surface like water colour paper. The hard crease, the dribbles and water smudges, seeing high quality parchment defaced this way made him queasy. Well, it made him queasier.

Dearest Rosie,

You are a special kind of idiot if you think you can avoid me.

You're needed back in Cherrywood. I have some paperwork that needs to be signed.

Mom's dead.

Your Sister,

Sundew Gareau

The paper fell from his hands.

Chapter Two

Heart Attacks of the Physical and Metaphorical Variety

Claire visited Rose Gareau the day before she died. When Claire entered Rose's bedroom, she found her looking better than usual. She sat in her bed, propped up by many quilted pillows. The surface of her comforter was covered in discarded papers scratched with black ink. It was the same black ink that clouded the tips of her frail fingers. She floated in a vast sea of her discarded drafts, trying to write something perfect. Righty, her portly grey cat, swayed to life. He was the first to pay attention to Claire, purring loudly and cocking his head for a chin scratch.

"Are you two doing well?" Claire relinquished her hand to the cat.

"Oh? Claire!" Rose jerked focus from her page. "I forgot you were coming over."

"Oh dear, I hope I'm not interrupting." A blush flared in Claire's cheeks. "If you're busy, I can come back."

"No, no, stay." Rose patted the mattress, inviting Claire to sit. "I've only got so much time left, it's much better to spend it with company."

"Don't talk like that." Claire took a seat at the end of the mattress, continuing to stroke the cat. "I think you're looking better. You'll be up and dancing before you know it."

She laughed slightly, her hand tensing around her pen. Rose still looked young, the wrinkles and laugh lines were brought out only by her gauntness. The sickness carved age into her, but she wasn't much older than Claire's own mother. Her dark red hair was brushed with patches of grey, a graceful transition from autumn to winter. But not close to death. Not by Claire's reckoning.

"Are you working on anything new?" Claire asked.

"Well…" Rose looked around at her papers. She turned them over, searching for an answer. "I'm trying to work out an ending for Oxnard's story."

Claire smiled. She'd grown particularly fond of Rose's stories about Oxnard. Rose wrote them for her own children about a stuffed hedgehog, the titular Oxnard, going on endless adventures. When she was young, Claire was pretty sure she met the hedgehog Rose based her stories on. It was rooting around in Rose's garden, far from home and probably someone's lost pet. Claire hadn't realized this at the time, or she would have brought him home with her.

"I think this is his last adventure," Rose said.

Claire's smile broke.

"He's had a lot of adventures, but I think he might finally reach the Sky World." Rose bunched one of the nearby pages. "He can make his own life from there."

"But does he ever find his friend? It better not end before he does."

Rose fell back into her pillows, sinking into the airy down as she relinquished herself. "I don't know, I haven't decided."

"He *has* to find his friend." Claire scowled. "It'd be so disappointing if after all those books — I might just write my own book and fix it if that's the case."

Rose snorted into a laugh before she wheezed, coughed and sputtered. She struggled to breathe, eventually falling back, weakened by the episode. There was nothing Claire could do but watch her weather it, absently holding her hand as she fought against her body.

"You know I'm only joking." Claire squeezed Rose's hand. "Cherrywood is only big enough for one writer, and I could never hold a candle to you. Whatever you choose for Oxnard's story will be perfect."

She shook her head. "The stories will continue long past I'm gone. I can't exist forever."

Claire felt a lump harden in her throat, a pressure building in her eyes.

Rose tightened her hand around Claire's, returning the comfort back to her. "Do you want my pen?"

"No!" Claire jumped to her feet. As she pulled away, tears fell free. She struggled to stable herself, the world spinning beneath her feet. "It was a joke, Rose. You know I can't write. I sell books, that's it. Nothing else."

Rose looked out over the valleys of blankets and paper. Stretching a hand out, she grabbed a fresh sheet. "If that's the case, it'll have to be Rosie. I'm dying, Claire. There's no stopping it."

"Not with this attitude. Have you seen a doctor in months?" Claire wiped snot from her nose. "Why have you stopped fighting?"

"There's never been a fight."

"No, it's always been a fight. You were supposed to finish the disease."

"No. Finish my stories," Rose said. "Things need to change in this town, and that can't happen with ghosts like me lingering."

"You're not a ghost."

Rose moved her pen across the page like a stream breaking a drought. "At my funeral make sure Rosie gets this." She didn't look up from her work as she spoke.

● ◈ ◑

The letter weighed heavy in Claire's hand as she left Rose's room. Righty followed her into the living room, sashaying along and bumping his head against her legs. He made it harder to do anything but amble. But it didn't matter, she felt drunk, shambling at a loss for words.

Maybe she'll fight harder tomorrow. Claire kneeled, petting Righty. *She's not the type to give up.*

A shroud fell over the living room, breaking Claire's attention. It stretched across the hardwood, over the dusted pink couch, then settled over Claire and Righty. Its long and wilting shape took root at the end of the hall. It was unmistakeable.

Sundew.

The woman stood in the door frame with her back to the kitchen light. She was an otherworldly presence. Her long burgundy hair trailed behind her, dragging across the floor as she stepped away from the light.

"What are you doing here?" Sundew sneered.

"Just helping with Rose." Claire hid the letter behind her back. She didn't know why she did it, but Sundew always made her uncomfortable. Her eyes were always intense, unravelling what she looked upon. "I made her lunch, so you can relax."

"Relax?" Sundew asked.

"For a bit, yeah, I know you've got a lot on your plate." Claire inched away, making in the direction of the front porch. "I'm going now, though. See you around."

"Wait." Sundew continued across the hardwood.

Claire froze. It was difficult to read Sundew. Her expression was often cold, a miserable flatline to her lip beneath an intense yet empty gaze.

"Did she finish her story?"

Claire's mouth dried. "Almost."

"Ah." She turned away toward the living room. A visible tension bristled through her as she left Claire.

"Row? Are you okay?" Chrys followed him as he ambled to the living room.

There was a horrible pressure on his chest, like a violent intruder pressing her hand against him, trying to crush his heart. The only time he'd felt this awful was—*No, don't go thinking about that. That was a dream.* He groaned, collapsing onto the couch.

He needed to say something before Chrys called 911. Being a volunteer lifeguard made Chrys particularly jumpy when it came to calling for help. Her first-aid and CPR certifications were a constant nuisance when combined with his heart issues. She waited like a hawk for the inevitable heart failure. As a precaution, he'd pawed through the first-aid books, learning what symptoms to never mention. Chest pain, nausea, fatigue—

Row winced and said, "I'm fine."

"Liar." She stood above him with hands on hips.

The pressure in his chest felt stronger and stronger, that same invisible hand now wrapped around his heart. He felt the world blur in front of him. He looked through a hazy image of Chrys, finding it difficult to fully remember what he was looking at. She was like an angel under the sea, guiding him beneath the waves. Her face got closer to his. She caressed his chin, nearing his face for a kiss—

No. Never mind. Chrys just shoved a pill into his mouth. He choked on the medicine, sputtering forward as things became clear again. The phone was in Chrys's hand, thumb pressed to the nine.

"Wait. I'm not dying," he uttered, gripping her arm. "Don't make me go to the hospital. I've got client work."

"You're not risking your life for a client."

"It's… it's a usual… flare up." He struggled through his breaths; they felt harder the more he tried.

She glared at him, one of her classic "no-nonsense" glares. Then she finished dialling.

If Row was ever forced to make a top ten list of things he hated, hospitals would make the top five. Chrys never seemed keen on his "I'd rather be dead at home than alive in a hospital" mentality. She thought it was stupid. They thought a lot of things about the other was stupid.

She pressed her phone to her ear, first spouting off their address, name, number, before saying, "My boyfriend is experiencing chest pain."

He rolled his eyes before catching a glare from her.

She nodded along with the operator, offering simple answers. Even if he couldn't hear the other side of the conversation it was easy to parse.

Is he conscious?

"Yes, he looked like he was out for a few moments, but I gave him some aspirin and it seemed to work."

Does he have a history with heart problems?

"Yes, he's been in and out with undiagnosed problems. I don't think there's a family history with any of it. We really don't have a good answer. I guess, prepare to be baffled?"

Is he taking any medications?

"Mhm, he takes something for his low blood pressure."

Is he upset about his mother being dead?

"Aside from the heart pain he's really not feeling anything about it."

Row blinked, staring at Chrys. She stared directly back at him, waiting for some sort of response. *Had he imagined that? Maybe he really did need to go to the hospital.* He provided no answer before blinking again.

"Row, stay with me." She patted his shoulder, knocking him free of a trance. "Can you tell us what happened?"

What happened?... With Mom? He watched Chrys as he felt water fill the room. Once again he was dragged into an ocean. The hands which wrapped his heart gripped his neck, strangling him as he unlearned how to breathe. He gasped as the water filled his lungs. Chrys, the angel in the water, held him tightly, pressing her hands to his heart. She fought against the grasping and clawing ocean, becoming his pulse for a few long moments.

With a jolt he surfaced, coughing and sputtering, but not regaining his full breath. He and Chrys were no longer alone. A pair of paramedics were in the room, efficiently throwing down their ECG/AED pack thing beside him. He hated ECGs and cringed as he prepared for the embarrassment.

"I think this is all just a big overreaction," he rasped to the paramedic with the tight brown ponytail.

"I think it's great that your girlfriend called. " She gave him an assuring smile. "It's really smart to get things like this checked out. I need to remove your shirt so that I can attach this. It won't hurt, it's just to monitor your heart."

"I—I don't think that's necessary," he said, tugging at the bottom of his shirt to keep it snug.

There was a whole host of reasons he was against this. One: He wanted nothing to do with the hospital. Two: He wasn't in the mood to hear their shock when the unsuspecting (and well meaning) paramedics were face to face with his irregular heart. Three: Taking off his shirt wasn't something he ever enjoyed. No thanks to his heart, top surgery wasn't an option for him. He'd deal with breasts for the rest of his life. While there was some comfort in the rug of hair he'd managed to grow, he still felt he looked more like a fat, female bigfoot rather than a man.

He felt Chrys's hand tighten around his. As he looked at her, the pain felt worse. Tears dribbled down her eyes with frantic worry. It was a perfectly warm hearted and normal response. He wanted to hug her. Unfortunately, hugging would do nothing, the only real comfort would come from allowing the paramedics to attempt to help him. And if that would make Chrys happy...

"Fine." He used what little strength he could to swallow his breath and shut his eyes. *Let's just get this over with.*

Before he knew it Chrys was pulling off his shirt. He could feel the presence of the paramedics as they moved towards him, and then pressed down electrodes. They were cold, uncomfortably sticky. The wires draped over him and he anticipated the shock. Not a physical shock. There would be absolutely no shocking. He opened his eyes a moment to watch the tiny portable screen of the heart monitor. There was a long and quiet beep as a blip moved along a flatline.

The other paramedic stiffened. He looked between Row and the monitor, pressing a few buttons without avail. The flatline remained unchanged. The two looked between one another. They said nothing, the confusion taking both of them at full force. A split second after they both restarted, jumping to life and busying themselves with different tasks. The woman took her turn at the machine, adjusting the electrodes and coming no closer to an answer. The other paramedic busied himself with a stretcher. Neither could properly acknowledge the lack of heart activity.

How could they? It made no sense. If he didn't have a heartbeat he shouldn't be the slightest bit conscious. As they continued to do their best through the nonsense, Row tried his best to ignore it. All of it.

"Oh! I know what's happening," the ponytailed paramedic exclaimed as they wheeled him to the ambulance. "His emotions are spilling out. He's got too many because his mom died and he's got no heart to hold them."

"Who told you about my mom?" Row glared at the paramedics as they got him inside the ambulance.

"Your mom?" she asked.

There was a flurry around him. She said more words, very official sounding ones too, maybe questions? They didn't make any sense. He didn't answer. Then he felt them clip things to him, felt a sharp pain in his arm. It didn't make any more sense to anyone involved. His breath became shallow once again, drowning on land. But Chrys was gone from his side, unable to pull him out of the deepening sea. He tried to speak, but there was something on his mouth.

At least I won't have to go back to Honey Walls, he thought.

Even if hospitals were on the top five list of horrible things, Honey Walls was always number one.

When Row woke up, he was in the hospital, a *tap, tap, tapping* rousing him from unconsciousness. He groaned, looking around himself. He was in a hospital gown now, a blood pressure cuff on his arm, an oximeter on his finger, and the familiar flatline at his side. Watching the blips for a few moments, he groaned louder. It was hard enough to convince his last doctor to release him, he'd be forced into the same conversations he'd suffered through years earlier.

"You can't leave, you don't have a heartbeat," they'd say.

"But I'm fine otherwise," he'd reply.

"You don't have a heart," they'd repeat.

And it would go on and on until all the medical professionals would cave. Because as shocking and interesting as he was, he *was* in fine shape. Fine enough.

The tapping began again. He'd nearly forgotten about it. He tried not to blame himself, his day wasn't exactly ideal for focus. He craned his neck, following the direction of the sound. A chill ran through him as he met eyes with the craft feather crow. She was perched on the window sill and barely visible against the night sky. Barely visible, but definitely noticeable, tapping her beak against the glass over, and over, and over, and over.

Furrowing his brows, he forced himself out of bed. He tried not to mess with the tangle of hospital equipment. The last thing he needed was to alert a nurse and get caught talking to a crow. If that happened, there'd be no way he'd ever go home. As he reached the window, the crow stopped pecking. He messed with the window latch, eventually finding a way to prop it open.

"This better be quick," he grumbled.

"Oh? I was thinking the same thing," she cawed. The wilted rose lay between her claws, suggesting to him that she hadn't returned home. "Cherrywood is a long ways from here, so you better stop being dramatic and start moving."

"Ha! You think that I'll be able to get to Cherrywood from here?" He kept his voice hushed. "You see, Ms. Crow, in this world there are a lot of rules. You can't just up and leave a hospital. There's things to think about here, like insurance, bills. Boring, mundane, normal things. Just the way I like it. Tell Sundew that I won't be coming to the funeral. She can take Mom's stories. I don't want them."

"She can't just take them — like you take my advice without paying." Her feathers fluffed. "Honey Walls is in your name. There are a lot of rules in our world. You can't just steal a house that isn't in your name. There's paperwork, pens, ink, signing. You know, normal, mundane, boring things. Just the way you like it. If you want Sundew to take your responsibilities you have to go tell her yourself."

He bristled at her accusatory tone. "I'm not going back."

"You don't have a choice."

"And how do you expect me to leave here?"

The crow flapped her wings, kicking forward through the window. "Advice without a price? Who do you think I am?"

"What? No! Stop!" He jumped forward, trying to grab the bird before she flew further. He tripped, barely brushing a feather.

The bird cawed wildly, circling the ceiling of his room. Row stood beneath her, staring up in stunned silence as she made her mighty racket.

"Quiet, shush!" he whispered before he searched through the drawers in a panic. He stumbled upon a collection of syringe tips and then offered one up to the bird. "Here's a present. Now be quiet."

She landed on top of the heart monitor, extending her beak eagerly for the shiny piece of metal. She flapped her wings more as she secured it in her beak. Once it was in her grasp, she sorted it amongst the rose. "Oh! I like this present." She stroked the clear cap with her beak.

Row swallowed hard, checking the door repeatedly for movement. "I've got plenty more. So I better get some good answers."

"I'll try my best." She spoke softly, transfixed by the gift. "You wanted to know the best way out of here, right?"

He rolled his eyes. "Not actually."

"But you did ask, so here's my answer. Your angel from beneath the waves will free you, all you need to trade her is a recent secret."

"Secret?" he asked. "What's the point of a prediction if you wrap it in a riddle?"

"Maybe it's not a riddle and you're just stupid?"

He scowled.

"Or maybe that was another riddle, who knows?"

"Whatever." He pinched his brow. "If I sign this thing for Sundew, will I be done with Cherrywood for good?"

She motioned to the drawer, not answering until another syringe tip was snug between her purple pipe cleaners. "If you sign the paper, you will never have business in Honey Walls again."

Row watched the line beneath her feet. *You could be normal again. Forever.*

He pressed a hand to his chest. He hadn't even considered that his pain was gone. "And if I don't go?"

"Sundew will send more than a crow through the mirror."

There was a tingle in his chest. "She has that power?"

"All sisters have the power to annoy their brothers."

He nearly spoke before he heard steps approaching. He tossed a final tip in the crow's direction. She caught it in the air, flying back out through where she'd came. *What could be worse than a crow?* he thought as he climbed back into his bed. As he sat, he met eyes with a nurse.

"Mr. Gareau?" The nurse responded, looking at Row like he'd walked in on a ghost. "Is everything alright in here?"

"I'm fine, actually. I wouldn't be able to talk to my girlfriend, would I?"

Chapter Three

Oxnard and the Sky World
by Rose Gareau

Wherein Oxnard Begins a New Adventure

There was little in the world sadder than a hedgehog's backpack. Oxnard never made it to lunchtime with his juice box puncture-free. He waddled into the kitchen, taking a seat beneath one of the tall chairs. After a long stroll in the bushes, it was nice to take a load off. Prying his quills free of the fabric, he set his backpack down. As suspected, there was apple juice covering his punctured papers and cricket snacks.

"Why do you bother packing your bag?" a voice purred from above. "You always come back inside to eat your snacks anyways."

It was that scoundrel, Righty Grey Sock Cat. He lay on the dining table, draping one of his stinky sock paws off its side. Righty was an overstuffed sock that looked a little like a throw pillow. If he wasn't so lazy, he'd have been a real terror, but he got winded every time he tried chasing a mouse further than the porch. And that wasn't even considering that his big paws didn't fit into their burrows!

"You never know when you'll get swept into an adventure." Oxnard held his ground, ready to ball up if the cat tried to pounce. (Though honestly, Reader, that no-good cat would think twice about causing mischief in my house — not unless he wanted a flick on the nose!)

"Adventure?" Righty asked.

"Yes, there is definitely adventure brewing in the air." Oxnard crossed his paws. "It's been a long time since I've been on an adventure. I'm ready whenever it is."

Righty yawned. The cat hadn't adventured further than the ditch. The forest beyond the mushroom ring was a mystery to him. No. Not a mystery, a mystery implied that the cat cared about the answer. The world beyond was simply uncharted and disinteresting to him.

"You know, I think I might have heard something you'd find interesting," Righty said.

"Is it another one of your dirty tricks?"

"Tricks?" The cat meowed. "When have I ever played a trick on you?"

Oxnard scowled at him, he didn't have to answer that. Righty knew very well what he'd done.

"Look, this isn't a trick, I just overheard Mrs. Gareau talking with the Crow." Righty stretched his toothpick claws before dropping onto the chair. "They were talking about very, very interesting things." He grinned at Oxnard, his head hanging upside-down over the chair's edge.

Oxnard puffed out his quills, a little like someone bundling into their coat on a winter day. Righty was about as tolerable as sleet.

"Crow's found a path to the Sky World," Righty continued.

Oxnard's quills softened. "She has?"

"Mhmmm…" Righty stretched out his paw, poking Oxnard's nose with one of his toothpicks. "You better go find her a present, she's not giving up a secret like that for cheap."

A sparkle filled Oxnard's heart, a little like if he'd caught a shooting star. He leapt to his feet, securing his backpack back on. He knew exactly the gift to give Crow!

Oxnard rushed into the craft room and found a tube of purple glitter glue. Then he ran along, passing Righty as he wobbled down the steps. The cat had switched places but the position was very familiar, his paw draped over the step.

"Do you know where Crow is?" Oxnard asked.

"The mice said something about a crow in the bog?" He rolled over, covering his face with his paw. "Sounds like a load of trouble if you ask me."

Ignoring any further chats with the cat, Oxnard set off through the door. The entrance of Honey Walls opened out into my garden. He stepped out onto the front step, walking beneath the magnolia trees which hugged either side of the house. Their flowery boughs formed a canopy above him. For a hedgehog of his stature the garden beyond was an epic adventure, a floral forest of wonder.

He descended the wooden steps, tumbling down the last into the thick of the wildflowers. Petals and leaves stuck to his quills as he continued to roll (as a balled up hedgehog is prone to do). He didn't stop rolling, and rolling, and rolling, until he knocked into a lavender bush. The world continued to spin around him for a while, the smell of lavender swirling with it.

When everything decided to play nice and stop spinning, Oxnard got to his feet. The bog wasn't far from Honey Walls. It was in the direction of town, past the ring, past the ditch, just a turn at the bridge following the flow of the creek. For a little hedgehog it was certainly more immense. He spent a good long time in the wildflower jungle before reaching the mushroom ring.

The entirety of the property was circled by a perfect ring of white mushrooms. Beyond it was a steep slope that was known as the ditch. Oxnard peaked over the mushrooms. Mrs. Gareau didn't protect anyone that went past the mushroom ring. Only unsavoury sorts, hooligans, and brave adventurers went past it. It was easy to go down but almost impossible to get back up. Almost. In Oxnard's last great adventure, he'd narrowly escaped a wolf, grabbing a mushroom cap before it snagged him in its jaw.

Oxnard put the somewhat traumatic memory behind him. Taking a deep breath, he then tumbled down the three-foot ditch. (He really has become a tough little hedgehog. Don't you think so, Reader?).

Once again, he couldn't stop tumbling by himself. He had to wait for something else to do the stopping. This time it was a tree. He got a little stuck to the bark and felt a little bit of a scratch on his nose, but he was fine otherwise. He brushed himself off once more, continuing through the big woods all the way to the bridge to Cherrywood and then to the bog.

Now, Oxnard had never been a fan of the bog. The Bog of Banishment wasn't a nice place for anyone, human, hedgehog, or crow. The only living thing it was suitable for was a witch (or that's what Oxnard thought. The truth is, witches prefer friendship but only manage to make friends in bogs). Oxnard kept on the dry land, avoiding the stinky slime. The salamanders and frogs stared up at him with eyes that poked out of the goop.

Oxnard twitched his nose, taking in the stink. Unfortunately, sniffing was the only way a hedgehog could see far away. If it meant getting his nostrils stuffed with bog stink? Well, that was the price of adventure. He kept twitching his nose until he caught a whiff of the crow. She was up in the tawny branches of an elm, scarfing down a pile of unlucky amphibians.

"Ms. Crow!" he called. "I've got a present for you!"

One of the frogs croaked, managing to splash back into the bog.

"Oh?" She grumbled. "It better be a good present, because you just lost me a good catch."

"A wonderful present, but first I've got a question for you."

The crow gulped down the last of her meal before flying to Oxnard's side. She was a very large bird, but like most scary things, she wasn't so scary after he'd gotten to know her. She ruffled her feathers as she inspected the tube of glitter glue. "Oh!" she cawed. "That's actually a very good present."

"Good." Oxnard kept the tube close so she wouldn't steal it. "Now, I heard from Righty that you've found a way to get to the Sky World. I'll give you this glue if you tell me how to get there."

"Hmm… It might be a little difficult for you."

"Are you underestimating me again, Ms. Crow?"

"No, that would be foolish, but this would certainly be your most difficult adventure yet. The Sky World is very, very, very far, even for a bird or human."

Oxnard clenched his paws around the glitter glue. "I'm ready for anything, Ms. Crow."

"I don't know about anything…" she tapered off. "But the Sky World can be reached in a very specific way. First you must travel down Big Road."

"Big Road!" He gasped, Big Road was incredibly dangerous (I've warned all the stuffed animals and children about it).

"Are you still considering this adventure?"

Oxnard un-balled himself, he hadn't even noticed doing it in the first place. "N-no, I think I can go down Big Road."

"Alright, if you say so," she continued. "You must travel down Big Road until you reach the Mostly Invisible Ocean. It's impossible to miss. From there you will find the Island of Lost Socks."

Oxnard took out a paper and scribbled down the directions.

"No matter how you reach the island, you must follow the sun. You need to reach where the sun touches the land. That's Sky World."

"Thank you, Ms. Crow!" He offered her the glue. "This is exactly what I needed to know. I can do this." He smiled at Crow. "I'm going to tell Mrs. Gareau!"

Chrys ran to Row's side, nearly throwing herself into his arms. As she got closer, she slowed, carefully squeezing him as her tears dripped onto the crook of his neck. Her dark hair fell over their faces and the two found one another between the strands of shadow. Chrys met him with a smile but he failed to return her one. "I thought I lost you," she said.

"I told you I was fine." While he meant it as a comfort it came out more accusatory than he wanted. After talking with the nurse about visitor hours the night before, he'd thought long and hard on what he'd needed to tell Chrys. But being beside her erased the words from his mind. "Maybe." He stopped. "Never mind."

"No, what is it?" She pushed back, getting a better look at him. She wiped her eyes until they were clear, until every last tear was gone.

"I... um... I think I might know what all of this is about." He watched the flatline at his side. "But it's a bit ridiculous."

"You have a low standard for what's ridiculous, Row."

He rolled his eyes, though he knew she was telling the truth. He collected his thoughts, trying to sort out exactly what he wanted to tell her. *Only the normal parts!* The smartest part of him said. "Um... anyways... I meant to tell you what was going on before you sold me out to the hospital."

"I didn't sell you out to anyone." She put her hands on her hips. "I was worried."

"There you go again, not giving me a chance to say my piece."

She let out an exaggerated sigh before she pretended to zip her lips, locking them up and throwing away the key.

"Alright." His chest ached as he realized he'd have to say something. "I got a... text. Yes, my sister sent me a text before I came inside yesterday." He clutched his chest as the pain ached again. The words formed inside of him but didn't want out. They clung to his chest, burning his insides until he couldn't handle it. "My mom passed away."

Chrys's mouth hung open.

"I think it caused a bit of an episode," he said. "It's nothing major."

"Nothing major?" Chrys repeated in disbelief.

"Yes… I'd liken it to a panic attack."

"No, not the heart." Chrys gripped his hands. "I'm talking about your mother. Is there going to be a funeral? Are you okay?"

Row felt a tad lightheaded. He relaxed a moment, taken back by her reaction. "You're not worried about my heart?"

"Sweetie, I'm always worried about your heart. But if you're telling the truth," she tightened her grip, "I wouldn't want you to miss your goodbye."

His head sunk. If he was honest, he wanted to be in neither place. *The hospital. Cherrywood.* He'd much prefer to snuggle on the couch with his dear Chrysocolla until he forgot about everything. But Sundew wasn't going to have it, Crow had made that clear enough. "I need to head back home to sign some papers. I guess Mom gave me her old house."

"Oh?" Chrys's eyes glinted.

"No. We're not taking it, my sister lives there. I'm signing it over to her."

Chrys slumped, but a gentle smile parted her lips. "That's very sweet of you."

"Pff!" Row fell back. "Are you kidding? I want absolutely nothing to do with that town and neither do you."

She tilted her head, "I don't?"

"No. You don't, I'll go on my own. If I can get out of this place…" He grimaced at the flatline. "And that's a big if."

"I'll vouch for you." She smiled. "But you won't be going alone, if you had an episode while you were driving—" Chrys shook her head to send the thought away. "No, I'll drive you down."

He bristled. *Maybe waiting on Sundew's tricks would be better?*

"I've always wanted to meet your family." Chrys rested her head on his quiet chest. "I'm sorry that I never got to meet her."

"Me too," he said. "She would have loved you."

Chrys turned to watch his face as he spoke, but remained relaxed on him. "She would have?"

He nodded. His mother loved fiction, would have loved to get tangled in Chrys's tales of ghosts and spirits. He could almost imagine her sitting with Zelda and Chrys, giggling about some nonsense. Maybe it was a ghost. Maybe it was a fairy. Or maybe it was just their favourite flavour of tea. He grunted as the pain flared up once again.

"Alright, let me go try and get you out of here." She raised her head from its spot. "This is a miserable place to mourn."

By some sort of magic (no, not actual magic, be serious), Chrys was able to release Row from the hospital. There were many tedious aspects to it, paperwork, phone calls, payments of unutterable sums, but eventually he breathed the free air. Chrys led him to the car, an obvious worry in the way she draped a protective arm around him.

"I hope we find a cure one day," she said as she opened the passenger side door for him.

He didn't say anything, not wanting to start a disagreement after all her help.

"Have you ever thought about continuing to seek out treatment? I mean, it wouldn't hurt."

The door shut, giving Row some time to collect his thoughts on the matter.

In the meantime, Chrys crossed over to the other side of their car before opening the door. She slipped into her driving shoes, sparkles of mother of pearl glinting by the gas pedal. She pulled her hair back, adorning a pair of driftwood shades. "There's got to be an answer to this," she said. "Maybe Mama's right?"

"There's no demons in there, if that's what you're about to say."

She snorted as she started the car. "Sorry, we really, really don't mean anything by that." She went quiet for bit as she navigated free of the parking lot. Chrys did surprisingly well considering how little she liked to drive their "pollution machine".

"I just — I was on the phone with Mama while you were out," Chrys continued. "I was telling her about it and I never realized how much I love you, Row. I don't know what I'd do if you were taken from me."

"Oh..." He lowered his head. *Of course she felt that way.* She'd been in his corner since the very beginning. A lot of times, Row had difficulty understanding why Chrys still liked him. After all the doubt he cast her way. "I don't know what I'd do without you either." He shut his eyes, trying to quell the discomfort in his chest. "Thanks for worrying about me."

"Don't mention it," she said.

They escaped the hospital together, driving back into the relaxing clouds of autumn. Row found himself eased slightly as he watched the rolling haze of autumn foliage. The trees which lined every road were a rotating gradient of red, orange and yellow. Before long they were back home, filing inside one after the other and beginning to pack their bags for the trip.

We really are doing this, he thought as he folded his clothes away. It almost hadn't phased him after the dry parts of the day. He'd almost managed to completely forget he'd be returning. Chrys would be coming with him. His chest flared. She was going to meet... *them.*

It'd been so long since Row had been back to his home town. He tried to think of the number of years but couldn't remember. Maybe eight? Maybe nine? When he'd left it was long before his transition. He'd still been little Rosie Gareau at the time, that awful girl with her awful sweet tooth. It all made him feel gross in his belly — not his sweet tooth, that was the reason he had a belly in the first place. Remembering his old life, however? Well, that just about made him throw up.

Are you certain that what Sundew sends your way will be worse? a part of him pleaded.

"You know that Sundew makes everything worse."

"Sundew?" Chrys's head poked out of the bathroom.

Row shut his mouth, not uttering another peep as Chrys came into the room with a duffle bag of toiletries.

"Who's Sundew?"

"My sister," he replied, pressing a hand reflexively over his heart.

"Oh, right, I was going to ask about that." Chrys loaded her things into their single suitcase. "You never told me that you had a sister."

"Well, I don't like her much." He looked away, busying himself with packing, trying desperately not to think about Sundew.

But the memories creeped in like unwelcome visitors, slinking through the shadows of his thoughts. He tried to focus on the "better'" times with her, like when she'd locked Mom out of the bathroom and tried to drown him in the bathtub. He vaguely remembered the surface of the water being solid, so she pressed really hard to get his head beneath it. He shivered. Water really was an awful thing.

"We never got along," he said. "Sundew always played too rough, always pushing me down that ditch and making me eat dirt."

"I'm sorry," Chrys cooed. "I'm sure you're both a little too old for that now though."

"I wouldn't be so sure." Row packed with greater intensity. "I wouldn't be surprised if the first thing she does is push me into the casket."

"That's not going to happen." Chrys patted his shoulder. "If she goes for it, I'll push her first."

Row snorted a half-hearted laugh. He was running out of things to pack, the suitcase full enough with stuff for weeks rather than a few days. "I don't want to go, Chrys."

"You have to. Your mother will need you to say goodbye. And you need to say goodbye to her." She leaned in closer. "I've met too many ghosts held onto, or holding on. Some never get the chance to say goodbye."

Row wanted to roll his eyes, but found himself wincing at his chest pains instead. "They're not going to like me back home. They never learned about *Row*."

"If they're awful to you, I'll shove them in the casket with Sundew." Chrys grinned.

"I'll hold you to that," he replied.

"You better." She hugged him around the shoulders. "Let's get going, Sweetheart."

Chapter Four

A Series of Miserable Reunions
with Bakers and a Powdered Corpse

Even if Row detested it now, the fondest memories he had of his mother always involved her stories. Every minute with her was stories. She'd read them every night before he slept. Together they'd sit in his bed, him pinned beneath the sheets and she above silhouetted by the incandescent light.

Then he'd shut his eyes. The flickering bulb above him would become the pulse of some distant star. All of his mother's best stories were about the stars. The one he remembered most fondly was the one she told the least. He forgot how it began, only how it ended. It was about a little girl who everyday reached upward for the stars. Every day she got a little closer. Until... maybe he didn't remember the ending.

In the morning, when his eyes were open and he was scraping peanut butter on his toast, his mother would tell him, "If you stretch your fingers to the sky, day by day you'll get closer. One day, when your fingers finally scrape the stars, you'll catch them like confetti."

"Confetti?" Chrys asked as she remained focused on the road.

"You know, the sparkles thrown at parties and stuff?"

Chrys shook her head, her eyes tipping up to the rear-view mirror. "I know what confetti is."

"Okay," Row said back. The memory of him and his mom in the kitchen was still vivid in his mind, her eyes sparkled with the sunlight soaking through the mesh window. In the morning, Mom's hair was still tightly wound in her rollers, her robe loose around her magenta night gown. Her feet bare, clock ticking, the sticky rips of her steps. The wheezing.

Chrys flicked Row's side. "Didn't tell you to stop. After she catches the confetti what happens?"

He shrugged. "That's where the story ends. She just catches the star."

"Aw, that doesn't feel like an ending."

"Well, you know my opinions on stories," he said. "It's a load of nonsense that's not worth remembering."

"You don't think..." Her brow crinkled, glancing his direction for a fraction. "Your mom, she wrote the story?"

He nodded.

"Doesn't that make it worth remembering?" She drummed her fingers on the steering wheel. "If I was a writer, I think I'd want someone to keep my stories alive. I'd hate for my words to be forgotten."

A pain began in his chest, flaring with his mother's memory. "Aren't you the one always going on about how ghosts need to be let go of? Writers are no different and should be forgotten like the rest of us."

"Keeping a memory alive is different than holding a ghost back from rest."

"I'm not talking about this, Chrys."

Row looked away from her. The road ahead cut into an overgrown forest of autumn. The pavement abruptly became dirt road, a sudden, albeit familiar culture shock. Row's mind grinded gears, shifting painfully back to its old ways. Things didn't change in Cherrywood. Row swallowed his nerves, he was too different to return.

The road wound out into Cherrywood. The other side of the forest met them with orange foliage. The thick of the trees continued onward all the way uptown. The dirt road faded gradually as the piles of leaves obscured the gravel.

Main Street (a.k.a. memory lane) was really the only street that mattered in

Cherrywood. All the shops lined it, from the grocery to the barber, each with their own wooden sign. The whole place was diligently kept the same with fresh coats of paint. Most places were passed down through the same family. Barbers bred barbers, bakers brought bakers, and writers made ham-headed illustrator/graphic designers, apparently.

They reached the funeral home at the end of Main, nearly a block from the bed and breakfast they'd be staying at. The lot at the funeral home was packed, everyone in town ready to see off the Gareau matriarch. Row shuddered at the thought of meeting each and every one of them. With a deep sigh, he unloaded himself from the car. Chrys reached to the back seat for her bouquet, a trio of sunflowers she'd taken from the front yard.

She pulled herself from the car, kicking off her flats.

Even at a funeral, no shoes.

Row looked to the cars gathered around the outside of the funeral home. Old but familiar faces hung around the door waiting for Row, to view the corpse and make sure it was up to viewing standards. He searched the crowd for Sundew, but he couldn't see her anywhere. In fact, there weren't many faces that Row recognized and wanted to pursue further. Eventually they'd each make their way to offer condolences and inappropriate questions whether he was ready or not.

He lowered his eyes, staring down at Chrys's feet as if the answers were hidden somewhere between her toes. "Alright, let's get this over with." He waded through the crowd of curious faces.

The last time Claire visited the funeral home was for tea with Azalea Blackthorn. It was a lighter occasion then. They'd spoken about the beauty of autumn for a moment before Claire talked Lea's ear off about her latest read. Every time she read a book, she became enraptured by it. So enraptured she imagined herself as a story book character. So enraptured she could almost hear the words written about her and she let her tea go cold.

This time, the building felt dour. A foreboding gloom fell across the house, severing it from its duty as a home for the Blackthorns. It was only a place of business now. Of death. Claire mulled towards the door, hiding beneath the thorny trees that lined the walkway. Round, black berries grew where there was once little white flowers. A shiver ran through Claire and she bunched inward.

She approached the door where Lea waited, dressed in black with her gothic locks serving the mood well. Much like everyone else in Cherrywood, Lea was destined to keep her family business alive. Of course, Claire was no exception. She clenched her arms around the books that she'd brought from her family's store.

In addition to a bouquet of roses she'd brought a pair of books. Neither were for Rose, actually. If they were, she would have simply returned them when she was alive. Instead they were for Rose's daughter… or her son, she supposed. Her heart fluttered at the thought. Back when they were in high school "Rosie" had told her about it, her plans to leave for the city, become an illustrator, a man, and then never return.

Would he actually return?

Her hands stiffened around her books. She'd borrowed them from Rosie years ago. The first was a copy of *The Illustrated Man* she'd stolen back when they were dating. It was a short story collection that Claire was certain Rosie never read and only bought because he liked the cover. The second she'd stolen from him in kindergarten, an illustrated copy of *The Velveteen Rabbit*. On top of both books was Rose's letter for him.

An arm startled Claire as it swung over her shoulder. She looked up, finding it belonged to the impossibly tall Dandelion Fletcher — better known as Dan the baker, obviously. He pulled her in close and said, "How you holding together?"

"About as good as I could be." She sighed. "How about you?"

He shrugged. Along with being impossibly tall, Dan had a feel-good smile. It was hard to be anything other than genuine with him present. He ruffled a bag of boxed pastries in one hand, awkwardly trying to hold onto a pen and notebook in his remaining digits.

"You going to be writing the obituary?" Claire asked.

He nodded respectfully. Dan ran the volunteer paper as both journalist and editor. The biggest scandal in Cherrywood was the occasional burnt scone. "I'm hoping that Rosie shows up to this thing she—"

"He," Claire corrected.

"Ah… right…" He was thrown off track of his thought. "Um… yeah, I'd rather talk to *him* than Sundew."

"Sundew's not that bad," Claire lied.

"Sure. You keep telling yourself that." He rolled his eyes. "I don't know how you could stand visiting Rose with her lurking in the shadows."

"Dan." Claire crossed her arms. "We'll talk about it when we're not at her mother's funeral."

He lowered his head respectfully before haphazardly swinging the pastries over his shoulder. "Want to help me unload the truck? Grandma's brought enough cupcakes to feed a horde of school children."

"Bake away the pain?" Claire smiled. "I dig it."

"Alright, Homeslice." He snorted. "My shoulder's here if you need it — or if you can even reach it."

She nodded before being startled as sadness hit her. Hard. Tears forced their way out, running down her cheeks. While she couldn't reach Dan's shoulder, she found herself in his arms. "I don't think I'm ready to see her," she muttered.

"That's okay, hang back as long as you need."

In death, Row's mother hadn't changed. She was inhuman, a woman cut from yellow craft paper. No body, no face, a shadow puppet scribbled over in black crayon. Her casket was open, surrounded by a bed of magnolias. The cloud of petals looked to hold her up while origami butterflies stretched their wings and fluttered amongst the dying branches. At least, that's the way Row saw it. He was certain that everyone else saw a powdered corpse.

Chrys's fingers warmed in his hand. She'd kept close since they'd entered, shadowing his steps. He allowed her body to warm against his, for a split second the warmth welled like emotion, like sadness. But Row had always struggled with feeling sad. His chest hurt, but no tears came. It all felt mundane.

Chrys reached for his shoulder, moving like a ghost through his walls. "I'm here for you."

"You don't need to be, I'm fine." He glanced back at his mother, testing just how okay he was. No feelings came.

Chrys said nothing, giving him a small amount of space.

He allowed her to pat his shoulder. His mother slept, peaceful, yet disappointed in front of him.

"Sorry, I just—" He turned, only to find Chrys had been absorbed into an encroaching crowd. The lingering warmth was all that remained as she disappeared behind the old women of Cherrywood.

His mom's old friends circled the room like fruit flies. They took sidelong glances at Row, trying to place him.

"Aster, is that you?" Mrs. Fletcher asked. She squinted up at Row, her frail hand on his elbow. She must have been ninety, with skin dry and thin like rice paper.

"Oh, hello Mrs. Fletcher," Row muttered, scanning the room for his escape. A crowd of old ladies spread out in all directions, purposefully cooing to one another while remaining quiet enough to eavesdrop. They'd all taken Row's moment with the casket to block him in.

"You look so young," Mrs. Fletcher continued. "If you have a secret, you better not be hiding it in the city."

"N-no, I'm just young," he stammered. "I'm not Aster, I'm Row actually."

"Row?" Her glasses slid down her nose. The thoughts came to her slowly, like baking one of her cakes. Then it dinged. "Oh my! Rosie. You look like your father!"

"Oh... um..." He scratched at his beard. "I wouldn't know."

"It wouldn't matter," Mrs. Fletcher scoffed. "It's not a compliment."

Dressed down by her sharp glares, she picked every inch of Row apart. "Exactly like your father." She tsked. "Rosie, I'll never understand your nonsense, sure you were a little round, but you were such a pretty girl."

Row shrank, stepping back towards his mother. He scanned the scene for Chrys, his lifeline, but she was still lost in the crowd.

"It must be a city thing, your father loved the city too — though I'd hazard a guess he didn't... well there aren't words for this mess."

"Mrs. Fletcher, I'm just here for the funeral."

"Are you? I know your mother left you her house. If you have any brains left — which I honestly doubt — you'll know that house is not yours to take. We don't want you here. We don't want you selling it to some outsider either. Things work here because they stay the same. I don't care what you have to say on the matter, the house belongs to Sundew. Rose has no son."

Row choked on his possible responses, his chest burned, and then all settled. Mrs. Fletcher worked at the bakery her entire life. She never gave free sweets to the naughty boys and girls. Row's inability to respond was Pavlovian.

"Do what's right." She squeezed him with her sharp nails.

"Grandma," Dan Fletcher interrupted, stepping to her side. "Ms. Poppy wants a word with you about your buttercream. She seems desperate."

Her brow wrinkled, side-eying Row as she was pointed in Ms. Poppy's direction.

One more pat on her shoulder, and Dan successfully displaced Mrs. Fletcher. Dan was a very tall man, his black slacks too short and exposing his socks. Yet, he still looked more formal than Row who'd opted to wear a sweater rather than a suit. He really couldn't handle the constraints of a suit and tie after the episode with his heart. That and it was easier to hide in a thick, grey, sweater.

Dan shifted in his shoes, causing them discomforted squeaks. "Sorry about that."

Row shrugged. Scanning the room, he took note of each person with an interrogation poised on their lips. The people to avoid. It was an easy list: everyone.

"Have you seen Sundew?" Row asked.

Dan shook his head. "No, I think she's getting things ready at the burial. You know how particular she gets."

"Oh, good," the words slipped out Row's mouth. "I mean, never mind. Nice to see you again, Dan."

"Wait," Dan stopped him, "While I have the chance, I'm writing up an obituary for Rose. Could I get your number? Talk to you when you're less… when you're up for it, I mean."

"Email me, my website's not hard to find." Row backed away. Halting for a moment, he added, "If you can't find it. I barely knew her anyways."

Dan blinked, allowing Row his space. "Alright. Have you seen Claire yet? She was really hoping to see you."

"She was?" Row glanced around the room. "I'll talk to her if I get the chance. Um… I just need a minute."

Dan withdrew, allowing Row to make his way through the crowd. Row swallowed. He made himself sick in the stomach. The room spun, an empty chair meeting him in the corner. He sank into the overstuffed cushion. Leaning forward, he pretended to mourn. His skin buzzed, the overstimulation of all the eyes transfixed on him.

As little as it was possible, Row tried to shut off the world. He rested his eyes, imagined he and Chrys were in the garden. Her bare feet broke through the dew. Her smile beamed like dawn at sea. He could smell the mulch on his fingertips. The breeze of a distant ocean. But the static of the funeral buzzed through him. He didn't know how much longer he could take the haze. He wanted to retire to the bed and breakfast, avoid the burial all together.

When his eyes opened, he was met with Claire. Like everything else in Cherrywood, she hadn't changed. Her eyes were sweet, dark but golden like syrup, or maybe a cup of pure twilight. She wore no black, but a charcoal blouse and subdued autumn plaid for her skirt. His insides felt fuzzy and numb. He'd never actually broken up with her, just disappeared from her life without a word.

"Are you okay?" Claire took the seat next to him. "I mean, it is you, right?"

"Um… yes," he replied a bit too late.

She began to smile softly. "I'm glad you came back."

"I'm regretting it."

"Oh." Claire shrunk back. "I know everyone's being a bit moody and rude, but I'll have you know that I'd be happy if you moved back into Honey Walls."

"I'm not considering it."

"Ah right, but I do think Mrs. Fletcher would be able to get over it. I mean, if that's the problem." Claire sighed. "I didn't think I'd recognize you, but you're so much like how I pictured. I'm glad that it finally happened for you, I personally think the beard suits you. Dan's never been able to grow one, so I bet Mrs. Fletcher is just jealous."

Row grunted.

"I'm sorry. This isn't the time, is it? My condolences by the way, I know how much Rose meant to you."

Row raised his hand and said, "No, not this. You want to know what's on my mind? Beyond the funeral. Beyond gossip."

"What?"

"My hotel. I want to check in as early as I can. I want to sleep, get everything here done, then return home and never think about this place again. Oh, and I don't want to get the strawberry room." He bristled at the thought of staying in the bed and breakfast's least appealing room.

"Oh, right, I'm sure you'll make it after the burial." She perked up, pressing a finger to her lip. "You could call ahead? Maybe they'll let things slide given the circumstances."

"But Rosie," he mocked, "what's wrong with the strawberry room? Don't you like how the wallpaper moves? And the smell, don't you like being assaulted by strawberry, *Rosie?*"

"Ask specifically for the rose room then."

"I don't want the rose room."

"No?" Claire set her hand on his chair. "What about nightshade? Or plum?"

"Or broccoli? Pumpkin? Maybe asparagus? Oh, I know, vinegar. I recall a vinegar room. That's the kind of room I need. I feel pickled."

Claire let out a short puff of miserable air. The room was thick with it. "Ask for nightshade."

"I will." He glanced back at Claire. She'd stopped looking at him. "I'm sorry, I don't feel myself right now."

She nodded slightly, fingers clamping around her pile of books. Tears were beginning to form in her already red eyes. It was sudden yet expected. But Row didn't know what to say.

"I brought these for you," she said, handing him the pile. "The books are yours and she wrote that."

He glanced at the books, only vaguely recalling ever owning them, then he brushed the letter. "You keep the books, you'll appreciate them more." He pushed them back into her hands, wanting to do the same with the letter.

Her fingers quivered around them, as she nodded inward and small.

The paper was softer than Sundew's invitation, almost warm to the touch. Etched in the finest penmanship was the single word, "Rose." He slid his finger beneath the edge of the envelope, careful not to damage the contents. Inside was smooth paper, expertly penned in his mom's handwriting. It was like something pulled straight from a memory.

My Darling Little Rose,

In this card I have sealed as many hugs as I can, brief ones, long ones, sad ones, happy ones, and hopefully every other kind you might need. I do this because now that you are reading this, you need them the most. I have saved them everyday since you left, because it's all a mother can do with her worries. And now that I'm gone, I doubt it will stop.

If you didn't already know, I have left the house to you. I want you to continue to care for my magnolias, the animals, and the stories. You are my most precious and the only one I trust to keep the house safe. I know this will be difficult for you, to protect and keep the Stories of Cherrywood, but I know that you can do it, and will do it.

Please take with you this advice. Whenever you're lost, remember to consult the birds. Not all help has a price. Never gamble with ferrets (they cheat). Never hire a fox for a lawyer, they're well-meaning but don't know a lick about jurisprudence. And most importantly, stretch your fingers to the sky, reach until you hold the sun in your hands, and the stars are silver sparkles that fall into your heart. Remember that I love you.

Sincerely,

The Former Rose Gareau

Row slid the memory away.

The burial came later at the end of a dreary march. They found themselves in the cold graveyard. It bristled with the signs of early winter, bitter and stiffened with frost. The ground was too cold to be dug out, so the casket lay on the dry grass in a ceremonial manner. His mom's closest friends circled its perimeter, a shadow of swaying black fabric.

Across from Row, his sister remained quiet. Exhausted. Their first moments in years after she'd avoided the funeral home. Sundew's fists were white, her jaw clenched shut. For all her anger she still looked soft, tears still wet her eyes, sadness still quivered her lips. But frustration brewed in the spaces between sadness. Sundew looked at Row, causing him to jerk focus to his shoes.

For her final goodbye, Sundew placed a single red rose. A short stem, its petals wilted. It was the same rose that Crow had taken. Above him he found the crow watching mournfully from atop a tombstone. Everyone looked at Row suddenly. In a fluster he threw down his sunflowers.

He stayed to watch the priest bless Rose's passing. He stayed as his mother's friends parted the grave. He stayed until it was only him, Chrys, and Sundew. She stood as a willow, hair hanging like vines, twisting around her toes. Row squeezed Chrys's palm. Sundew wouldn't want them to watch.

They'd talk later.

Chapter Five

The Monster that Lives in Honey Walls

The mid-day memorial service was more in line with what Rose would have wanted. It was held above the bakery in the Fletcher's living room. Rose's old friends mulled about, sitting around and discussing their memories. Claire felt far more at ease, snuggly wrapped away in the smells of fruit and buttery pastries. The mood was further lightened by Row's absence. Whether he'd refused to show up or hadn't been invited, a weight was lifted from Claire's chest.

She held onto her books, listening to the tales told of Cherrywood's storyteller. They focused on older tales of her, from before Claire was born. Each was more endearing than the last. At least they were until Claire's own mother, Mrs. Waters, decided to mention Row.

"As lovely as she was," Mrs. Water's began, "I'd be remiss to not mention that *daughter* of hers."

Claire bit her cheek, trying to slip away between the crowd before the gossip heated up.

Mrs. Waters looked to her husband. "She was always troubled that one, wasn't she?"

Ms. Poppy interrupted. "You mean Sundew?"

"No, no, the other one," Mrs. Waters corrected, patting her husband's shoulder. "Heath, you used to babysit for her back when Claire was in preschool. You must have something to say about her."

Claire rolled her eyes, but didn't get into it. They were going to talk and there was little she could do to stop them. But that certainly didn't mean she had to listen. Instead, she parted the crowd and headed in the direction of Dan's old room. As she gained some distance the gossip became uninterpretable. Then as she swung open a door which read, "No Girls Allowed" and slammed it behind her, the noise stopped.

"Huh?" Dan spun around in his chair.

The room was a mix of his childhood things and an office. He sat in a blue swivel chair, crammed between his old bed and an antique desk. On top of it was his computer, another antique. The grey brick still ran Windows 95 and connecting to the internet required knocking his grandma off the phone line. But such was life in Cherrywood.

The rest of the room was decorated with spaceships and dinosaurs. It was far too small for Dan to live in anymore. While his initial plan was to move out and go to college, that dream died with his parents. After the car crash, he'd moved into their old room, staying in Cherrywood to help his grandma run the bakery.

"Wow, this brings me back." Claire dropped down onto his bed, snuggling atop a mountain of stuffed dinosaurs.

"What? You mean memories of how I used to lock you out?" He smirked.

"Nah, I'm talking high school here." She smiled at the thought. Back in the day, herself, Dan and Row had big dreams. They'd spent a lot of time imagining themselves away from Cherrywood. The three of them living various professions, living various lives.

"I'm talking about The Three Musketeers," she continued, "or whatever, there really aren't many other good allusions for groups of three, are there?"

"Three Stooges?"

She swayed her head back and forth but was no happier with his attempt. "Either way, really takes me back to you, me, Row."

"Did you get to talk with him, by the way?" Dan asked.

"Yeah but it wasn't exactly what I was hoping for. I think they might be right about him changing, becoming a city type." She buried her head beneath a diplodocus. "Why don't I just move out of here?"

"Don't know, nothing's stopping you." He poked her knee with his foot. "Besides, Row is probably just in a bad mood because of… well… it's a crap day for everyone."

"Yeah. Today sucks." She groaned.

"No kidding." His chair creaked as he leaned back. "I'm struggling to come up with anything to say for this obituary."

"Really?"

"Yeah, this whole day has me thinking, you know? Just seeing how much everyone cared for her, making this obituary simple, distilling her down to a few words seems impossible. I want to write something bigger, get into the heart of why she mattered so much."

Claire sat up, pushing the dinosaurs aside. "That sounds wonderful."

"It does?"

She swung her legs off the bed, orienting herself to better face Dan. "Yeah, I'm totally biased though. Rose meant a lot to me. She just always believed that I could do whatever I dreamed, even when no one else thought so."

"You're making me feel bad I didn't get to know her."

"You should feel bad! She would have loved to talk to another writer. I think it got lonely doing it all by herself."

He smirked at that. "I can believe it. Speaking of which, you mind helping me write this thing?"

Claire felt her heart flutter, causing her to bound forward and stumble to her feet. "Of course, I'd love to help out."

"I thought you could talk to Sundew for me?"

"No way in hell, Baker Boy."

Check-in was delayed, furthering the delay to Row's comfort. Rose's death rippled through the town, the bed and breakfast one of many shut in her memory. A feeling spread up Row's spine, the feeling you get when you know you haven't been invited to your mother's mid-day memorial. The one Mrs. Fletcher no doubt was holding above her bakery.

Chrys inspected the note on the door. They'd be open after dinner. With the average age of the townsfolk in mind, that would be around six. Row grabbed a pamphlet for Chrys, an illustrated guide to the flowers and birds of Cherrywood Gardens. The famed Cherrywood from which Cherrywood got its name.

"You should get to know the town," he said. "Me and my sister need to talk about the estate."

Her brow creased. "Today? It's a little soon. Wouldn't you prefer to watch the birds?"

"I'd prefer to drown in the river, honestly." He pressed a hand to her shoulder. "I'll get it over with, then I'll show you all my favourite spots."

"You don't have to show me Cherrywood." Her smile dampened but didn't disappear. "I just want to see you're okay."

"I will be when I'm done with Sundew."

Shadows cast over her eyes, the pools like deep sea. Then she kissed him, quiet like the night. As they finished, she looked inside of him, scraping away the dreariness with the subtle light that glinted in her eyes. Her body always so warm compared to his.

He let her go.

"I promise, I'll be back as soon as I can."

Just behind a thick of amber leaves, Row could see the gold glint of Honey Walls. Thankfully, Chrys allowed him the car for the short trip. Walking the slope leading to Honey Walls was not something he was prepared for, nor was introducing Chrys to Sundew.

The car climbed over the ditch at the end of the woods. The path he'd walked many times before. The brush was tight and Row wasn't sure if a car was meant to fit, since his mother never owned one. She and modernity were like oil and water. They may have briefly had a truck. But it definitely wasn't his mother's, the whole thing embodied his father, a man made of memories. Clunky, harsh, discordant with the countryside. It pulled out one day and never came back.

Row's car broke apart a line of toadstools, rolling into the brush that surrounded Honey Walls. He parked it in the wildflowers. The uncut lawn was to his knees. The stems of grass were long and yellowed, while blue, purple, and yellow daisies sprung up amongst the growth.

Honey Walls itself was overtaken by the magnolias. The bushes were bigger than he remembered, arching over the doorway, and growing upward onto the roof. He approached the building, trying not to disturb the bees on the flowers.

"Excusez-moi!" shouted a mouse at his foot.

"Oh, sorry." He shifted away from the little lace mouse.

"I'd have thought your mother taught you better." The mouse shook her head, tightening a ribbon around herself.

"She did, um, do you know if my sister's here?"

"Inside I think, but I'm not a house mouse anymore. Not the life for me, I'm starting a nest with a field mouse. There's a tree with golden apples we're moving into. They're better than any pastry."

"Congratulations."

"Thank you, but I really don't have a choice. You're an awful cook. Being a house mouse is no longer a lucrative life choice." She shivered, appearing to puff up at the thought of Row's overly sweet pastries.

"I'm letting Sundew take the house, actually."

The mouse gasped. "Non, non, non, your mother really has taught you nothing! Sundew absolutely cannot, for any reason ever, watch this house. Do you know how much more trouble she could cause?"

"She'll do fine," he said. "Do you need help to the apple tree, that's a load of ribbon you have there." He lowered his hand to the ground and the mouse climbed onto his fingers.

"Rosie, have you talked to Oxnard about any of this?"

"No, where is he?" Row looked around for the hedgehog in the grass all the while avoiding any more mice.

"What? You don't know! Mon deiu! I thought he left with you to the city."

Row shook his head.

"Oh dear, he left looking for you about a year ago. Here I thought he was the one that sent you! I bet you feel bad now, don't you, Rosie?"

Row set the mouse down at the foot of the apple tree. The golden delicious were ripe, heavy on the branches. "I'd have talked to him if I saw him," Row mumbled.

The mouse scoffed, burying herself in the roots of the trees. Row walked back to the porch of Honey Walls. The steps were old and in need of a repaint, though the railings were so tangled in flowers it was no wonder why his mother hadn't. He wiped his feet on the welcome mat, and then opened the door. Cherrywood wasn't a town for locked doors.

Inside was the past. Rose's gardening gloves sat on a bag of mulch, her rain boots caked with a layer of dry mud. Row pulled his shoes off, stretching his toes like Chrys and walking onto the familiar carpet. The couch was the same, an old pastel pink thing with a chocolate frame. The walls were honey gold (of course) and the carpet soft and beige.

The far wall was lined with Rose's bookshelves leading out into her studio. The studio was cramped, but organized. She'd taken to writing in a walk-in closet where she could surround herself with her notes. Everything was in her reach. Row pushed her cabinets shut, making room to walk to her desk.

The room smelled most like his mother, like ink and honey. Yet it didn't feel like her. The chair was uncomfortable. The walls weighted with papers pressed their shadows down on Row's back. A piece of prose lay unfinished on the table. Her ink well still exposed, drying up, pen sat in a puddle of spilled ink. *The Keeper of Cherrywood's Stories*, the familiar phrase echoed through Row's head.

He stumbled backward, tripping over the chair with the grace of a hurricane.

The lights in the living room turned on. "What are you doing?" Sundew asked from the other side of the room.

"I-I just tripped." He moved the chair out from under himself. Sundew extended her hand and helped him to his feet.

"You were looking at Mother's stories?" she asked, wiping her finger across Rose's books. "Did you see something you didn't like?"

Row shook his head, taking a moment to get himself reorganized.

"No? Then let me guess. You don't think you can continue her stories." Sundew made work of cleaning the ink well. Row's sister moved like a shadow. Her hair was unbraided dragging across the floor.

"You know I want nothing to do with them. Let's just get this over with."

"*Rosie.*" Sundew cleaned the ink from the table. "It's good you know your place. You're not a storyteller, you never have been."

Row stiffened, trying to wade out Sundew's games.

"I've always had to tell myself stories, you know?" She held onto his mother's pen. It fit perfectly in her hand. A fine branch, light like a dry vine. "Mother never told me stories."

Sundew stared into Row's eyes. His breath was short, wavering like there wasn't space in his lungs. He'd spent too much of his childhood on the wrong side of the water, his sister above him, holding him under. "I've been watching you, Rosie." She reached out to him, touching her finger to the sorest part of his chest. "Waiting for things to change."

Row flinched back, suffering through a hotter sensation than before.

"I didn't think you'd be brave enough to return. I thought this would take more effort on my part. *Rosie.*"

"It's Row."

She stopped, clasping her hand before relaxing once more. "Row, Rose, Rosie, they're all just words. Aren't they? And if you take this house from me, become the writer instead, what power would my words ever hold over you? Nothing."

"No, they matter. I'm not Rosie, so stop calling me that."

Sundew scoffed and rolled her eyes.

"I don't get why you're so angry." Row scowled, though he was acutely aware of how lacklustre his tone was. "After what *you* did to me? Honestly, it should be me tormenting you."

"Don't lie to yourself." Sundew took sweeping strides around him. "You're as incapable of anger as you are every other emotion."

Row choked a bit on his breath, darting to the safest topic. "Let's just figure out the estate."

"No, I like this conversation. Does Chrys know you can't love her, or do you plan on stringing her along like Claire?"

"Sundew, I'm not talking to you about this nonsense." He huffed. "And quit spying on me, it's not normal."

"You'll never be normal." She sneered. "Normal humans have emotions. Normal humans feel pain. Normal humans cry when their mother…" She hesitated. "We cry."

"Where are the papers I need to sign?"

"Is busy work how you cope with being a freak? That's so sad." Sundew followed him as he tried to find some sort of escape in paperwork. "You don't even know how sad it is, and that just makes it sadder."

"Fine, I don't have emotions." Row stopped and looked her in the eyes. "Is that what you want me to say? I don't get what the point is in teasing me about it."

She leaned forward and pressed a hand to his chest. "I just hate you. Simple as that."

Row kept silent as her hand remained against him, utterly still.

"You don't even know what hate feels like, do you? I hate that."

"Let's just sign the paperwork, Sundew."

"Ugh!" She threw her hands to her sides. "Fine, let's just sign this stupid house to me. Maybe then I could teach you a thing or two about hate."

Row sighed, unable to keep up with her ferocity. Talking about *it* out loud always made it seem stronger, like it wasn't all just a bad dream. He became aware of the flatness of his expressions, the insincerity of his rare smile.

Deep down, he knew everything about him was fake.

Deep down, he knew that he felt nothing.

Deep down… there *was* nothing.

Row didn't have a heart.

Once upon a time, Rosie had a heart that ached. She lay alone in her mother's bed, tears rolling down her cheeks. The room was dark and creaky, the window open so that the howls of wind and wolves entered unchallenged. She pulled her covers right up to her nose and watched over the folds for monsters.

Shadows ran across the floor, the tangles of tree branches casting down into monstrous hands. Shivers buzzed through Rosie as footsteps creaked at the edge of her bed. She brought her feet close (the safest procedure for dealing with monsters of most types since monsters notoriously feared floral quilts). But this monster was different.

It lifted the quilt and climbed under the sheets.

"Go away," Rosie pleaded.

But the monster moved closer, and snatched at her feet. Rosie screamed, calling for her mother… but no one came. No one heard her at all. She flailed and swatted at the shadow, but it kept getting closer and closer. The monster, still hidden beneath the sheets, pinned Rosie down.

Slowly, the monster became familiar. The quilt rolled down its shoulders and revealed a girl like Rosie. A girl named Sundew.

Rosie whimpered as Sundew press a thumb against her eye. She wiped her tears with force, pushing so hard Rosie felt her eye might pop out. "Don't cry," she said.

She pressed her body down harder, squeezing the air from Rosie's lungs. As she did so, another monsterly plot began in her head. Sundew hid a hand behind her back so that Rosie couldn't see. It became colourless and glassy all the way up to her elbows. By the time the magic reached her shoulder, Rosie had finally noticed. She attempted to struggle and scream once more, but Sundew didn't care.

With her glass hand she reached right into Rosie's chest and grabbed her aching heart. Her body twitched and convulsed as Sundew struggled with the heart. It was incredibly painful and very, very, very, stuck inside. Sundew yanked and yanked until the hurt ripped free. And that's when Rosie finally stopped screaming.

In her hand, Sundew held Rosie's heart. It was dusted with light, fragile, but thorned, a single red rose. Rosie lay still beneath the monster, the covers draped on its shoulders. The moonlight tangled in its mess of hair. The monster ate the flower petals as Rosie's last tears dried on her face.

You see, the worst thing about someone taking your heart is that it's the worst pain you ever feel…

And then you feel nothing ever again.

Chapter Six

Oxnard and the Sky World
by Rose Gareau

Wherein Oxnard Learns About Adults

Oxnard found me after his harrowing journey back up the ditch. This time there were no wolves to chase him, but every time he neared the top, he found himself grabbing a loose rock or twig. Then he would roll all the way back to the bottom. This happened five or six times, so when he made it to my garden he was covered in dirt and scratches.

"Good heavens! What happen to you?" I exclaimed as he made his way out of the tall grasses.

"Just adventure, Mrs. Gareau," he said as he patted dirt from his knees. "You know how it is, and it isn't the biggest thing on my plate either. I'm going to Sky World."

"You are?" I gasped.

"Yes!" He hobbled forward and patted my crocs with his tiny paws. "It's a dangerous adventure, I know, but I've already spoken with Ms. Crow. I think it'll be my best adventure yet."

I sighed one of my motherly sighs. Oxnard, like all the stuffed and craft animals, was like a child to me. "The way to Sky World sounds very dangerous," I said, "and very, very, very adult."

"Oh, you must believe I'm tough by now, Mrs. Gareau."

"Of course, you're a very brilliant and talented hedgehog, but this is a different kind of adventure." I bent down onto my knees so that he could see me better. "If you make it to Sky World, you're going to become a different hedgehog."

He crinkled his snout, trying to figure out what I meant. "Like… Boxnard?"

I laughed a little bit. "No, you'll still be Oxnard, but you'll probably become an adult like me and Ms. Crow."

"What does that mean?" He puffed out his quills, readying for adultness to sneak up on him. "Is it dangerous? Should I be worried?"

"Yes and no. It happens to all of us at different times." I sighed once more, this time an everyday sigh (the same sigh that all us somewhat old people do when we look in the mirror). "But it's a harrowing journey that you can never return from."

He balled a bit, but his two little eyes sparkled beneath his quills. "What makes becoming an adult so different than other adventures? Does Sky World turn everyone into an adult?"

"No, no, it's not Sky World that does it — though big adventures are often the cause. There are just things waiting for you there. Things you won't quite understand until you're an adult." I bent down and lifted him up. "When you become an adult, all your big adventures will become very small. Those wolves that chased you will seem like tiny poodles! But that's only because the world will become so big… and tricky. Things you thought were small will grow with you and maybe turn to monsters. You'll be tangled in so many quests without a map to turn to."

"Oh…" Oxnard's head sunk. "That sounds horrible."

"Not always." I smiled at him. "There are endless adventures out there, and millions of new and wonderful things. But I want to warn you of the bad stuff, because if you're not prepared to become an adult, well, there's very little fun to be had."

"But if I'm prepared, will the bad stuff go away?"

I shook my head. "Being an adult means being surrounded by the bad and the good all at the same time. It's the difference between drawing with one crayon and the whole box."

He let the thought bounce around in his head a bit, and he started to understand. "I suppose I won't know until I reach Sky World."

I nodded, bending down to give him a kiss on the nose. "You're so brave."

He balled up in the embarrassed equivalent of a hedgehog blush.

"Goodbye, Oxnard," I said, bringing my arms in to hug myself (I'm a very worrisome adult these days, Reader).

"I'm not going away forever, Mrs. Gareau." He unrolled himself to show off his smile. "I'll bring back Rosie too!"

The Cherrywood Inn check-in was covered with knickknacks. Snow globes lined the shelves, most of which were Grandma Betty's princess and angel collection. A neatly printed sign on the desk read, "Ring a bell!" Beside it was a line of themed bells. Chrys snatched the bluest of them and rang it. Row stayed back, not feeling up to much after his meeting with Sundew.

You'll never be normal. Sundew's words echoed through his mind, resting like a heavy weight on his empty chest.

From the back room, Barry Cobbler dragged himself out. His hair stood on end in a mess of bedhead and his TV could be heard when the door opened. "Hello, welcome to the Cherrywood Inn." He yawned. "What can I do you for?"

"Nightshade," Row said.

"Nightshade?" Barry squinted. "Okay, cool, I'll get you Nightshade, one sec."

Row had babysat Barry on a few too many occasions. He wasn't a smart kid, but was far more tolerable than his mother. He took the key to the Nightshade Room from the cubby behind the desk and handed it to Row.

Row pocketed the key along with an itinerary printed on salmon paper. As he did so, Barry headed to the backroom.

"Wait, I didn't pay you." Row stopped him.

"Nah, it's cool, Mom said she wants to give you the night free, like friend and family discount plus 'dude your mom passed away I'm so sorry' discount comes out to like zero-ish dollars anyways."

"No, I'm paying, how much is the room?"

"Zero."

"Before your discounts. I don't want a pity room."

Chrys pulled Row from the desk. "We'll take it. Thank your mother for us."

Barry gave a dumbfounded nod.

Chrys kept pulling Row towards the door, then pushed on his back as they neared the steps. His feet scraped across the carpet — the ridiculous fruity patterned carpet. Then he tripped on the stairs. He fell forward and hit his head on a step. It didn't hurt too much, but nothing really hurt anymore. *Have you just been faking pain this whole time?* He lay on the step and accepted his fate.

"Row, are you okay?" Chrys frowned as she pulled on his arm.

"No, I feel nothing. Pity me. This is my free pity step."

"Quit it, people just feel bad."

"I hate it when people feel bad for me." He reached for the railing, though it felt incredibly distant.

"Well, that's something you need to work on." She held out a hand for him.

He grabbed her hand and lifted himself to his feet.

"There we go, just a few more steps and I'm going to swaddle you in blankets and get you a scone."

"A scone?"

Chrys inhaled. "Don't you smell that? I saw someone in the kitchen, she was making scones and a million other delicious things. I'm going to get you every sweet thing I find." When they reached the last step, Chrys's fingers were pressed together with devious delight.

"I'm not really in the mood for sweets."

She gasped. "You're always in the mood for sweets!"

Row shrugged, continuing to the Nightshade Room, the only thing subdued about the house. He slid the key into the doorknob, the brass creaking when it moved. The frame disagreed with opening. Once inside, Row hit the light, then hit the bed. It was far more comfortable than the stairs.

The whole room was dark. Cold air leaked through the cracks in the windows. Chrys threw her things down on the floor, then she laid down half on Row half off the bed.

Her hair rested so close he could smell sea breeze. Just like when they'd first met, she was water, sea foam, and shadows. She lifted herself above him, her hair a waterfall cascading down. She rested her hand on his cheek, leaned forward and kissed his forehead, lips, nose.

"Row," she said, the purest version of herself, the one he thought even a heartless man could love. "Row, I want scones."

"Go get us scones, Chrys."

"Thank you," she whispered and she hopped to the door.

Chrys's touch lingered on Row's skin as he sank into the sheets. The whole day had left him weary, thoughts of the funeral, his heart, his sister had become an intangible haze. Soon he found himself unable to remain awake, drifting off into neither restful nor comfortable sleep.

When he woke, the quilt was covering him. The TV was on at the foot of the bed beside a clutter of old VHSs, *Beauty and the Beast* playing out quietly on the tiny screen. Chrys sat in the space beside Row with a plate of scones, among other things.

She smiled at him and handed him a small plate for his own scone. Beside him, she pointed to a cup of fruit tea and a jar of honey. While Row said nothing, he thanked her. He sweetened his tea and nibbled on the scone. Exactly as he remembered, the pastry was perfect. It almost made up for the detestable film. Almost.

The movie was one of his sister's absolute favourites. She'd watched it on repeat for years of their childhood, always kicking him off the TV when he was trying to watch *Art Attack*. He supposed it was far from the most reprehensible thing she did, but it hardly endeared her.

"How'd things go with your sister?" Chrys asked.

"About as well as expected." He looked away, not interested in pursuing the conversation. Yet it weighed down on him, a haze of numbness. "Chrys... I have a weird question."

"What sort of question?"

He stared at the crumbs on his plate, searching for his words. "Do you know that I love you?"

She smirked, nuzzling his neck. "I love you too."

He pushed her back, looking into her eyes. "No, I'm being serious. When we talk, do you feel that I love you?"

Her brow tensed, not angry, confused.

"If anything bad ever happened…" He shook at the thought. "If anything bad ever happened, I'd want you to know that I love you."

"What?" Her mouth hung open, eyes wide with shock. "Of course I know, Sweet Heart. Is this about your mother?"

He shook his head but couldn't help but be reminded. "I haven't cried a single tear," he mumbled. "What if I didn't love her? What if I can't love anyone?"

"Everyone handles things differently. That doesn't mean you didn't love her." Chrys pressed her feet against his. Her eyes rested and she snuggled closer. In the silence Row could feel her heart beat, feel it pound. Sundew's words returned to his head. He needed to leave this town, maybe then he could rid himself of the awful memories.

They left early the next morning due mostly to Row's insistence. They'd fallen asleep to the movie like pigs in blankets, covered in pastry crumbs. At some point Row rolled onto a fork but otherwise he couldn't complain. Well, he didn't complain at least, he was too busy thinking about leaving.

Their drive home felt shorter. It started to rain when they left, a drizzle that didn't stop no matter how close they got to the city. Chrys kept her window open the whole while, enjoying the water splashing on her face. Paved roads and highways and worn away billboards found them again.

They stopped at a burger joint on the way back. Row stuffed his face with the deep-fried cardboard passing for French fries and a burger squished into a yellow tissue wrapping. The bun was dry and dense, and the burger was thin, more grease than meat. But he ate every bite. The bitter, chemical taste of fast food was a cleanser.

Chrys didn't find the meal as cathartic. She ate a bowl of tomatoes and iceberg lettuce they were trying to pass off as a salad. As a thank you, Row promised to take her to the all-day breakfast after church.

After finishing their burger and "salad", they headed back on the road. The rain looked to have let up, though that may have been the dark. They drove in the direction of the suburban sprawl and found their teal house. Chrys hopped out of the car and danced across the driveway puddles. Row rolled his eyes and ducked to the front door. He got there relatively dry, while Chrys stood in a puddle with eyes closed and head tipped back.

"You feel that Row?" She smiled. "The city missed us so much it's crying."

Row unlocked the front door and went in, Chrys and the city clearly were having a moment. They were like two old friends meeting in an airport. The house didn't appear to miss Row. They acknowledged one another, then Row went to check emails. He and the house's relationship was more akin to jaded spouses. Row paid the bills while the house cost money and looked pretty.

Once inside, Chrys embraced the first wall she could. "I know, I missed you too!" She giggled. Her feet were wet from puddle jumping, she left footprints everywhere she pranced. "Lucas! Markus! Claudia!" She kissed the fish tank. "You wouldn't believe the trip we had!"

The fish said nothing back. They were just normal fish.

Normal. It almost brought a smile to Row's face. It would be normal for a very long time now. Honey Walls belonged to Sundew and slipped away from his memories.

"Éclairs for a Claire." Dan met Claire the afternoon after the funeral. In his hands was a box of his grandmother's hearty éclairs. They were closer to an apple fritter with a cream cheese glaze, but Claire appreciated puns more than French culinary standards.

"Don't mind if I do." She smirked, taking a pastry before sitting on the bookstore steps.

Dan took a seat beside her, leaning back on his palms. Notebooks were piled into his delivery bag. Serious small-town journalism was afoot.

Claire snatched a book from his bag, reviewing the notes he'd made on Rose. "How's the obituary going?"

"Claire!" He grabbed at his notebook. "I don't have copies, be careful."

"Oh, don't be a big baby. I'm not going to ruin anything. I'm making sure you're not making any mistakes." She jabbed his side with her elbow. "I mean if you mess it up, this whole town will chase you out. We're talking pitchforks and torches. The town loved her."

"No kidding." He laughed, but sweat collected on his brow. "It's harder than I expected. You'd be surprised by how little people know about her."

"How so?" She took a bite of pastry and could feel cavities forming. "You still too chicken to talk to Sundew?"

"She creeps me out."

"She's not *that* creepy," Claire tried to say with a straight face.

Dan snorted in response. "Everyone's suggesting I talk to you. You're the only one that tolerated Sundew enough to visit Rose."

"Pardon?" Her brows tightened. "No one else visited her? But she's been sick so long…"

"Yep." Dan looked away. "It was just you, and your dad before that." His concern shifted into a gentle smile, offering up a fresh eclair.

Claire refused the pastry, the intention behind them abundantly clear. Buttering her up for the sake of his story. It almost brought a smile to her cheeks, but the idea of Rose spending her last days alone left a dreary feeling.

"Why would no one go to visit her? Are they really that opposed to Sundew?"

"I know, it really doesn't add up." His arms crossed over his bag, his chin resting down on the canvas. "The whole town was there for the memorial, and yet everyone I talked to… they all hadn't seen her in years."

"No one?" She looked down at the notes and skimmed. Dan's notes were a mess of shorthand, his cursive slurred. "Rose never told me people didn't visit, I would have dragged them by the teeth."

"I can believe it," he said. "I've been trying to get hold of Row, but he's not answered." He flipped the pages, from Azalea to Ms. Birch, no one had visited. "And forget getting hold of Aster. No one knows where he disappeared to."

"The deadbeat?" Claire choked. "As if he'd be useful."

"True, but I'm really grasping at straws." Dan shut the notebook.

Claire pressed a hand to his knee. "You really only have to write what people want to hear. I was kidding earlier, Cherrywood will eat up any schmaltzy piece you write." She closed the box of treats before she stuffed her face further. "That or you talk to Sundew."

Dan stood up, the worry washing over his face. He smoothed the crumbs from his sweater. "It looks like I'll have to. Does she have a favourite flower? That might help things."

"Not that I know of, but you can't go wrong with roses."

He nodded. "Roses, sounds good."

"Oh!" Claire stood. "If you are going to Honey Walls, would you mind getting a story for me?"

"A story?"

"Yeah, Rose's last story, she was working on it before she died. I want to read the ending." Claire hung her head. "If you could save me the Sundew thing, that'd be great."

"Fine." He slung his bag over his shoulder. "But you owe me, Book Girl."

Chapter Seven

Boring and Depressing Places to Spend a Sunday Afternoon

The Man and the Mermaid

by Sundew Gareau

Once there was a man who lived by the sea with his wife. His wife was tall and fair, with dark hair that moved like liquid. The man, however, was fat and ugly, and only loved by his strange wife. Together they lived in a small house so close to the sea it splashed their deepest dreams.

In the mornings, his wife would raise the sun with her voice. She would dance by the water, and start the waves. The man, who was nothing special, would watch his wife from their window. He'd prepare fresh fish for her breakfasts, lunches and dinners. When she came back inside, she'd bring the sunshine with her, tangled with her hair.

And so, every day was happy.

At least, every day was happy until they weren't. The man woke late one morning to find there was no sun in the sky, no wife in his bed. He ran to the window and through the darkness he couldn't see her dance. The man ran, and on the beach he found his beautiful wife.

There were dark clouds caught in her hair which now lay in the sand. The night had stirred the waves and she'd been carried under the sea. Dragged deep into the shadows. She drank the dark waters with her lungs, and his wife was now dead. As he reached to touch her, the clouds began to rain. The sky so dark and rain so thick, it was the last he saw his wife again.

It was exactly what he deserved.

The rain was getting stronger, and there weren't any signs of it letting up. Row woke a little later in the morning and found Chrys pacing around downstairs. Her feet were wet again, from early morning puddle jumping, but her hair seemed dry. She often got anxious before church. She said it was from letting herself open for the spirit world.

Row sat at his desk, glancing up occasionally at Chrys as she paced. Work had piled up in his absence, an endless parade of illustrations needed for some detestable project. He'd much preferred to format text, but found himself drawing hedgehogs for some sort of children's book. He really was not in a hedgehog mood.

"Row." Chrys stomped down in front of him. "I think I'm going to do a sermon today."

"That's nice," Row said, but focused on his sketches.

"I need you to come, for moral support."

"You'll do great. I'm busy."

"It's Sunday. Please, then we can walk down to breakfast afterwards."

"I need to work or we won't be able to pay for breakfast."

Chrys scowled, "We'll be fine."

Row rolled his eyes.

Chrys latched onto him. "Please, please, please, with chocolate chips and honey and a really super delicious cherry on top."

She rocked Row back and forth as she pleaded. With a sigh, he gave in and set his pencil down. "This better be the most amazing sermon you've ever done."

She hugged him. "I'll try, but no promises."

The name of their denomination seemed to always be changing. It was one of those new age places, more focused on meditation than the words of Jesus Christ. In fact, Row didn't know what their standing on the holy trinity or anything was. It may have had to do with his tendency to fall asleep.

By the time they reached the church, Chrys was soaked. She'd walked in front of Row the whole time, and splashed through the puddles. Meanwhile he'd stayed safe under his umbrella. They snuck inside the church as the morning hymn began. Row took his seat far in the back, while Chrys made her way to the altar.

There weren't many more than twenty of them, and near all of them regulars. It was a makeshift church inside a studio flat. The chairs were the uncomfortable plastic kind, lined up into about five rows and an aisle. Up front near the podium, Chrys sat amongst three other speakers.

Reverend Samantha took the podium, engaging the crowd in yet another song. The crowd stood, mumbling words. Chrys's voice was the clearest and most beautiful, ringing louder than the rest.

Another song followed.

And another.

Row squinted behind Chrys at the chalkboard, their scrawled out itinerary. The last song would lead into the guided meditation and healing portion. This was the part at which Row usually fell asleep. They all sat, eyes closed as Reverend Samantha told them to imagine they were trees expelling the negativity from their leaves. Row managed to stay awake long enough to "cleanse the throat chakra."

A few minutes later, Chrys roused him.

"Huh?" He looked around. Everyone's eyes were still shut and there were now four chairs at the front of the room. Three were filled with older ladies and a gentleman receiving healings. Reverend Samantha was quiet now, letting the background music do the work.

"You're sleeping," Chrys whispered as she grabbed Row's arm.

"Meditating."

"Snoring." She pulled him to his feet. "It's time to get your healing."

"You're going to heal me?" Row scoffed. "It would be less embarrassing if we did this at home."

"You need healing to keep evil spirits away. They love feeding on grief, and you're so susceptible"

He rolled his eyes. "What a load of nonsense."

She rolled her eyes back at him and led him to the front of the room. The firmness of her touch put him on edge and she sat him in a free seat. "Fox is going to heal you." She motioned to Fox. "Ze's been studying under me, you know? I think ze has a gift."

Then Chrys abandoned him, headed back to her seat. She looked rigid, maybe stage fright as her time for predictions approached.

"May I put my hands on you?" Fox interrupted his thoughts.

"No," he said and closed his eyes (more from embarrassment than for relaxation).

The healing didn't feel like anything. Row had watched healings before and easily pictured zir moving zir hands around his body. Ze would hover over certain parts, imagine ze was magically fixing them. As the healing service concluded, Fox whispered into his ear, "You should see me later, there's something definitely wrong inside." Then he was sent back to his seat.

The knots of tension he felt went away the further he got from the front of the room.

"As always, we send healing thoughts to the names placed in the healing bowl who are not able to be with us." Samantha concluded the healing service. "We now welcome our resident medium Chrysocolla for today's sermon and readings."

Chrys smiled and walked up to the podium. She looked for Row in the audience, and when their eyes met, she appeared calmer. "Thank you, Reverend Samantha. If any of you are new to the service, I hope you can bear with me. I don't exactly have anything prepared." Chrys took a deep breath, shutting her eyes. "I was channeling a spirit this morning, and they—" *Cough. Cough. Cough.* She covered her mouth but kept coughing. "Sorry."

"Do you need water?" Samantha offered her a glass.

Chrys nodded and took the water. She sipped as she clasped onto her chest. "Sorry, what was I saying?" She looked pale, falling onto her hands. Row leaned forward on his seat, as did everyone else.

"The vision… it's coming through clear now." She tightly closed her eyes.

"There's an ocean, it's so deep. I can see shadows beneath me." Chrys's fingers dripped with the water she'd coughed up. Her face was pale, her brow glinted with sweat.

Chrys sniffled and coughed again, then she retched. Clear water spilled into her hands, and dripped on the floor. Her breaths were short, warbled and choked. Gasping, she grabbed onto the podium and she tried to say something. But nothing came out. Her lips were faintly blue.

Row reached for his phone, but other hurried hands beat him to it. For the second time in only a few days, an ambulance was on its way.

A long time ago, Rosie was sitting in a hospital waiting room. She spent a lot of her childhood in hospital waiting rooms. This was because Rosie's mom was very, very sick. Sometimes, she would get out of school early to visit her. The adults in her life kept acting like she would disappear one day.

So Rosie would sit, bunching her dress in her hands, fidgeting as the clock ticked and she tried to remember her numbers. Most times, she brought craft paper and crayons. But it made her saddest that she couldn't bring flowers. It was against policy, but she knew if her mom saw flowers she'd be better.

Hospitals were like dungeons, the kind princesses are taken to by ogres. Rosie would hold Oxnard close, hoping the brave adventurer would protect her. She'd squeeze him so hard his stuffing would come out. Then Mr. Waters would come back and lead Rosie inside.

Her mom would be lying there under a thin white sheet, tubes in her arms, in her nose. Rosie had a little chair by her bed. It was just tall enough for her to rest a bit on the mattress.

Quietly her mother would say, "Come closer, Rosie."

And Rosie would. She'd shift her seat and look right in her mother's eyes.

Her mom would shake her head, a smile always starting. "I mean even closer."

And Rosie would move even closer, right up until her head was in her mom's hand.

"My darling Rose," she'd say, and Rosie would close her eyes. "Did I ever tell you the story of how the stars got in the sky?'

"No, how'd it happen?"

"Come lay with me, and I'll tell you," she'd say with a smile.

Rosie would crawl into bed and rest in her mom's arms. Oxnard would squish between them and her mom would tell the story. Rosie would draw her gardens to make her happy. And her mother would teach her things, like to make paper birds, butterflies and flowers. At some point her mom would fall asleep and Rosie wouldn't follow.

Adults said their time was precious, so Rosie wouldn't sleep until Mr. Waters took her home.

The hospital felt larger from the other side of things, more mechanical. There was a buzz to it. Not life, just movement, electrical currents. Row sat in the waiting room. Though bigger and fuller, it still felt like the old times. It was the most relatable room, where air always felt like sludge.

He dropped his head in his hands, covering his eyes, in hopes it'd dim his thoughts. *It was just a cough,* he persuaded himself. She hadn't choked on the water. No one choked on water. Okay, people choked on water all the time. But no one choked on a sip… but the choking wasn't the problem. It was something before "her vision"—No, that thought was just as ridiculous.

"You miserable, rotten, heartless, boy! What did you do to my daughter!?"

Row was struck on the head. He'd never seen Zelda outside of her apartment. She was short, glowering at him with her hand tense around the closed canopy of her umbrella.

"I said, what did you do?" Zelda raised her umbrella menacingly.

"Nothing," he replied, rubbing the sore spot on his head. "She was just channeling one of those spirits of yours when she started to choke."

"My spirits? Don't you even joke, we've only ever channeled good spirits." Zelda glared down at him, prodding him in the chest with her umbrella. "This is you. Your fault. I know the kind of nasty creatures that nest where that heart of yours should be."

He felt the empty spot. *Did Zelda know about his heart? Or was it an expression?* He didn't have time to ask and answered with, "I didn't hurt Chrys."

"You better not have hurt Chrys, for your own sake. If Chrys is hurt, I will never forgive you, I will never ever forgive myself for not convincing her to leave. I will curse you and hex you!" She kept prodding him.

"She's fine, Zelda." He backed up. "How about you take a seat?" He offered the chair beside himself.

She glared, but took the seat. She was bundled in a shawl and scarves. Her skirt was long and rested on the ground. That was the thing about Zelda, no matter the weather she was always bundled in layers. Her fingers clasped around the canopy, water drying in her hands as she stared down at her feet.

"She's my only daughter," she said. "You're not a parent, you don't understand. One day, when you have kids, you'll understand."

"I think I do," Row said, quietly, not as bold as Chrys. "I mean, I have my own mother. And it's not as though I haven't known Chrys for a long time now."

"You know Chrys?" She huffed. "I, for one, have a heart. So please, let me be the one to explain this to you. You don't know Chrys."

His mouth dried. She sounded like she meant it this time. "What do you mean I don't have a heart?"

Zelda folded her arms. "You haven't noticed? It must have happened when you were young then, and if that's the case, I almost feel bad for you." Her eyes shut as she searched for her next words. "I've known since the moment I met you, that's a man with no heart. That is a husk of a human being, a puppet, an emotionless robot. I'd imagine a spirit took it."

"I… I have feelings, Zelda." He felt the weight of his emptiness once again.

"Really?" Her eyebrow cocked. "Or do you believe that because you've never known anything else?"

He glanced at the familiar faces of the hospital personnel. He'd hardly noticed them staring at him. The heartless man. People couldn't exist without hearts. The notion was ridiculous. *That night was nothing more than a dream.* He failed to convince himself.

"If I were in your position, I'd traverse the world to find that spirit that stole my heart. Though I suppose that'd require passion."

"I love Chrys. I wouldn't be here if I didn't," he muttered in vain.

"You don't believe in spirits, prediction, meditation, how can you know Chrys when you don't even believe in her world? You can't."

"There's more to her than all of that."

"Hm, true, but do you even know that? Tell me, put my mind to rest and I'll leave you be. What kind of person is my daughter?"

The question was ludicrous. Chrys was… Chrys. She didn't need an explanation. She was soft, but excitable. She loved to dance and dance loved her. There didn't need to be a purpose to it, any more than there was, she was there simply to be. She liked to watch movies to watch Row's reactions, to lie with him and… Chrys didn't need words. She didn't need Row to define her.

"Nothing? Hm… What about you, Row? What's beneath all of your pleasantries? What kind of man are you? And does she know?"

Row had never spent so much time with Zelda, and he imagined he never would again.

It was creeping up on one o'clock. Neither Row nor Zelda had heard anything. Row's stomach was starting to growl. He leaned back in the stiff chair, imagining the breakfast they had planned at Tina's Diner. The greasy spoon was one of their favourite places. On Sunday, it was all day breakfasts, over thirty different pancakes and waffles, each more delicious than the last. It wasn't Cherrywood bakery level good, but it was humble.

Chrys liked to eat this one waffle with a tower of coconut whipped cream, strawberries, chocolate chips, and a drizzle of hot fudge. While he didn't have a go-to, he felt like today was a good day for honey on waffles.

He yawned. Zelda had dosed off beside him. The woman and Row at least had that in common. They both were roused awake at a pattering of footsteps. A familiar doctor approached them with clipboard in hand. Her eyes looked heavy, jaded, or maybe just tired. "Mrs. Piper?" she asked and Zelda sat right up.

"Yes, that's me, do you have any news on my daughter?"

"I'm her boyfriend," Row offered and Zelda glared.

"Oh… well, Mrs. Piper, we have some bad news. Your daughter didn't make it."

"Pardon?" Zelda scowled. "What do you mean she 'didn't make it'?"

"She stopped breathing. There was too much damage from lack of oxygen, and she didn't make it."

Row stood from his seat. "Oh… um… thank you for your efforts."

"No! Excuse me, but this is ridiculous." Zelda pushed the umbrella against the doctor. "Did you even go to school for this? Fix my daughter."

"Zelda, don't assault the lady," Row said, pulling the umbrella from her hands.

"Of course! A heartless man and an idiot doctor! Oh! The company I'm in,

I swear." Zelda snatched at the umbrella but Row kept it far from her.

"Zelda, you need to calm down, I'm sure that everyone here has a thorough and rigorous education."

The doctor nodded. "My condolences. I can take you to see her if you want."

Row nodded. His mouth was dry, head spinning and sorting the details.

"This is nonsense," Zelda uttered, before she followed the doctor anywhere.

Row tried to remember the feeling of reading the invitation to his mom's funeral. He imagined his "heart attack" as if it were his emotions bubbling and boiling. But now there wasn't bubbling, there wasn't even heat. If he ever had emotions, they were now evaporated.

The hospital hallway felt longer with each step. He dragged his feet along, eventually turning to find Chrys. Zelda ran to her but Row held back. There was a long-held disagreement amongst the old ladies in Cherrywood on whether corpses look asleep. After seeing Chrys, Row now sided against Mrs. Applegate. Corpses, especially the fresh ones, look exactly like they are asleep.

Chrys's eyes were shut, fingers entwined with Zelda's. Row stood far from the bed in the shadow of the doorway. As Zelda wept, everything about him drained. Everything. Chrys was as empty as he was. She rested on a bed of her dark hair, her cheeks pale. Row's fingers trembled to touch her, but what was the point?

He left for breakfast. What else was he supposed to do?

Chapter Eight

Consolatory Flowers, Waffles, and Kidnappings

The Fletcher bakery lined its windows with rose-themed pastries. Apple rose tarts, rose water cupcakes, and a wedding cake with sweeping boughs of magnolia sugar flowers. The bell chimed as Claire entered the building, causing Mrs. Fletcher to look up from a tray of chocolate cupcakes.

"Claire, did you have an order?" She swirled pink frosting into closed petals.

"No, I'm here for Dandelion."

The icing fell to the counter, a wild smile taking over Mrs. Fletcher. "You and Dandy have a date?"

"God, no!" Claire snorted. Dan's hairy arms made her skin crawl. His grandmother didn't appear to think the same way, her brow twitching. "Er... I mean, I'm here to check on his article and maybe try one of those cupcakes."

The diversion hardly worked, Mrs. Fletcher's lip curling in. "He's really got a crush on you, you know? And the pair of you would make some handsome children."

Claire shuddered. "I'll talk to him about it. Where is he?"

"He's not here. He went to Honey Walls to console Sundew." She returned to the cupcakes, frosting them with swift circular movements. "I haven't seen him since yesterday."

The cupcakes rested on the plate, judging Claire. They wanted her to go on a date with Dandelion. Claire, however, didn't have anything to say on the matter. The option of being the baker's wife was hardly a new prospect. They'd practically been betrothed since the day Claire had offered him a purple crayon — clearly a pinnacle moment in a romance for the centuries.

"I hope Sundew is okay." Claire sighed. As creepy as she was, she didn't want her to be hurt.

"Sundew will get through it, I'm certain." Mrs. Fletcher's hands were steady, sturdy. She'd been the town's rock a dozen times over, ever since the death of Dan's father — her son.

"I already miss Rose," Claire said. "I can't imagine what Sundew's going through."

"I imagine that's where Dan still is, he's a gentleman to all damsels in distress."

Claire nodded. Dan was as soft as spongecake. "I think I'll go down too. And maybe you could give me a discount on some cupcakes?"

"Discounts?" she said, tilting up her nose. "Maybe, if you're thinking of dating Dan."

Claire paid in full.

White flowers bloomed along the road to Honey Walls. The edges of each petal blushed pink. The little flowers were soft and mourning, their stems sticky, sprouting off of barbed vines. Claire picked a small bouquet, tying them together with a pink ribbon she found in the wild grass near the apple tree.

Honey Walls stood at a distance, looking greyer than usual, the golden glint diluted. Claire made her way to the door and stood beneath the canopy of magnolias. The wilting petals fell as she knocked. After three or so knocks, silence followed. She waited in the shadow of the house, bathed in an apparent dreariness (though perhaps it was in her head).

Sundew opened the door. Her hair was now in a braid, but she didn't look any less haggard than when she'd been at the funeral. A scowl, as always, was plastered on her face. "Oh." She groaned. "More flowers, I couldn't have guessed."

"Huh… are you at capacity?" Claire handed her the flowers. Sundew's grip was limp, allowing the blooms to fall to the floor.

"It's fine, at least they aren't roses." She pinched the bridge of her nose. Vases and pots of roses covered the tables, the overflow spotted along the carpet.

"Oh wow, you're not kidding." Claire craned her neck to peer inside, while Sundew blocked most of the view. "I'm not exactly sure what those flowers are, it's the first time I've seen them."

Sundew bent down slightly, bringing the discarded bouquet to her nose. "Sundews." Her breath drew the flowers to her skin, the silken petals brushing her cold features. Then she dug her nail into the stems. "They've always grown here."

"I never noticed." Claire strained to remember them, but all she could remember were marigolds and forget-me-nots.

"Of course you didn't." She grimaced. "What are you doing here?"

"Looking for Dan." Claire looked over Sundew's shoulder, skimming the roses for one that looked most like a gift from Dan. "He never came back to the bakery. Did he bring you roses?"

"I don't recall. But I wouldn't be surprised."

"I'll check." Claire attempted to push past her, and sort through the roses.

"I'd prefer you not." Sundew's hand clasped Claire's wrist, blocking her out of the house.

"I'll only be a—"

"No."

"Sundew." Claire huffed. "I don't see what the big deal is, I just want to know if he stopped by here. It's not like I think you kidnapped him or anything."

She didn't respond. The loose strands of hair shadowed her face, escaping her braid as if by magic. There was perfume to her hair, dry like pollen. Her lips heavy and dark, eyes brushed raw at the edges.

Claire felt the coldness of Sundew's expression run up her spine. "Dan's not in there, is he?"

"Do I look like I'm hiding something?" she snapped. "I have no idea where he could be, and I'd have no reason to keep that idiot around."

Claire furrowed her brow. "Well, that sure doesn't sound suspicious."

"What?" Sundew gasped. "Honestly, what kind of person do you think I am?"

"Fine." Claire sighed. Maybe she was jumping to conclusions. "But there's something else, Sundew."

Sundew's lip twitched.

"Rose said that she was finishing a story, and I really would like to see it. You wouldn't mind if I had a quick look around?"

"Absolutely not."

"I wouldn't disturb anything."

She clasped Claire's arm with nails like thorns, pushing her through the doorway. "Can you not just leave me to mourn?" The intensity of her conviction burned in her irises.

As Sundew pushed her forward, she left an opening to view beyond her. Inside the living room, Rose's writing closet was shut. The door hadn't been shut as long as Claire had been alive. One of the oakwood dining chairs was wedged beneath the doorknob. Claire's mouth dried, darting her eyes from the detail. "My apologies, Sundew, I'll leave you to your mourning."

Sundew didn't wait a moment, slamming the door in Claire's face.

Righty, the large grey cat, guarded the back entrance to Honey Walls. He sat on a lawn chair next to a stone urn that spilled over with petunias. Sniffing casually and yawning, his tail swayed as Claire approached. He licked the dust from his fur and looked into her eyes. His irises were pink, as if he were a really dusty albino.

"Sorry," Claire whispered to the cat. She'd caught Rose's bad habit of talking to animals. "I don't want to bother you, but I need to get in there. Front door's locked."

The cat understandably said nothing back. His eyes softened and his tail wrapped around his front paws. Behind Righty was a seldom used metal door. Vines coiled up along its mesh window, with flowers that bloomed like a magenta waterfall.

Claire sidled past the lawn chair as Righty growled. "I'm breaking in for a good reason, I swear."

The cat didn't care, swatting at her as she passed.

"Hey, I think your friend in there kidnapped Dan." Claire scowled. She couldn't imagine any reason why someone would kidnap Dan. Yet, she didn't put it past Sundew to do something so strange.

Vines broke as Claire pried open the door. The back entrance led in through an indoor garden storage. Cobwebs draped over bags of expired fertilizer, rusted trowels, and old rakes. The storage was packed wall to wall, with a narrow path connecting the doors. The tight fit reminded Claire of her family's bookstore, and she moved through it quite naturally.

Claire expected the dark of the hall to end when she entered the kitchen, but even inside things were gloomy. The only light came in through the windows, sunlight dappled by the plants which grew on the building. Claire entered slowly, dispersing the weight of her feet as carefully as she could. The steps softened the creaks of the hardwood, but the whole house settled in discomforted moans.

Claire made her way back to the living room, heading straight to the den. The chair was still jammed under the doorknob of the closet. The movement of the handle had worn away its varnish. She removed the chair quietly and gently, as if it were a sleeping puppy she didn't want to play with. Then she rattled the doorknob… but it was locked.

Rapping softly, Claire whispered. "You in there, Dan?"

"Claire." Papers rustled. "Is Sundew gone?"

"Gone-ish." She checked over her shoulder. "I think she went upstairs. What are you doing in there?"

"Writing a story." He made a little sad laugh. "Sundew's as crazy as I remembered."

"Writing?" The keyhole was too dark to see through. "Odd timing, Dandy."

"It's not my idea!" He strained to keep to a whisper. "Sundew's obsessing over it. She asked me to look it over and next thing I knew I was locked in the cupboard."

"Give me a second." Claire attempted to force the door. She threw herself against the wood. It barely rattled. "Yeah, I'm no help." She ran a finger across the keyhole. "I'll have to find the key or get some help."

"You're better off getting help. There's something off about her, Claire, like more than normal."

Claire huffed and looked out into the living room. Honey Walls was far from endless. Through the darkened corners and streaks of sunlight, the key couldn't be that hidden. "I bet it's in Sundew's room," she said, ignoring Dan's idea.

"Claire, if we both end up in the cupboard, then what?"

"This is silly, I'm not afraid of Sundew." She glared at the door. It looked about as patronizing as Dan probably did.

"Claire…"

"Fine. I'll go get help. Just wait and don't touch any of Rose's stories."

Claire turned away from the den and made her way for the stairs and Sundew's room. It's not like Dan could tell the difference.

The railings that led upstairs looked straight down into the main hallway. Claire slid her hand along the rail, winding up into the top floor where the bedrooms were. Below her, shadows rose along the walls, clawing upward like evil spirits in a children's cartoon.

Light pooled from a window at the top of the stairs. The magnolias filtered the light, softening the edges of shadows. Claire's last steps creaked. She stood still to regain the silence, listening for Sundew—

"Meoooow!"

Claire jumped. The cat followed her up the stairs, stepping in front of her. As large as he was, he walked relatively silent.

"How'd you get in?" Claire scowled, reaching out to pet him as he approached.

He leaned into her with all his weight, seeming to want to push her back. While strong for a cat, it didn't set her off balance or anything.

"I don't have time for cuddles."

He continued to push up against her, rubbing his head on her leg with force.

"You wouldn't happen to know where the cupboard key is?" she asked.

In a snap, Righty darted down the stairs.

"What are you doing in here?" Sundew loomed from the top of the steps, a shadow filling the house like a breath.

"I've got a better question, what are you doing with Dan in your cupboard?!"

Her lip twitched. "He's writing a story."

"Voluntarily?" Claire folded her arms. "Because that's not the way it looks."

Sundew's cheeks paled. She postured herself like a willow, her glowering figure nothing more than a defence. Her eyes were redder than earlier.

"What's so important about this story?" Claire asked.

Sundew used her hair as a curtain to hide her expressions. "If I'm to keep the stories, there are some loose ends I need to tie up."

"And you think Dan can do that?" Claire rolled her eyes. "He's only interested in reporting. Fiction isn't his thing."

She twisted her bang into a thin braid. "I'm not looking for a complete fiction."

"Unless it's an article, I don't think it matters."

Sundew grimaced. "What about you? Do you think you could do a better job?"

"I know I could." She scowled. "But I'm not going to."

"What if I let Dan go?" The way her lips softened without smiling set Claire off balance.

"What do you mean? You weren't planning to keep him forever, were you?" Claire gripped the railing.

"If I let him free, do you think he'd come back?"

Claire paled at the thought. "And what, you didn't expect people to get worried about him?"

"You'd be surprised what you can make people forget."

Claire backed up. As more shadow washed over her, she felt paler and sicker. "W-what are you talking about?"

"Do you want to find out?" Sundew's hand met Claire's on the railing. Her thorny nails dug in deeper. "I don't care which one of you it is. But I need a writer here to finish these stories."

Claire yanked at her arm, but Sundew's grip was unyielding. "Can't you write your own stories?" She glared back.

"That isn't important." She hissed. "Who will it be? You or Dan?"

Claire felt her heart flutter. Dan was too soft for something like this, too unequipped to deal with Sundew. Claire could escape on her own. And if she couldn't, she could at least find the ending to Oxnard's story.

"Fine." Claire glared up at Sundew. "I'll write your stupid stories."

Row sat across from Chrys's decadent waffle. The whipped cream was melting beneath the hot fudge. The chocolate chips rested in pooled cream, while he nibbled on a slice of brown bread with honey. Something felt inappropriate about skipping the breakfast he'd promised Chrys, so he'd taken a taxi down to the restaurant.

It rained harder when he left the hospital. He wasn't in a rush and allowed the cab to meander. The rain was thick, blurring every second after the wipers swiped. It wasn't until he reached the restaurant that he realized he still had Zelda's umbrella. His stomach sank when he looked at it. He didn't want to face Zelda again.

Water puddled beneath him where his shoes and pants dripped. He set the honey toast back on the plate, stirring his coffee absently. The rain pelted on the windows, obscuring the outside world. It was as if he was underwater.

"Row!" Fox appeared from behind him, worming zir way into the seat across from him. "Is Chrys okay? I've been so worried about her."

Ze looked entirely stiff, leaned on the palms ze placed on the table.

"You know, it's kind of funny," Row said, despite not knowing what was funny about the situation at all, "but she's not okay, she's dead."

"What?" Fox froze. "Are you serious?"

"I wouldn't joke. I think she asphyxiated, but I didn't stay for the details."

Fox's eyes brimmed with tears. It was strange to see, ze usually was filled with passion. Self-confidence. Though, maybe ze was just normal... unlike him.

"Fox." He offered his hand. "Please don't cry, it'll be okay."

Fox nodded and sniffled, trying to stop zir makeup from running.

Row offered zir his clean napkin, "Please don't cry." He swallowed and cleared the dryness from his throat. "Help yourself to some waffles, I don't think I can eat all that."

Fox blew zir nose into the napkin. "I don't want to eat your waffle, it's yours. You need it."

"If I needed it, I wouldn't offer it. Go ahead, I don't even know why I ordered the thing."

"Because you're sad, you need the most cheerful delicious food on the planet right now. Oh my god, Row. I'm so sorry."

Ze slid the waffles forward, but Row stopped them with his hand. "I'm not sad. I don't want the waffles, those are your waffles."

"What do you mean you aren't sad?"

He shrugged before sliding the plate towards zir once again. "I'm just not. If anything, I'm a little amused by the coincidence of it all."

Fox narrowed zir eyes. "Coincidence?"

"I just came back from my mother's funeral yesterday. It's like a practical joke from the cosmos."

"That's... that's so messed up." Fox lowered zir head, searching the plate. "I can't imagine — can I pay for the meal? You know, it's that or I'll get you flowers."

"You'll get me flowers anyways, everyone's going to get me flowers."

Fox leaned forward and cut a chunk of the waffle with zir fork. Cream and syrup spilled from the broken pool. Ze offered him the forkful but he turned his head away. Fox ate it. Ze chewed the bite slowly, contemplating. Then ze continued wiping zir nose on the napkin and cleaned the chocolate syrup from the corners of zir lips.

Outside, the rain was getting heavier, running down the windows, and painting them silver like mirrors.

"I was really afraid of water when I was a kid," he said, pointing to the reflecting surface. "Drowning and stuff."

Fox set the fork down.

"My sister used to hold me under the water. When Chrys started to choke, it felt like she was holding me again. I just couldn't do anything."

Fox trailed zir eyes to the window, trying to understand. But ze couldn't, not even Row could.

"Fox, you have to walk home, don't you?"

Ze nodded.

Row offered Zelda's umbrella. "I'm taking a taxi back, the last thing I'd want is for you to get sick."

"I can't take your umbrella," Fox gasped.

"Don't worry. I'll be fine."

Fox bit zir lip. "Okay, I don't want to strand you out in the rain. But if you're sure, I'll make sure get it back as soon as I can."

"Don't worry."

Ze nodded back, and reached out for his hand. Fox was warm, lingering for a moment as ze let out fresh tears. "I'll get you flowers," ze promised, "and your umbrella."

Then Fox left, following Row with zir eyes as ze disappeared into the opaque downpour. The melted cream dribbled from the corner of the leftover waffle. Row rested his chin in his hands, contemplating a shave while he waited for the waiter to clear his plates. The waiter offered to pack the waffle for Chrys to eat later and Row couldn't say no.

The wait in the hospital had eaten up most of Row's day. It was around five o'clock when he left the diner. He waited for a taxi outside under the lip of the roof. Chrys and him had a car but, mostly because of Chrys, they walked places. They rarely touched it until a road trip, or when the weather got way too cold, and of course when there was shopping to be done. The back seats got most use transporting new plants and worms for the compost.

Had they ever planned for more? They'd talked on the rare occasion about one day getting married and having kids, the typical end to the modern fairy tale. But Row didn't mind the way things were. Flowers and fish, and his beautiful Chrysocolla… though maybe that was just another symptom of his heartlessness, that he'd never considered proposing.

A car drove through the puddle in front of him, splashing him in a wave from head to toe. Even the more cautious drivers were rippling waves in the deep puddles flooding the parking lot. Row's cab was no doubt stuck in the same clustered chaos. He checked his phone for the time. It was about six-thirty. Already half soaked, he squished his toes around in a sock swamp.

Row couldn't wait any longer.

He hopped off the curb into the thick of it, the rain blurring down so strong even his glasses couldn't protect his vision. Only a foot from the curb, he felt lost, deep in a maze. He shielded his eyes from the water dribbling down his forehead. Crossing the road to the pathway home, his feet sunk into an ankle-deep river. The streets were flooded.

The further he got from the diner, the worse the weather got. Lightning cracked the sky. It spread out above him like spider webs. When he was younger, his mom used to tell him not to be afraid of storms. She said that the more scared he got, the worse the storm would become.

Most of his times in storms were spent safely inside Honey Walls. He wasn't afraid of the thunder or lightning, just the water falling and falling forever.

He always imagined a biblical flood, and finally being drowned. But then his mother would take him into the cupboard without windows and they'd draw animals. Just him, Mom, and Oxnard.

Row wasn't afraid of the rain anymore, just the lightning and the tree branches rattling above him. His feet were pruny and chaffing in his shoes. The water level crept past his ankles. The walk was regretful, regret for ditching the taxi, ditching the umbrella, rain boots, and other things.

The rain soaked through his jacket, pants and shoes. He shivered as it pelted him. It felt icier. The house felt distant. The sky was dark, covered by the grey clouds. He tightened his hands around Chrys's waterlogged waffles and power walked the rest of the way home.

His fingers shivered around his keys, and he forced himself inside. Row's eyes still blurred with raindrops. His feet peeled from their shoes and socks, a mushy wet version of their former selves. He tried to wring himself out and not make a mess on the floor.

"Lukas, Markus, Claudia," he said "You are lucky to be fish."

He made his way upstairs, finding something warm to wear and a towel. The house was dark — Row wasn't the person that turned on the lights. He set the Styrofoam container onto Chrys's wardrobe. That smell, her clothes light with her ocean smell. He pulled one of her sweaters out of the closet.

"Please, just come home." He stood alone in the empty house, still damp, still cold. Water hit him from above. "No." He looked up. "No, not today."

There wasn't just one leak, the whole ceiling was dripping.

Chapter Nine

This Might be a Good Time to Admit Something Magical Could Possibly be Happening

The Man and the Mermaid

by Claire Waters

Once upon a time, there was a man who lived by the sea with his lovely wife. His wife was tall and fair, with dark hair that moved like liquid. Together they lived in a small house so close to the sea it splashed their deepest dreams.

In the mornings, his wife would raise the sun with her voice. She would dance by the water, and start the waves. The man, who was nothing special, would watch his wife from their window. He'd prepare fresh fish for her breakfasts, lunches and dinners. When she came back inside, she'd bring the sunshine with her, tangled with her hair and seawater.

And so, every day was happy.

At least, every day until the night grew jealous. The man woke late one morning and found there was no sun in the sky, no wife in his bed. He ran to the window and through the darkness he couldn't see her dance. The man ran, and on the beach he found his beautiful wife.

Dark clouds were caught in her hair which now lay in the sand. The darkness had stirred the waves and she'd been carried under by their anger. Dragged into the deep of the sea. She drank the dark waters with her lungs, and his wife was now dead. As he reached to touch her, the clouds rained. The sky so dark and rain so thick, it was the last he saw his wife again.

Day by day, minute by minute, the rain filled the sea. The water grew higher and higher, and the man's house flooded. He moved into the attic, then to the roof. And then he faced the dark sky. As the sea swallowed his home, he closed his eyes tightly, trying to remember his wife, her songs. Maybe her memory would be enough.

"Please come home," said the man to the sea.

There was silence. And then there was a song.

The sun rose slowly to the song of a mermaid. She, unlike the man's wife, was slow and subtle. The sun was skeptical of the shadow that shrouded her heart. The man ran to the shore, to the side of the beauty. She lay at the edge of the splashing waves, eyes sharp. Her face, for however distant, was that of his wife.

"Your face, your beauty, I know you," said the man, approaching the creature.

"And I know you." She reached up to the man, her fingers frail and cold.

"I thought I'd lost you," the man cried, embracing the beauty. "You're so cold."

"I was swept beneath the waves by the jealous ocean." She held the man in her frigid arms. "But I remember your face. Even when the darkness filled me, I remembered you."

"I'm so glad you remembered me." The man's eyes filled with tears. "I thought I lost you."

The mermaid stroked the man's cheek. "You haven't lost me, I'm right here."

And she was. They sat in the rising sun, waves splashing her scales and his toes. Her hair was wet, hanging over her shoulders. Her eyes rested past him, looking out on their little house. She was beauty, the light caught deep in her eyes. She ran her fingers through her hair and watched the man she loved.

"There is one thing I need to say," said the man. "Your tail, your scales are all so beautiful, but I fear that with our differences now we'll grow apart."

The mermaid nodded, continuing to caress the man.

"We're now of completely different worlds," he continued, looking deep into the mermaid's dark eyes.

"I understand, but it doesn't need to be that way. Two sides of the same coin, water and land. Take your hand in mine and follow me into the ocean."

The man stared deep into her eyes, looking for the trust he'd once held for his wife. The woman was different.

"If you follow me, I'll take you deep into the ocean, where shadows change mortal souls."

The man hesitated. In part he understood that his love was long gone, that no soul could shift its form. The jealous shadow overtook him.

"I don't know who you are," he said, finally taking her hand from his face. "Even the sun shows its trepidation, and I am nowhere near as wise as she." The man's fingers entangled in the mermaid's. "My love would never take me into that darkness, she would never suggest it. She is the light, she is my love."

At that moment, the spirit noticed once more a passion in the man's eyes. The spirit was a creature made of jealousy she had mistaken for love long ago. The man still holding onto her hand, she tugged on him. "You're so mistaken," she said, dragging him towards the wave. "I am your love, maybe not as she was, but I am at least her reflection. I at least deserve you."

The mermaid pulled and pulled but the man refused to budge.

"I don't want a reflection. I know better than to cheat myself."

The mermaid sneered, looking away from the man as she did. "Is there nothing I can do that can prove I am, at heart, your love?"

The man shook his head, while the mermaid thought of the sun. She thought of the girl, and of light, and of how she'd tricked it. And in these thoughts, a plan formed. She closed her eyes and sang. As the sun rose, the man faltered.

She trailed her fingers away from his, her touch lingering, a trail leading him. The man, so entranced by the song, followed her lingering path. The water surrounded her and the song continued to pierce through. The light and the man both entranced by her song.

And then, the shadow swallowed the light. Like any other light a mermaid steals, the man became a reflection, trapped beneath the water.

A reflection, the only thing worse than being drowned. He, a man with a mortal soul, never learned to escape. Trapped from reaching the other lights, he looked up at night, distant from the stars, his home, and the love of his life.

"Sundew!" Claire rattled the doorknob of the writing closet. "The story's done!"

She'd written the story in the writing cupboard. The tight walls reminded her of the bookstore, the perfect thing to kickstart her creativity. She wrote a mermaid story as Sundew instructed. Her rules were liberal. All she wanted was the man to drown, the rest was up to Claire.

The pen she'd given was formed for Rose's hand. The angle it preferred was steeper than Claire was used to. It fought quick movements, trying to savour the words. The stem bent in Claire's hand. It was soft, or maybe Claire pressed too hard. So hard she could feel her pulse. She swore she saw the pen glisten gold when she was most absorbed into her story. And when she lay it on the desk, her hand became cold.

Sundew took her time responding. For a long time, Claire was left to the silence of the dismal room. She took the time to skim Rose's notes. On every scrap was a new outline, paragraph, or idea. She searched for something that screamed "Oxnard's last chapter" but nothing popped out.

More time dragged by.

"Sundew!" Claire started pounding on the door. Sundew didn't respond, and Claire was no better at breaking down doors than before.

She needed to think about door destruction in a different light. The door faced outward, so the joints weren't anywhere near her reach. Based on her short intimate experiences, she knew the door was made of solid wood. There weren't any places it showed signs of give.

Her next attempt involved pretending she could pick locks. She shoved a pencil into the key hole until the lead broke. Shortly after, she retreated to the drawing board.

Rose's calligraphy was top notch. The tools for the job were precise, the nicest ruler Claire had ever seen being the most notable. It was thin enough to hug the table, and the lines it made required very little give. Claire jammed the fancy ruler between the door and the frame.

A few strikes up and down and the door jimmied open. She laughed, not expecting it to work. She hit the ruler to the door to show it who was boss.

To Claire's surprise, Sundew watched from the stairway. Her hair looked slept on, her eyes puffy from dried tears.

"The door was stuck." Claire smirked. "But the story is all finished. Now what?"

Sundew passed Claire, entering the story room. She skimmed the story, flipping the pages too fast to be reading but slow enough to care. Claire held onto the doorknob. All things considered, she was curious for a critique.

"It might need edits," she said without emotion. "I've made a room for you." Her hair coiled around their feet. The unruly locks looked longer.

Claire glanced to the front door. It was no doubt locked. "So, did Dan get home safely?"

"He did." Sundew glowered, snatching the ruler from her hands. "You're staying in Rose's old room. I don't want to see you snooping around."

Claire nodded. The window in Rose's room looked out on the lip of the roof. She could easily slip out and be done with things. After living under her mother's thumb, Claire was thoroughly equipped to escape a house. In the worst case, she'd need to break some glass.

"What's so important about these stories anyways?" she asked, humouring Sundew.

"They keep this town alive."

Claire tilted her head. "Keep it alive?"

"Yes, though honestly I don't know why I care." She rolled her eyes. "That story you wrote will just finish something I've been looking to do for years."

Claire scowled more. "Yeah, what?"

"Get rid of my sister."

Row went to bed with pots and pans. On his bed, on his floor, they sat catching drips with loud pings. Sleep came slowly, when the drips and thunder stopped bothering him. In a way, it was nice to have something else to think about, something other than the empty bed.

In a dream, he was back at Honey Walls. Across from him was a telescope, a midnight colour, that peered out the front window through the magnolias. When he approached, he felt how small he was, too short to reach the window. He stretched on his tiptoes, trying to look through the telescope, but the more he reached, the smaller he got.

The ceiling stretched taller, disappearing into a midnight sky. Above him were a thousand tiny stars, glinting far out of reach. The floor was gone from beneath him. There was only darkness. He grabbed onto the telescope, feeling tears warm on his cheeks.

"Just a little higher," said his mother. Her voice stung in his chest.

"Shush, you're safe where you are, Row," said a voice in the wakeful world. She pressed her hand to his cheek, cold.

"Chrys?" Row groaned, pushing himself up. The room was completely dark.

Chrys leaned closer, pushing him down into his bed. "It's late, Row, go back to bed."

"Am I dreaming?" He wiped his eyes, making out Chrys's face, her eyes bright and sharp. "Or... did I just wake up now?"

"You just woke up. You were having a bad dream, I think."

"Why wouldn't I be?" He lay back on the bed and rested his eyes. "Do you know the kind of week I've been having?"

"I know, I'm sorry." She kept petting his arm, her skin damp. "Was it about your mother or me?"

"No, it was about my dad's telescope. The thing never worked... and the stars..." He muttered. "Stars aren't like confetti, they burn you when you touch them."

"Burning confetti? That'd cause a lot of lawsuits."

"Not if they add a warning label or something," Row joked. "Star dust, burns right to the soul."

Chrys held onto him with her wet fingers. It was so dark. She squeezed his hand and he let her go.

"Chrys," Row said, looking at her eyes, which glistened in the shadows. "You're not here, are you? I want you to be here, but you can't be."

"Why can't I be?"

"Because..." he said, but the rest was too much to say.

"Yesterday morning? Yesterday, I had a vision. I was pulled into the sea, down into the deepest parts where the sea monsters and spirits live." Chrys hummed to herself. "I heard a voice. It's been calling to me for a while, but in the vision I could hear her clearly. She kept telling me to breathe."

"You were choking."

She shook her head. "Not then. That happened after I listened and I breathed the ocean in."

"But it was a vision, how could it… you know? Kill you."

"Because my visions are real, Row. Mom used to tell me how lucky I am, that I've never run into a malicious spirit, but yesterday I did. When I breathed in that water it was thick, something alive. It crawled inside me and my soul dissolved into the ocean."

"But you never went to the ocean." Row scowled. "Things don't happen like that. It's nonsense."

"I know, you don't understand. But please, Row, believe me. Believe me and get some rest, you look so tired. I'm going to ask my mother about this."

As Chrys retreated from his side, he sat up. He grabbed her hand as she turned to leave. "Wait." He pushed away his covers. "I know, I've never given your ghost talk the time of day, but if there's a way I can help, I'll do it." He stepped out of bed and his foot landed in a pot now full of water. "Shoot!" He put his other foot down, and when it got soaked too, he realized the whole floor was flooded.

"It's okay, Row!" Chrys gasped, grabbing his hand, pre-empting a panic.

His bed was standing in a pool of ankle-deep water. He pulled back, drying his feet on the bedsheets. Around him, the dark water gave its subtle glints.

"It stopped raining. You aren't going to drown," she said, pawing his arm.

"Drowning? What about our house? We're under water!" His chest tightened, the pang of over-boiling emotions beginning to burn.

"The house is fine, this isn't a normal rain."

"Well, that's obvious." He glared at the abnormal amounts of water.

"No, no, it's stranger than you think," she continued. "There are cars driving along the streets like the water isn't even there. It's completely ethereal. Like a ghost ocean. A ghost-cean."

Row groaned, pulling the sheets over his head.

"Welcome to my every day," Chrys pulled at the covers. "You'll be okay if you take a nap, I promise. You just sleep and I'll go see Mom, okay?"

"No." He held the covers over his head. "We'll go together. I don't want to lose you. I don't want to drown."

"I'll come back, and I promise you won't drown."

As she started to pull the covers from his head he turned away. "No, I'll go."

"Sorry, what did you say?" She tugged on the blanket more. "I can't hear through all your covers."

The blanket slid off of him and he turned back to Chrys with a playful glare.

"My beautiful Row."

"I'm already dead, aren't I? This is where the drowned people go when they die." He squished his cheeks, feeling for aliveness.

Chrys cupped his hands in hers. "I think you're very alive right now. And very, very cute."

"Cute? Excuse me for a very realistic fear of drowning."

Water dribbled from the ceiling still, quietly tapping down. The freshness of rain water twisted with sea salt. His bed rocked gently with the faint currents.

The part of water he feared most was its surface. When his sister used to push him under, he noticed something awful about it. From the right side of the water, you can see your reflection. But on the wrong side it was an endless, inescapable wall of silver.

Chrys sat on the floor by the bed. She stared up at him, her body lost in shadow.

"Do you really think your mother will know about all this?" Row asked as he tested walking away from his bed.

"Yes, she's wise. Careful, Row, downstairs is completely flooded."

He stopped by the door frame, hesitating at the light switch. "If I turn the power on do you think I'll die or something?"

"No but—"

The room filled with light.

Chrys sat still in the water, unclothed, her hair pushed to one side and hanging over her shoulder. Wading in the water was, not her legs, but a tail. It was scaled and teal… with fins.

"I didn't know how to tell you." She flinched.

"I can imagine." His back fell against the door. His girlfriend was a mermaid. He was awake, and his girlfriend was a mermaid. "How…?"

"I don't know." She stretched her fin, letting the water run off. "I remember what I told you, and then it feels like I was in the water a hundred more years. Then I saw you, my love. You're sunshine. I followed your light and found my way home."

"Ah." Row glanced at the floor, not sure what to say. "I hope we don't have water damage."

She dragged herself through the shallow water, headed towards the stairs. "It's not normal water, remember?"

"Ah." He nodded. "…Of course."

"Row, are you okay?"

"I don't know about okay, but I suppose things could be worse." He looked behind himself. The hallway was dark, and on the other side of the railings the water was deep. "Here. Let me help you."

He bent down beside her and lifted her, cradling her back and tail. He'd never been on the muscular side, as much as he wanted to be romantic and kiss her, he couldn't. He heaved and sweated until he set her down onto the steps. Then he sat in the water, panting and recollecting himself.

"Thanks, Row." She smiled, resting her chin on his knee. "You're taking this all very well."

He cleared a strand of wet hair from her face. "About as well as I take everything else."

"Row, don't be so hard on yourself."

He swallowed a dryness in his throat. "I think this might be my fault."

She tilted her head. "How could it possibly be your fault. I summoned the spirit."

Row felt sick, forced to remember his least favourite places in the world. Here he'd thought that giving Sundew the house would give him his freedom. *Had he really thought it'd be so easy?*

"There's no such thing as an evil spirit," Row said. "This stinks of my sister."

"How would she—"

"She's not normal!" he blurted. "Nothing about Honey Walls or Cherrywood is normal and she is the least normal part of all of it." He groaned, feeling relieved to get the words out. "My mom was a magical wizard or something, and my sister's a monster. There. I said it. Can I please, please, please just get back to my boring life now?"

"Row… wizards aren't real."

"What? You're a mermaid! You believe in ghosts! How on earth could you not believe wizards are real?"

She paused, staring at her fin. "You're right, sorry, tell me about your wizard mother."

"My mom is not a wizard," he said, still somehow clinging to his pretend normalcy. "She just… when she wrote stories, they'd become true. That's it. She brought my crafts to life and my stuffed animals. It was a mess."

Chrys nodded to herself.

"But who cares about her, she's dead. This isn't about my mother, it's about my sister. She's a monster."

"What kind of monster?"

"I don't know." He slumped his shoulders. "She just showed up one day and ate my heart."

"How did she—"

"She just reached inside me and took it. It sounds so ridiculous, sisters don't just eat hearts — and if they do I figure it's a bloody mess and it makes the six o'clock news." Row groaned. "You know what? I'm delirious, this is all just silly."

Chrys pushed herself up, patting his knee. "It's not silly."

Row avoided her eyes. "That's it, there's your answer. We can stop going to the hospital, there's the answer to the mystery. It's why I can't cry. I can never love anyone."

"Don't do that to yourself. You love me."

He shook his head, wishing it was true. "Only if we pretend that none of this is real."

She smiled, stroking his cheek. She was cool but warmed against him. "Or we could fix this."

His chest felt hot. He brought her closer, wrapping her tight in his arms. He thought he lost her. He thought he'd never hug her again. Maybe she was right. Her body felt like ice.

"Let me get you a sweater," he said.

Chapter Ten

Oxnard and the Sky World by Rose Gareau

Wherein Oxnard Discovers an Island

After travelling all of Big Road and exploring several islands, Oxnard was looking a little rough. His paws were dirty and his heart a little battered. He was beginning to miss his friends (yes, this included the Mean Pigeons of Big Road). Mostly, he missed me, Righty, and Craft Feather Crow. He thought of home as he rowed his boat towards a new island.

He'd become an expert at boat hitching. Oxnard walked onto the new island, no longer afraid of sneaky crabs. His knots were so excellent even the sneakiest of crabs wouldn't be able to cut through them. With this certainty, he waddled away and onto the island.

The island reminded him a lot more of his home. There were large green trees and soft soil. It had a good earth smell, and a stinky sock smell too. *Had he finally found The Island of Mismatched Socks?* He tightened his scarf and knapsack, walking on his way to explore the island. If he was where he thought he was, his adventure was nearing a close.

The further down the path he went, the less familiar things got. The willow trees looked down at Oxnard and made him so scared he balled. Oxnard balled further from embarrassment. He'd been doing so well, but sometimes scary things still overwhelmed his bravery.

"Look!" shouted a treetop monster. "Thar be a spiny!"

The monster's friend shook his head and approached the spiny. "No, no, no, not a spiny. This is a delicious, yummy, scrumptious hedgehog." He grinned and snickered, placing his paw down on the poor shivering Oxnard.

"Ar! Why's it always have to be land food? Land food at breakfast, land food at lunch. All I be asking is for one crunchy, juicy sea spiny."

"O-oh, I suggest that t-too." Oxnard stammered. "I even have a boat you could borrow. Provided that you don't eat me." For a brave moment Oxnard stuck out his nose and sniffed. One whiff and he coughed. The creatures were pungent, definitely sock monsters. The one smelled like a musky weasel and his friend an otter.

"Or," the otter began, "and this be just a thought, but we could sniff yer spiny trail all the way back to yer boat. Eat ya and the sea spinies."

"Oh, but I'm a master of knots," Oxnard said in his bravest voice, taking a peek at the two meanies.

The two were long with button noses and sharp teeth. The otter was made of a red and white striped sock with a felt patch where one of his button eyes should have been. The weasel was spotted with pink flowers, but still had a menacing face.

"You two would never untie the boat," Oxnard continued. "And catch urchins? Oh no, I am a master at that. I'd have to teach you."

Otter watched his friend, eager for the go ahead.

"Sounds like a bother when we could just eat you." Weasel rolled Oxnard closer.

Oxnard tightened into a better ball, while Otter looked through his backpack. "What are these?" he asked as he pulled out Oxnard's directions.

"They're directions, and meanies aren't allowed to read them."

Weasel grumbled. "We're hungry, not mean."

"No, you're mean. If you eat me, you'll make my friends very sad. And that would mean you're mean."

The *maybe* mean weasel huffed. "If *I* starve, all *my* friends will be sad."

"That's not my fault, I could teach you all about finding food. I've become an expert."

Weasel continued to huff and sigh (he didn't like his way of life to be questioned by hedgehogs, though I suppose no one likes their lunch to give them a guilt trip). They all stood at a standstill.

And then Otter cleared his throat. "So, little matey, ye said these be directions. Where to?"

"The Sky World."

"The Sky World?" Otter awed and rolled Oxnard away from Weasel. "What be the Sky World?"

"It's a magical place where all the fallen stars are collected."

"Fallen stars?" Otter bounced, rolling Oxnard around in his excitement. "Ya mean wishing stars!? Magic wishing stars?"

"Yes, exactly like that." Oxnard smiled, though he was getting dizzy. "My best friend went on a quest to find one and she never came back. That's why I'm going. It's all going to be in my memoirs."

Otter scrunched his snout. "Memoirs?"

"Oh, I'm writing all of my adventures down. I'm about nine chapters in but I'm certain that my editor will hack at least half of them. A lot of time meandering, you know?"

Otter shook his head, then Weasel swiped the ball from him. "I'm still hungry," he said.

Otter swiped him back and Oxnard started to feel a bit sick. "No, we'll find something else. If he can write, ya think he could teach us to read?"

"You're too dumb to read." Weasel hissed.

"Ar, ye be the dummy if ya eat our teacher." Otter rolled Oxnard ahead of him with the tip of his nose.

Weasel groaned but followed his friend.

"'Sides, if we found a wishing star, we'd never go hungry."

Weasel groaned more.

"Right, Spine Friend?"

"Of course!" Oxnard smiled at his new friend. "But no eating me, not even a nibble!"

"Ar! We can do that, right, Weasel?"

Weasel scoffed and said a pouty, "Fine." Then he bounded ahead. "But before we go anywhere, we need to talk to Pillow Bear."

"Pillow Bear?" Oxnard asked.

Otter nodded. "He be right, Pillow Bear is in charge around here, she'll want to know about this stuff."

Oxnard nodded a little bit, hoping the bear wasn't as scary as she sounded. As frightened as he was of his new friends, he knew I'd be very proud of him, and that kept him going. When he felt a little safer and a lot more dizzy, he unrolled himself. "Alright, take me to Pillow Bear."

Not wanting to test the waters, Row let Chrys scope the area. She drenched the navy sweater in her first moments of wearing it. She assured him it was still comfortable, but he didn't entirely believe her. Soon after that, she disappeared into the pool.

An hour later, Chrys's head surfaced. Her hair dripped and drained, a dark curtain over her eyes. "You'll never believe it." She grinned as he moved her hair away. "I found the perfect boat."

"You found a boat?" Row gasped, literally taken aback.

"It practically found me. I just took a swim outside and there it was, nestled in some low hanging clouds. I'm going to bring it to your window, okay?"

"Okay." He left when she did and looked out the bedroom window. It took Chrys a while to leave the house. But then, he saw a little brown row boat floating toward him from the distance. He leaned out the window, looking the boat over as Chrys brought it close.

"See!" she exclaimed, throwing her arms in the air. "It's the perfect boat."

"But how did it get here?" He looked across the shore, and at the tree tops peeking out of the deep water. Everything was your normal underwater city, and then there was a boat. He looked down at it in the water. It wasn't quite level with the window, leaving a bit of a drop.

"I'm not sure. Why is there a sea to begin with?"

"True," he said as he began to pull himself out the window and onto the lip of the roof.

He grimaced at the water. Whether it was there or not, he wasn't excited by the idea of climbing in the boat. Jumping out his window because of some fevered fantasy seemed as likely as everything being real. And if it was real? His fear of drowning was also real.

He steadied on the roof's lip, took a deep breath, and hopped in. The boat rocked on top of the water, and Row cowered inside in hopes that it wouldn't tip. It sloshed and swayed, but eventually it settled and he slowly sat up.

Inside the boat was a set of paddles and a pile of papers. He leaned forward, nervous as the boat rocked. "There's stuff in here." He shuffled through the blank papers, finding a red scarf beneath them. It was a very tiny red scarf, only about a foot in length and an inch wide.

"Are there paddles?" she asked. "Or am I going to have to push you?"

"There are some, but I think pushing might be our best bet. I've never rowed a boat in my life."

"You're a disgrace to your name." She laughed and grabbed onto the side of the boat, nearly flipping it.

"Watch out!" He counter balanced with his weight. "I really can't swim."

"Sorry, I'll be careful." She backed away from the boat and disappeared under the water. Then the boat began to move. Under her control, the boat rocked less, but Row held tightly onto his seat. They drifted toward downtown effortlessly.

Beneath them, the city looked its usual self. No one noticed them, let alone the water as it carried the fallen leaves in lazy patterns. The city buildings reflected the same teal light of the ocean. The trees poked out above the water, the last of their leaves contrasting against the sea with orange and deep reds.

Row glanced beneath the water, hoping to see Chrys surface. Only when the boat was pressed right to Zelda's window did he see her again.

"There we are." She smiled, looking over at the thick drapes. "I told you it wouldn't be bad."

"I suppose it wasn't the worst." He huffed. "Do you think her window's open on a cold day like this?"

"Wouldn't hurt to try," Chrys said, panting between breaths.

"You okay?" Row asked.

"Oh no, I'm fine. I wanted to get here as quick as I could." She swam towards the window and pulled on the panels. They didn't budge. "You're right, that's not opening. Do you want to go down and try the door?"

"I'll drown," he said immediately. "Let's just knock."

"I don't want to startle her."

"And barging in through her window wasn't going to startle her?"

"True." Chrys reached up to knock on the window. She pounded her fist on the glass, but there was no response. She pounded again, waited, and still no one approached.

"She must be out."

"Mom doesn't go out," Chrys said. "She probably isn't paying attention, we just need to knock louder."

In an attempt to appease Chrys, Row reached a fist to the window. The curtains flung aside, and Zelda screamed.

"Zelda, wait! I didn't mean to startle you."

A tea tin came flying through the window, knocking into Row's head. "What sort of trick is this you awful, awful, boy!?"

Chrys bobbed forward, clinging onto the window sill, "Mom, it's me! Row saved me."

"He what?" Zelda's mouth hung open, hand reaching to touch her little girl's cheeks. Once Chrys was in her hands, she looked out at the sea. "What is this I'm seeing? An ocean. That wasn't there this morning."

Row groaned, rubbing the sore spot on his forehead. "Yep."

The woman glared at him, before Chrys turned back to her mother. "Oh Mama, I thought you'd be able to help us."

Zelda blinked. "Chrys, tell me what's happened, are you safe? Are you well?"

"I'm very well, Mama, but not entirely myself."

"Clearly." Zelda looked down beneath the water at her mermaid tail. "What happened?"

"I don't know, Mama. I was preaching at the church when I got in contact with some dark spirit."

"A dark spirit?" Zelda hummed. "Yes, now that you mention it, there is something ominous about this."

"You're just noticing," Row muttered beneath his breath.

"Do you have something to add, Row?"

He shook his head, fidgeting away from her glare.

She then let him free with a roll of her eyes. "Alright, come inside. I was just about to make tea."

"Mama, I don't think I can come in."

Zelda nodded. "I know my dear, I need to speak with your Row. That shadow... I still feel it around you."

Chrys paled in response, looking down beneath the waves.

"It's not your fault," Zelda consoled. "But whatever is tangled in your heart should best be left from this conversation. Come along, Row."

Row swallowed a dry lump in his throat. Zelda stared directly at him, window open and inviting him inside. He crawled along the boat, steadying himself the whole way to the window.

To his surprise, Zelda took his hand at the edge and helped him inside. Her gloves were itchy and her hands small. She didn't help him much, but it was a gesture.

To Chrys she said sweetly, "I'll get you a cup of tea. I'm sorry for the trouble."

"It's no trouble," Chrys said, all the while looking very troubled.

And then the curtains were closed on her.

Row almost smiled at the solid ground under his feet. Zelda walked ahead of him, reaching her stovetop to take off a whistling kettle. Then she continued on. Following Zelda through such a small space didn't sound difficult in theory, but he did lose track of her. The woman quickly disappeared behind a few too many beaded curtains. Eventually he opted to wait for her at the dining table.

He took a seat on a sequin green pillow. When Zelda made her way to the table, she was carrying a silver tray. She set it down in front of them, then poured a cup for Row to let steep. He sniffed, discerning a snap of ginger from the blend. "Ginger tea?"

"Yes, we're coming on cold season. Though I imagine you don't have to worry, stealing my umbrella and all."

"Sorry, I didn't mean to. I'll get it back."

Zelda raised her brow in disbelief. "Whatever you say, Row." She took a spoonful of sugar and stirred it into her cup.

"No honey?"

"We're out," she snapped.

Row took five or six spoonfuls of sugar, watching Zelda's glare grow tenser the more scoops he took.

"Are you done?"

He nodded, stirring the sugar until it dissolved. He pressed his hands around the cup. It was exactly what he needed on such a cold and miserable day.

"So, it was your spirit that did this?" Zelda glared.

He took a startled sip, burning his tongue. "My spirit?"

"I knew it was your fault."

"I didn't do anything to her."

Zelda rolled her eyes.

"What? You didn't want to save your daughter? I thought you'd be ecstatic, I mean, she's a little different, but you love weird stuff like this."

Zelda pinched her brow. "You don't honestly believe that's my daughter, do you?"

"Pardon?"

"That creature… you really do have something wrong with you. That thing isn't Chrys. Not anymore at least."

"I… if that's not Chrys, what is it?"

Zelda shrugged. "One of the many nasty evil things that tricks heartless boys. You're so foolish, Row. I'm glad it took you here first."

Row fidgeted with the cup of tea.

"I'm not trying to make you look like an idiot, this is just my professional opinion. As someone who's seen spirits all her life, you're being fooled."

"But… it's clearly Chrys." Row shook his head in disbelief. "Everything about her is — she's Chrys."

Zelda shook her head, lifting herself from her cushion. In the corner of the room she had a bookshelf, all the books laying on their sides. She took a black book from the shelf and began sifting through the pages. When she found the right page, she put it in his hands. The book was discussing sirens. On the page was a detailed description and on the other page a sketch of a mermaid on the rock, combing her hair with a sea shell.

"I imagine, based on your knowledge of everything else, you think that mermaids are whimsical carefree beauties." Zelda watched him watch the book. "They aren't, they are cruel deceivers."

Row closed the book and handed it back to her. "I'm not lusting after some siren." He scowled. "It's actually Chrys, she said it herself. There was a shadow in the ocean, something about breathing it in. Her soul... became sea foam?"

"Sounds like a clever lie for a stupid boy."

"Don't be like that, Zelda, you have to think there's a way to save her. If you really want to hold having a heart over me, have one."

"You want me to just change the truth? I'm a seer, not a witch." Zelda's fists were balled as she looked at her books, searching for answers.

"Please."

Zelda sighed, releasing the tension. "You believe me when I tell you that you don't have a heart?"

He nodded, glancing away.

"There is a chance that thing you found is Chrys. But even if it is, there is shadow twisted up inside of her."

"Is there a way to fix it?" he asked, quieter this time in hopes to keep Zelda calm.

"Yes."

"How?"

"Love." She looked at Row, waiting, watching as he tried to comprehend her. "Not just any love, true love, exactly like the fairy tales. She needs you to love her with all your heart, and you with hers. But you have no heart to love her with, so I won't hold my breath on this."

"Why don't you just love her with all of your heart? She's your daughter."

"Because that's not what we're talking about, of course I love my daughter, I love her more than anything I've loved. I'm talking about the kind of love that happens when hearts beat as one, where souls become intertwined so tightly that immortals become mortals and are allowed passage into the eternal bliss beyond death."

"Oh." Row paused. "And I need a heart for that?"

"Yes."

He looked down at his tea. "If I find a heart, then I'd be able to save her?"

"Maybe. Again, I'm not certain that's her. But if it is, yes."

He let the weight of defeat set in. "And where would I find a heart?"

"Everyone has a heart, you're not just looking for some random one. It'd have to be yours, because that's the one Chrys loves."

"I don't think I can find it…"

Zelda crossed her arms. "That's exactly why I won't get my hopes up."

"My sister ate it," he said, looking up from his tea. "Do you think it's possible to get it back?"

"Asking her would be a good start."

He nodded, his legs felt heavy. "Does it have to be me? Could I set her up with someone else?"

Zelda hit him with a teaspoon. "You awful boy!"

"What?" He winced. "You wouldn't want a better man to replace me?"

"What are you talking about? You're perfect for Chrys. I've never seen her so in love."

"Never?" He set down his tea, now empty. "But you're always trying to get rid of me."

Zelda set down her tea cup. "I can't stand the mess around you, but you're not intolerable."

Row helped her lift the tray and followed her through the winding mess of her house, back to the kitchen.

"You," she began, "as angry as you make me, bring out the best in my daughter — even as a sea harpy."

He stopped, thrown completely off guard.

Zelda set the tray down on the kitchen counter, scurrying off to find her stepladder. "Now stand still, I don't want you wandering off just yet." Zelda climbed up the ladder and then onto the counter. She stretched up into the highest shelf, pulling out a selection of zip locked bags. "Hold out your hand."

Row complied and she dropped a clover into his hand. It only had three leaves.

"It used to be a four-leaf clover. I lost a leaf, but that doesn't make it any less lucky!"

"Oh. Thank you."

"I'm not finished," she snapped, then dropped a bag full of crystals into his palm. "These are healing crystals, mostly quartz. It's a very versatile stone."

"What do I do with it?" He stared down at the clear crystals, each on the small side.

"You use them for healing." She forced his hand closed.

"Right." He pocketed the stones. "Is that it then? Do you want to go out and say goodbye to Chrys?"

"I'll say goodbye when my daughter's safe. That or when you tell me how you tried and failed." Zelda set the empty bags down on the table.

"Right…"

"Wait, I keep forgetting to give you these." Zelda ripped through her kitchen drawers, sorting through more stones and baggies. From the back of the drawer she scooped a handful of dirt, then stared at him, waiting for his hand to accept.

"These are rose seeds," she said, as she dropped the little brown specks into his hands. "I think you mentioned something about wanting to start a garden sometime back? Chrys loves roses."

He smiled, trying not to spoil the moment with some sarcastic comment about already having a garden. That or commenting how hard it was to grow the fresh rose seeds. Instead he thanked her and took up a travel mug of tea for Chrys.

"Now go," she said, pushing him back towards the window. "Surprise me."

Chapter Eleven

The Unavoidable Call of Adventure, Freedom, and (Obviously) Snacks

Row waited in the silence for Sundew to pick up the phone. His cellphone felt hot against his face. He hung on his nerves, the nausea as he anticipated her voice. But it had to be done, Zelda was right. Sundew was the only person that would have an answer. He glanced at Chrys for some support and she smiled back from the side of the boat.

And then there was Sundew's breath, her voice following, flowing like venom. "Hello, this is Sundew."

Row bit his lip. As usual, Sundew rendered speech difficult. "It's Row."

"Rosie." She preened. "I hope everything's well."

"It's Row, and everything is not well."

"It isn't?" She hummed. "That's no good, I'd hate to hear that my dearest sister was trapped beneath the ocean. I'd be so, so, so sad."

Row crinkled his brow. "I'm not trapped anywhere."

"What?" Her voice sharpened, losing her taunting lilt.

"You didn't drown me— Yes, I know you caused this so don't start playing coy."

"Caused what?" Her playfulness returned.

"This ocean, and what you did to Chrys."

"Ocean?" He could hear her grin. "I sure hope that nothing happened to your girlfriend. I mean, it's bad enough you can't love her, and now to have her turn into a mermaid."

Row huffed. "Just turn her back, Sundew. I'm not bothering you anymore, so get out of my life."

"Not bothering me?" Her tone turned severe. "Who said that you don't bother me? And who said that I'd leave you alone once the house became mine?"

"You did." His chest ached. "In your letter. I wouldn't have showed up if it wasn't abundantly clear I'd be done with this stuff forever."

She laughed. "The only thing I made abundantly clear was that I'd show you the meaning of hate. That's exactly what I'm doing."

"That's stupid." Row rolled his eyes. "You ate my heart. How am I ever supposed to learn the meaning of hate without it?"

"Once you're trapped, I'll show you," she said. "When I was in that awful place, I didn't have a heart either. But I learned a thing or two. I'll fill that empty space in your chest with misery and hate, and then you can rot. It'll serve you right, Rosie."

Row clasped his phone tighter, not knowing what to do or say. "What did I ever do to you?"

The phone cut off.

Row sighed, laying down in defeat. The pain in his chest quieted slowly. He looked to Chrys who remained staring at him from the side of the boat. "That was a waste of time." He groaned.

"It was a long shot."

He nodded. A long shot, but his only shot.

"Do you have any other ideas?" Chrys asked.

Row shook his head, laying his arms over his face to hide the shame.

"Aw, Row, did she at least give you some sort of idea?"

"Nothing I didn't already guess. She's started all of this to get back at me for *something*." He rolled his eyes. "Though, honestly, it becomes more hopeless the longer I think about it. Even if there was a way to get my heart back, it'd be impossible. Sundew would make it impossible. She hates me."

"I bet she doesn't actually hate you." Chrys smiled, trying to bring a bit of hope.

"She ate my heart. She turned you into a mermaid and is now trying to drown me. If she hadn't even said it outright, I think it's pretty clear at this point."

Chrys pushed herself away from the boat's side, circling it as she thought. "You have no clue why she hates you? Or what she's trying to get back at you for?"

"No clue. Everything about her's so weird. I don't even know if she was around until that night with my heart. She seemed so familiar, but I couldn't place it." Row sat up slowly, getting a better view of Chrys. "I think Mom felt it too. Whenever me and Sundew were together, she'd ignore her. Like, act like she didn't even exist. Maybe Mom knew she was a monster too."

Chrys gasped. "That's horrible."

"You get used to it."

"What?" Chrys scowled. "Even if you are a monster, if your mother never acknowledged you... how do you think that'd make a little girl feel?"

"But—"

"But nothing." Chrys put her hands on her hips. "I don't care what kind of monster she is. I saw her at the burial, she clearly loved her mother just as much as you did."

"But she—"

"You need to be better than her. Even if she is a monster, her feelings have been hurt."

"But—" He stopped himself. "Are you really Chrys?"

"Maybe I'm not." She scowled. "But you don't need to be a monster to empathize with one."

"I know," he muttered, not wanting to even consider his sister in a positive light. He looked to the ocean, to Chrys, felt the pain of his empty chest.

"None of this forgives what she's done." Chrys petted his hand. "But maybe all she needs is a little understanding. You'd be surprised how far that can go."

"So… we should go back to Honey Walls then?"

"I don't see any other options."

Row nodded, running a hand through her hair. Her hope and compassion rubbed off a little on him, but it wasn't potent enough. He could feel his sister's fingernails still pressed on his shoulders. Above him, silver glass. A prison beneath the waves.

Row and Chrys made it back to their house to prepare for their long boat trip. He made sure to pack himself warm sweaters and human-sized scarves. Clothing, food, first-aid, and his medications, but there was no way they could pack enough in their tiny boat. Chrys calmed him. They'd follow the road and stop in towns, maybe attempt to get down to street level if they absolutely had to. Chrys said nothing bad would happen.

But half an hour in the boat and Row was already nauseous. "I'm going to get scurvy and die."

"No, you won't," Chrys snorted.

"I'll starve, and die."

"Nope."

"I'll drown."

Chrys swam to his side. "We'll be okay."

Row grumbled, lying down and trying to forget where he was and how ridiculous his life had become. He'd never thought he could hate fiction any more than he already did. *Your mother had to be some sort of word wizard, didn't she?* A part of him lamented as he heard Chrys duck beneath the waves. She pushed the boat through the city and into the ocean mist. His mother hadn't told him a lot of stories about the ocean. The ocean was new.

Row groaned. He should have brought his sketchbook. His clients would have a fit with all this ignored work. Well, there were the blank pages. He sat himself up, picking up some of the paper. Underneath it and the scarf, he found a set of pencil crayons. They'd have to do.

He turned off the awful world around him and sketched. He still had to design a hedgehog for that story book. He was supposed to be a brave adventurer, a main character in some sort of LGBT friendly children's book. It was typical work for him, yet uncomfortably familiar. The design kept coming out the same. *This has nothing to do with you,* he thought as he scribbled over a red hedgehog he'd drawn. The little hedgehog wearing a backpack and scarf disappeared behind a scribble of green. Row almost felt bad (but he obviously didn't because he didn't have a heart).

Ahead of the city was still in mist. The closer they got to the highway, the closer they were to the misty clouds, the deep fog. *Please don't let us get lost.* He searched his pocket for the three-leaf clover and found that it was now a two leaf clover.

"Luck's running out, be careful." He joked, though worry panged inside of him.

The clouds closed around them as they floated into the darkening of dusk. The sun set through the mist and Chrys relaxed. She raised her head above the water and sang to herself. As she did, Row offered her a break and paddled.

But eventually, the songs made his eyelids heavy. He lay down in the boat and rested. But he couldn't sleep. The rocking of the ocean made him nervous and extra seasick. "I can't do this," he grumbled.

"Doesn't look like you'll have to."

"Huh?" He sat up, slowly because everything was spinning. Through the mist he saw trees, trees not in the water but in the ground. "An island?"

"Yes." She grinned. "Let's hope this isn't the last."

He nodded, squishing out the last of the clover's luck. One wilted petal remained. Chrys pushed the boat through the clouds and mist. The island was a while away, the anticipation killed. It was many long minutes before Chrys pushed the boat to the shore, scraping it across the sand.

Row stepped out of the boat and stretched his legs, while Chrys rested on the shore. She lay down in the sand, letting the water splash over her. She was the picture of beauty, her scales glistening under the caressing light of the moon. Row sat next to her and held onto her hand. It was one of those moments, one of those times, he felt he could almost cry. He held where his heart would have been and looked up at the distant stars.

He lay down and they watched the light together.

Chrys fell asleep beneath the stars, exhausted from pushing the boat. Row sat up, looking out at the sea and back to the shore. He still couldn't find it in himself to sleep. He stood up and decided to take a short walk, leaving Chrys to rest. It was better for both of them that he stay up and watch. With Sundew writing stories, who knew what could happen next?

And Sundew or not, falling asleep on a strange island (especially a strange, fictitious island) was not a good idea. He walked across the beach looking through the trees. The forest was deciduous with what looked like willows. There were mixes of other low trees but nothing populated enough to stand out. The spaces between the branches were small, filled with twisted vines, plants, and mushrooms. Row squinted through the dense brush, darkness, and trailing sea mist.

A little voice cooed in the distance. "Hello?"

Row furrowed his brow, in the glint of moonlight he could see a stripe of yellow. He squinted trying to get a better look at whatever it was. The yellow stripe was far from the shoreline, lying on a patch of grass. The grass and shrubs were flattened, like they were walked over.

"Hello?" he replied through a yawn.

The little voice didn't reply. He continued forward, approaching the yellow stripe. As he approached it, he became even more confused. Lying in the middle of the woods was a yellow envelope with childlike letters scrawled on it in black. "Good Monstar Snaks" it read.

Row bent down, picking it up to get a better look. As he pulled it, he heard a snap. Beneath him, the ground became unstable. Before he could react, he slid down a deep dirt hole.

The tunnel scratched along his side, bumping and battering him until he hit the bottom with a thud. Above him the light of the opening was distant.

"Good job!" he heard someone shout. "I knew monsters couldn't resist a snack. Nobody can!"

Claire waited for the silence of night. A bitter chill rolled in, carrying with it the first flecks of snow. The glints of ice interrupted the black night as sudden white specks. She'd spent the day in Rose's room. It was imprinted in her memories. The sheets were still indented where Rose had spent her remaining months. A vase of roses wilted on the bedside table. The windows were covered by thin grey curtains. Claire flicked the light on, giving the room a much needed dose of life.

She remained vigilant as she listened for the last sounds of Sundew. As her footsteps dulled to nothing and her cries became faint, Claire approached the window. While she felt a pang of guilt for Sundew, she could hardly sustain it. With Sundew's behaviour, how could she?

She looked out the window at the front of the house through the canopy of magnolias. The plants grew up against the wall, the vines pressed tightly in a way that looked climbable.

Claire fussed with the window. The frame was stiff. It hadn't been open in years, perhaps never at all. Though the idea of Rose never letting in a breath of fresh air didn't strike her as possible. The window scraped open. The gap, while on the tight side, looked like she could fit through with a little shimmying.

She removed the mesh from the window, setting it up against the bed frame. Before thinking anything out, Claire was straddling the window. Her left leg dangled outside, a few feet from the awning. She squished her right knee against her face, wriggling until both legs hung outside.

Petering above the awning, she measured her next move. If she wanted to land above the door, she'd need to put faith in the structural integrity of the magnolias, or jump blindly. She tested the magnolias with slight pressure from her foot. They felt securely rooted.

She slid from the window sill, putting her trust in the branches. They were nowhere near as sturdy as she expected. They snapped in succession, sending her tumbling down. She grasped the branches that passed her fingers. Her foot hit the ground first, rolling over as the rest of her landed, scraped and battered, at the base of the bushes.

"Crap." She hissed as her ankle flared with pain.

The light lit from Sundew's window.

"Double crap." She hissed again, struggling to get herself to her feet. Bruises flared on her shoulder and back, adding to the already impossible ache of her ankle. Her body caved as she attempted to put weight on her foot.

"Triple goddamn crap." She hobbled forward on a light tip toe.

The walk through the wildflowers was excruciating. It felt much further than it ever had. Icy winds cut across the open area, stinging Claire's nose and fingertips. She hardly had the time to think about it, reaching the mushroom ring. She sat herself down and slid down the ditch, stumbling at the bottom into the woods.

Howls of wolves cut through the silence of night. They sounded like screeching claws across a glass pane. Claire bristled, considering climbing back up the ditch. The moonlight and starlight were swallowed by the tangle of branches above. It was a tunnel without an end. She shook her head, braving the passage.

Chapter Twelve

Oxnard and the Sky World
by Rose Gareau

Wherein Oxnard Braves a Bear's Den

Pillow Bear lived in the sock caverns, the large tunnels beneath the Island of Lost Socks. Oxnard followed Otter's lead into the mouth of the caverns. He expected the insides to be spooky and dark, but things were mostly just smelly. Little lanterns lit the way along the path, providing more than enough light to guide him forward. However, all the light in the world didn't make the twisty tunnels easy to navigate. Signs scrawled with squiggles and wingdings marked the multitude of parting paths. Without Otter's help, Oxnard was certain he'd be lost.

They passed the occasional sock ferret and sock cat, each watching Oxnard and licking their sharp teeth. Fortunately, none of them picked a fight, and before long they reached Pillow Bear's den. The den reminded Oxnard a lot of his and Rosie's room back home, especially when he and Rosie used to make blanket forts together. Quilts lined the walls while throw pillows were thrown about the floor. Otter hopped ahead, over to where Pillow Bear sat.

"Greetings Cap'n," said Otter as he approached.

Pillow Bear was the largest stuffed animal Oxnard had ever seen. She stretched out her pillow paws, each the same size as a rolled up hedgehog. She wasn't a fluffy bear, her fur amounting to a lavender pillow case, her face scribbled on in permanent marker (you know, the kind of marker that kids aren't supposed to use! Especially not on their pillow cases when their mothers say, "No drawing on the furniture!")

"Evening, Lefty Red Striped Sock Otter," said Pillow Bear in a very official sounding way. "What brings you to my den?"

"Thar be a visitor on our island, and me and Righty Pink Flower Weasel wish to go on an adventure with him."

"Visitor?" Pillow Bear sniffed, finding Oxnard amongst the sheets.

"U-um, hello." Oxnard waved.

Pillow Bear didn't wave back. "What brings a visitor to the Island of Lost Socks, hm?"

"Well… you see, I've been looking for your lovely island, Ms. Pillow Bear, because it is the next stop on my way to the Sky World."

"The Sky World?" She raised her brow. "What business does a little hedgehog have in the Sky World?"

"I-I…" Oxnard took a moment to find his bravery. "My friend disappeared a long time ago and I believe she's in the Sky World."

"Disappeared?"

He nodded. "I think she went on an adventure without me… and never came back."

Pillow Bear's face contorted into a very mean and scary scowl. "That's no good."

"Oh please, don't eat me!" Oxnard balled up. "Weasel and Otter promised I wouldn't be eaten!"

"Eat you?" She stopped sounding so angry. "I wouldn't eat you."

"You wouldn't?"

"Of course not. I much prefer honey and custard." She smiled. "I'm certainly not mad at you. We here on the Island of Lost Socks are very sympathetic to your plight. You see, we've all been abandoned and forgotten by our other halves, and the one that owns us. Abandoning your friends is one of the most serious of crimes on this little island."

"It is?" Oxnard looked back at his friends. "What happens if you're caught abandoning your friends? Do you get a time out?"

Pillow Bear shook her head. "If you're caught, the matter is taken to court."

Oxnard's mouth hung open (you see, Reader, he was thinking about the kind of court with kings and princesses, since he was a good hedgehog who'd never had a run in with the law).

"If you are found guilty of willingly and purposely abandoning your friend, you are sentenced to something way worse than a time out."

Oxnard shivered, unable to think of anything much worse than a time out.

"That's all well and good, Pillow," Weasel interrupted, "but we've not even found the bad friend. Is it okay for us to go on this adventure?"

Pillow Bear glared at the weasel. "Yes, you may go on this adventure, but mind your manners."

Weasel scoffed and rolled his eyes.

"But before you leave, I haven't gotten the name of your friend."

"Oxnard," said Oxnard.

Pillow Bear blinked, seeming to recall an Oxnard (though she really knew a lot of stuffed animals). "And Oxnard, what is the name of the friend you lost?"

"Rosie," he said, though it made him a little sad. "Little Rosie Gareau."

"Oh." The bear grumbled. "We've been looking for her for a very long time."

A sock fox poked her head over the edge of the hole and stared down at Row. She was a small thing, about the size of a ferret with a body made of grey socks. Her button nose twitched as she sniffed.

"Hello?" Row asked and the fox jumped back.

"It's talking to me," she whispered back to her friends, who remained out of sight.

"Yes, I'm talking to you." He scowled. "I'm not a monster, I'll have you know. And I need to get back to the ocean, my girlfriend is waiting for me."

"I-I don't believe you," she stammered.

"I'm not a monster, I don't even have claws." He held up his stubby human fingers. "And my teeth aren't good for biting, I don't get good dental coverage. I'd be in trouble if I chipped one."

The fox stared at him entirely perplexed, as if he was speaking another language.

"Look, I'm not a monster. I'm actually friends with a fox," he offered. "I let her borrow my umbrella."

"An umbrella?"

"It's like, um, it's a thing you hold to keep rain off your fur."

The little fox gasped and did a little jump, knocking a bit of dirt onto Row as she did. "Let me see! Do you have another?"

"No, sorry… Maybe if you let me go?"

The fox kneaded her paws on the ground, scratching the dirt up. She was perked up a little more, ears alert. "I don't know, you still might be a monster."

"I'm not a monster." He huffed. "My name's Row."

"I'm Lefty Grey Sock Fox."

"That's a long name, Lefty."

"It's a better name than Row. What's that even supposed to mean?" Lefty scowled.

"Ummm…." He sighed. "It's short for my birth name, actually. I like it better, a lot less girly."

"Why? What's it short for? Roll? Rooolling? Rolly-Polly Monster?"

"No, it's short for Rose. Like the flower."

"That's not girly." Lefty scoffed.

"It's not?"

"Yeah, roses are tough! And sharp! My friend Righty Red Striped Sock Otter, he got caught in a rose bush and got ripped up in it."

"Oh, I'm sorry." Row fidgeted. "Was he okay?

"Mhm, he lost some stuffing and an eye, but he's okay now." She hopped again. "Roses are very, very tough — not to say you're rose-like at all."

"I'm not tough?"

Lefty shook her head. "No, I'm just saying you're not like a Rose. I knew a Rose, and she wasn't like you." She scoffed. "She was nice, wrote stories, grew flowers, and kept all the matchless socks happy. Every time she found a sad and lonely sock, she gave it a new life. She brought them to life with a story and a name."

"Rose Gareau," he uttered. "You're talking about my mother."

Lefty gasped. "You're Rose's son!"

"I am."

Lefty Fox thought long and hard, scratching the dirt. "I need to talk to my friends about this," she said in a rush, hopping away from the hole.

Row hit his head against the dirt wall. He hoped she'd be back soon, that she'd convince her friends he wasn't a monster. All the while, he tried to remember the sock animals. His mother had made so many crafts. He vaguely recalled them making sock puppets when his socks got old and had holes. He remembered the lace mice, the yarn cats, and paper butterflies.

When he was little, the thought that his mother was in some way magical never crossed his mind. Well, that she was more magical than other mothers, that is. All mothers felt a bit magical, not just his own. The magic of a mother's kiss was well known to him. But the fact that stuffed animals and crafts came to life? That was just normal.

Normal. He cringed.

One day, he was out on recess talking to a squirrel. He didn't remember what they were talking about, but his friend Lea came over. She gave him the most concerned look he'd ever been given. The years got worse, the more he realized what he thought was normal wasn't at all.

There was a cacophony of sock feet from above. When he looked up, he met eyes with a parade of sock weasels and ferrets, one after the other beginning to squish and climb down the hole. They bounced and wriggled around each other trying to get a good look at Row. Some squeaked and others yapped. They were the loudest group of mischievous sock animals to ever co-exist.

"No way! That's not Rose!"

"Lefty Fox never said he was, Spotty!"

"He's Rose's son!"

"Rose didn't have children!"

The bundle exploded with loud gasps. It was impossible to tell exactly which of the wriggly, noodle fluffs was speaking.

Row corrected them. "Rose had two kids, actually."

"No, no, no, you're thinking Rose's mom Rose. We're talking about Rose

Rose. You know?"

"Oh…" He paused. "I'm Rose's Rose."

The ferrets stopped the haphazard wriggling.

A small one in the corner broke out into laughter. "You're not Rosie. You're a giant!" This set off some other ferrets into their own laughing fit.

An older, larger weasel squeezed out of the tunnel and approached Row. He sniffed his face. "If you are Rosie, why do you look like this?"

"Humans get bigger if you give them some years."

The big ferret nodded as he pondered this. "You do smell faintly of her, I'll admit. But maybe that's just because you ate her."

"I don't eat people." Row rolled his eyes. "I'm Rose. I grew up and now I'm Row. My girlfriend is waiting for me to go back to shore and see her. It's very important that I keep at that, so would you just let me go?"

The ferret continued to ponder. "If you're really Rose, what's my name?"

"Um…"

The ferret was large and made from white socks. Holes in the cloth were sewn together with pink threads. He stared back at Row with blue button eyes.

"I don't remember," Row admitted.

The ferrets whispered amongst themselves in loud hissy voices.

"What do we do now?"

"We'll take it to a cell. Whether it's a monster or Rosie, you know Pillow Bear will make us do a trial."

"Oh! You're right!"

"Shush! It'll hear us!"

The large weasel turned back to Row while the others scurried off in every direction. "You're going to the slammer for the night until we can hold a trial."

"Trial, for what?" Row frowned. "I don't have time for this."

As he spoke, the socks returned with balls of yarn. They rappelled down the hole, beginning to circle and tangle Row in their strings. While he tried to stop them, it quickly became impossible. They circled him so fast that in seconds his arms were tied to his sides. He couldn't move his feet any better, and the ferrets kept climbing and tangling him.

"If you don't have the time, don't do a crime!" giggled a ferret as she began fastening the yarn in expert sailor knots.

"I didn't do anything." He scowled at her. "This is just ridiculous. At the very least, I have the right to know my charges, don't I?"

The ferret looked to her friends. The socks shrugged.

"I think he's right," said one at the top of the hole.

The little ferret harrumphed. "You're getting tried for being a bad friend, Rosie."

"What?" He furrowed his brow. The ferrets began securing ribbons on all sides of him. "The only thing making me a bad friend is leaving Chrys at the boat — and mind you, that is all your fault."

The crowd gasped. Again.

"Rolly!" A voice hissed from above, it was Lefty. "You're just giving the prosecution more evidence."

"Prosecution?" He faltered, looking around him at the ferrets. *What in the world had his life become?* He stopped himself from further self-incrimination as the socks pulled on the ribbons and dragged him from the hole. It scratched and scraped until he was out. Then, once he was out, he was carried on the ferret's backs, disappearing into the dark of the forest.

The forest surrounding Honey Walls had never been so dense. Claire felt that she may have strayed off the path at some point, as she now found herself stumbling through piles of frozen leaves, and shivering against tree trunks for support.

Shadows hid in every corner, no longer yielding to her approach. She stopped moving and listened to herself pant. The rest of the world was silent, frozen. *What do you do now? Wait for morning?* She could no longer feel anyone on her tail. Maybe even Sundew wasn't crazy enough to brave the forest in the howling night. But would it be wise to sleep where she was?

She winced at the pain in her ankle. As her adrenaline died down, it had started to ache more. She leaned against a tree, eventually lowering herself to the ground. The bounds of the swelling pressed against the sides of her shoe. She loosened her laces, feeling very little comfort from doing so.

"Oh my god, what is going on?" She groaned into her palms.

The oddity of it all was only beginning to catch up with her. The kidnapping, the stories, the looming threat of nobody searching for her? It didn't make sense, and felt a little like the sort of weird games she'd played in elementary school.

A crack sounded in the dark behind her. She stiffened.

Whether it was Sundew or a wolf, she remained quiet all the same.

Goosebumps ran up her spine as a new breeze blew past. The rustling sound of wind accented the steps of her pursuer. It was an invisible threat, a mere idea until its paw pressed down beside her.

The wolf was silver, moonlight trapped in its fur. It stood at her eye level, sniffing a foot from her. As she watched it, another one pulled itself free of the dense forest, ruling free in her peripherals. They were silent, cautiously circling her and sniffing.

Claire copied their slow movements in all but her heart. She tried to make herself taller, becoming the same strange and threatening human they usually avoided. But they didn't look the least bit perturbed. They embodied the oddity of the day, entangled in shadow like the rest of the forest.

"Shoo!" she yelled at them, clapping her hand against her thigh.

The nearest lowered its head, flaring its teeth and began to growl. From the distance, more wolves approached, each glinting with the same silver coat.

Claire's heart quickened and she became louder, yelling and clapping. But the wolves were no more dismayed than before. They gnashed their teeth and snapped at her hand. And when nothing happened, they grew bolder. One lunged for her ankle and she reacted on impulse, kicking it square beneath its jaw. It whimpered, teeth smacking into one another.

They froze a second before lunging at her with fangs ready. For a split second, Claire watched them, then ducked. She fell to her knees, curling herself tight so that they would have little to grab. And then she just screamed in hopes someone would find her.

She felt their teeth hook onto her sweater, brushing her skin by a thin margin. And then she heard one squeal, whimpering like a little puppy. She looked between her fingers as it fell to the ground. It smacked down with force, causing the other wolves to still. They and Claire looked up.

Sundew stood at the opposite side of the wolves, the whimpering one rolled onto its back at her feet. She stooped down, grasping its neck. The other wolves cowered at her feet, backing away from both her and Claire.

"What do you think you're doing?" she asked the wolf. As her grip tightened, her hand bled. Somehow, it was her own blood. "If you think hunting people is going to endear you poodles to me, think again."

Claire relaxed, sitting up to watch the scene. Some of the wolves already parted with tails between their legs. While others remained, growling and barking at Sundew.

"Did I not make myself clear?" she said, continuing to glare. "Or do I have to shatter every last one of you?"

Shatter? Claire grimaced at the word, but the wolves appeared to respond. They looked to their fallen friend before turning away in defeat.

Once they were gone, she released the last wolf. Sundew staggered back, holding onto her bloodied hand. "You idiot…" she muttered as it staggered away, running after its pack.

Claire stared at her. "How did you do that?"

"What kind of fool jumps out a window?" she snapped at Claire. "Do you realize that you could have been killed if I didn't notice?"

"And what? I'm supposed to let myself be the prisoner of some wolf whisperer lunatic?" Claire retorted. "I'm not writing anymore stories for you, Sundew. I thought I'd humour you a bit because of your grief, but things got too far too fast. This isn't cute."

Sundew glared back at her, long since past the end of her rope. "What are you even talking about? This isn't some game to me, I need a writer here."

"Why?"

"Because someone has to keep the Stories of Cherrywood going, and it can't be me." She squeezed her bloodied hand tighter. "Can we just go back to Honey Walls? I can explain things better there."

Claire considered things as she felt her foot throb. "I'll hear you out. But if this is insane, I'm leaving and you're not kidnapping anyone to replace me, okay?"

Sundew shook her head. "It's too important for me to chance it."

"I'm not unreasonable, Sundew. Try me."

Chapter Thirteen

Plastic Prisons and Laundry Lawyers

The cell Row was carried to was deep inside a series of twisting caves and tunnels. As they threw him in, they replaced the tangle of yarn with a pair of crocheted cuffs. They were tight but soft, reminding Row of wearing a pair of mittens which were one size too small. He sat against the wall of his cell, flinching back as the ferrets slammed the door shut.

When the socks grew bored, snickering and bounding away, Row made himself acquainted with a pile of pillows. One corner of his cell was packed with them. It was all what was to be expected of sock animals. The bars were made of pieces of plastic laundry baskets hot glued together, the floor carpeted with a quilt.

"What you in for, Kid?" rasped a voice from the cell next to him.

Row sat up, looking over at the creature. He was an argyle sock ferret with the voice of a gangster. "Being a bad friend?" Row replied. "What about you?"

"Teaching kids to gamble." He shrugged. "Not a crime as far as I'm concerned, but I've got a month behind bars."

"Ah…" Row acknowledged the ferret but hardly sympathized with his plight.

"Socks around here call me Chester. Feel free to do the same."

"Alright, but I won't be here long. I've got to get back to my boat soon."

The ferret snickered. "You better hope your trial goes well. There's a mandatory minimum on being a bad friend, we're talking five years after a sincere apology."

"What?" Row went rigid. "I can't spend five years of my life here. I've got a lot on my plate."

Chester shrugged. "The law's the law. You better hope a good lawyer takes up your case."

"Yeah." Row fell back onto the pillows. "Where will I get one of those?"

"I don't know, but you better hope yours is better than mine was."

"Who was your lawyer?"

Chester groaned. "Lefty Grey Sock Fox, she's the only one that takes guilty parties because she's real gullible. Yeah, you don't want her as your representative. Better off going it alone."

"Duly noted." Row replied. "Anyone you would recommend?"

"What? You think I've done more than one offence?"

"Umm... no?"

"Good." The ferret harrumphed. "I'm a first-time offender, but I've heard a few good things about Righty Rainbow Toe-Sock Axolotl and Lefty Green Sock Snake — prefers you call him Alphonso outside of court though."

"I'll try to remember that."

"Good, bad friendship is not something socks take lightly. Everyone here's been abandoned by a someone," he said. "But that's neither here nor there. Hope your trial goes well, friend-o."

"Thanks, Chester."

Sundew dropped Claire down onto the couch before disappearing into the kitchen. Claire winced, setting her foot up on the coffee table. The swelling certainly hadn't gone down after all the action and movement, but it felt much better to no longer be struggling to stand. She watched Sundew carefully, waiting for her answers.

When Sundew returned to the living room her hand was wrapped in a floral tea towel. In her opposite she had a plastic bag full of ice. She pressed it onto Claire's ankle, the cold sensation startling her. She jerked back before settling back on the table. All the while Sundew remained agitated and impatient.

"So," Claire prompted. "Start talking."

Sundew grimaced, remaining quiet as she neared an empty chair. She brushed her long hair aside, resting it on her lap. The strands fell down as diverging rivers, pooling amongst the chair legs. Her already long hair appeared longer than usual, moving as if it were almost alive. "I don't know where to start," she responded at last.

"Well, I'd like to know how you're a wolf master or whatever. Start there."

"I'm not a wolf master." She scowled. "They're just a bunch of cowards."

Claire rolled her eyes.

"You can't see them for what they really are, so they took advantage of that." Sundew said. "They're fragile creatures made of glass."

"Glass?" Claire blinked. The idea was familiar, straight from Rose's story books. "Sundew, don't pull my leg."

"I'm not," she snapped back. "They're the wolves from my mother's stories. The wolves made of reflections and broken glass." Sundew held up her bloodied hand. "You can't see them the way us Gareaus do, but that isn't your fault."

"Why?" Claire furrowed her brow.

"Because we're the ones with the magic, not you."

"Magic?"

Sundew crossed her arms. "Yes, magic. That's the big secret, alright? My mother's stories are magical, they become true. They keep this town together."

Claire stared in disbelief. "How so?"

"Far be it from me to care about this town, but without my mother's stories, it wouldn't exist." She tightened the towel on her hand. "What does our town provide the world? What jurisdiction are we in? This place stopped being anything other than a storybook years ago."

"You…" Claire paused, allowing herself a few more moments to drink everything in. She tried to think past her idyllic small-town life and into the real world. But the world and its consequences were a mystery to her. Her world was defined by a role which felt inescapable, the book keeper's daughter. "That's not possible."

Sundew shrugged. "I've never known a world different than this."

Claire swallowed a lump in her throat, all the while staring at Sundew's bloodied hand. "You're saying that if the stories stopped being written… what would happen?"

"This town would likely die off the way many places like this do. People like you and Dan will tire and leave. And those older… well, they may remain until their ends. Either way, Cherrywood will likely fall apart."

Claire's body felt heavy. She struggled to look back at Sundew. "And why don't you write the stories by yourself?"

"I can't."

"Why not?"

"It's Rose's pen where the magic comes from." Sundew sighed. "And the thing detests me as much as she did."

"Oh." Claire softened.

"Even if I wanted to do the right thing, I doubt I could make it glow."

"Glow?" Claire paused, vaguely remembering the golden glow of Rose's pen. "Wait. Does that mean that story I wrote actually became true?"

Sundew nodded.

Claire jumped forward, knocking the ice from her foot. "Who did I drown?! Oh my lord, what did you make me do?"

Sundew straightened out in her chair. "N-nothing." She sputtered. "It didn't work out like I planned. She's still alive."

"She?" Claire grimaced as she pieced it out. "Wait, do you mean Row?" She gasped. "How could you do something like that? He better not be drowned."

"He's not." Sundew stood. "I'll show you."

Claire glared at her, trailing her as she neared the coffee table. Stooped over the table, her reflection faint on its surface.

"Look into my reflection."

Claire grimaced, staring at the reflection. It was still Sundew. She glared up in response, only to be motioned back by Sundew's eyes. When she looked back down, the image had changed. It was Row, asleep on a pile of pillows.

"See." Sundew scoffed. "He's fine."

Claire blinked, glancing back up in a dizzied shock. "How did you…."

"Do that?" Sundew rolled her eyes. "It's nothing. I don't have a reflection, your eyes play tricks on you. That is what's in the mirror if you pay attention."

"Oh god, my brain hurts." Claire groaned. "How in the world is any of this real?"

"What does it matter?"

"I don't know, because I want to know if I'm out of my mind?" She gripped onto the couch cushion. "Wow."

"Are you going to stay and write the stories?"

Claire's whole body tightened as the question blurred through her. "I don't know," she said. "I need to think about this. That won't destroy the town or anything, right?"

"No."

"Okay, cool." Claire rubbed her temples to relax the beginnings of a headache. "Just let me sleep on all of this."

"Morning Rolly!" Lefty shouted through the bars.

Row rolled over and Lefty jumped. The little grey fox was as bouncy as he remembered. She skipped from side to side, unable to still her tiny body. Row yawned, sitting himself up. "What are you doing here, Lefty?" He looked around. The den was still dim, but since there were no windows he easily believed it could be morning.

"I wanted to start working on your case!" She hopped.

"My case?" He scowled, glancing over at a sleeping Chester. "Lefty, you seem nice and all… but… I don't really want you as a defence attorney."

"W-what?" She stilled. "But I've really been practicing, and practice makes perfect!"

Row scowled. "Practice on some simpler cases, Lefty. This is really important for me and I don't want to lose."

"B-but, I don't want to lose either." She whimpered. "And… Mr. Gareau…"

He raised his brow as she trailed off. "What is it, Lefty?"

"S-sir, I was talking with my other lawyer friends and nobody wants to take your case — in fact, everyone's fighting to be prosecution!" She dug the dirt floor beneath her paws. "You see, to a lot of us here think everything you did was inexcusable. You're basically the definition of the worst friend ever."

Row froze. "Everything I did?"

She nodded. "I mean, Rosie, you abandoned every single one of your friends. At least, that's what everyone thinks. But I'll give you a chance! Maybe you got lost on your way to pick us flowers?"

"I don't see what's so wrong in leaving." He avoided the answer as to why he left in the first place. "You all seem to be doing fine without me."

Lefty gasped. "Don't say that. You can't leave someone's life without telling them, it's illegal."

"Says some kangaroo court." Row scoffed.

"Oh, no, Pillow Bear is judging and if there's a jury it'll likely be seventy percent ferrets." She tapped a paw to her mouth. "I don't think there are any sock kangaroos around here."

"Oh, wonderful, here I was worried that this would be a load of nonsense."

Lefty paused in confusion before resuming her bouncing. "The point is, unless you plan on representing yourself, I'm your lawyer."

"Great…"

"That's the spirit!" She bounced about. "I've been thinking about different witnesses to bring up to the stand. I was thinking your other fox friend would be a great idea! I mean, lending an umbrella is a very friend thing to do, very unmonsterly."

"I don't think I'd be able to get zir here."

Lefty slumped. "Well, there goes that idea."

"What are you two yammering about?" Chester barked from his cell. "Who in the world wakes up at six? This is a sleeping hour, Lefty. Wait. Lefty?" He looked at Row. "Oh no, you didn't listen to my advice, did you?"

Lefty scowled in Chester's direction. "Wait, were you the one that said I was a bad lawyer?"

"Course I was, you lost me my case."

Lefty gasped. "Mr. Argyle! You started gambling with the bailiff mid-trial. You don't think that had anything to do with our loss?"

"Pff!" The ferret stuck out his tongue. "It got so boring in there. What's a ferret supposed to do?"

Lefty shook her head, turning back to Row. "I'm going to build up a really strong defence for you, Mr. Gareau! And if you don't cause trouble, I could see you going free!"

Chester yawned. "Don't listen to her, she believes anything is possible."

Row looked between the socks as they argued. It was hard to believe that everything was real. There was a reason why he'd left all them behind, and while unfortunate for them, it wasn't criminal. He crossed his arms, waiting for a lull in their bickering.

"What sort of case needs to be made?" he interrupted before Chester could fire a retort to a comment about his sneakiness.

Lefty looked up, struggling to get back on topic. "Um, we need to make it seem that you left for a good reason, or that you're a good friend."

"Well…" Row considered why he left. "I went to start my own life."

"Why didn't you say goodbye or visit?"

He shrugged. "I just forgot."

"Hm." Chester piped in, "Maybe you can make a case that he hit his head and forgot about everything?"

Lefty scowled. "We can't make up lies, Chester."

"Fine." Chester scoffed. "But he never said it wasn't true, right Mr. Gareau?"

"I didn't hit my head," Row replied blandly.

The socks sighed in unison, returning to their pondering. They scratched at their chins while Lefty bounded back and forth. Then she jumped higher than he'd seen yet. "I know!" She bounded and bounded. "I can find that friend of yours, the one at your boat! You *are* still friends, right?"

"She's my girlfriend, but she might be hard to get to the witness stand. She's a mermaid."

"I'm sure we can make accommodations." Lefty grinned. "If we can make a case that you've changed, we're well on our way to getting you free."

"Right." Row paused. "How close exactly?"

"A couple hours?"

"Hours?" Row stumbled back. "You're not saying that the trial starts in a few hours, are you?"

She stopped bouncing. "What else would I be saying?"

"Can't you ask for more time? How will you come up with a solid case in an hour?"

She flinched back a little bit, because Row was a little bit scary. "Well, everyone was really excited to start… so I didn't say no."

Row gave himself a moment to still his aching chest. As the pain built and dispersed, he found his words again. "Fine," he said. "You hurry up and get Chrys, she'll be able to fix this."

"Alright!" Lefty bounded away. "I'll see you at the stand, Row!"

Row groaned, falling back onto his pillows once more. He sure hoped that he was right.

As Lefty had suggested, the trial began a few hours later. Row found himself arraigned by ferrets, the fluffy noodles leading him down the complexities of the tunnels. Even for a short man, Row found himself ducking and hunching over for the entire walk. It wasn't until he walked into the courtroom that he finally could stretch out.

The room was packed with more sock ferrets and sock weasels, sock snakes, sock kittens, and sock any other small animal Row could think of. Quilts were pinned to walls like the forts he'd made as a kid, serving as hammocks and cozy tunnels for the sock creatures. Sat in the centre of the cozy fort was a small bear, about three feet long. She was, as her name suggested, made of pillows.

Row was led to one of the two tables in front of her. He swallowed a nervous lump in his throat as he looked up at the stand. The last time he'd been in a courtroom was to have his name changed. He'd been dressed better at the time, and his only real fear was the embarrassment of admitting his old name to strangers. Somehow that ridiculous little fear nagged at him the same way a five-year prison sentence did — it probably had something to do with not being able to take any of the stuffed animals seriously.

A few seconds after taking his seat, his lawyer came bounding forward. She grinned at him, scrambling up onto the tall chair. "I've got us some character witnesses."

"Did you find Chrys?" he asked.

"Boy did I!" She bounced in her seat. "This is going to go great!"

Row looked behind himself, back at the sneering socks in hopes of finding Chrys. Unlike Lefty had suggested, he couldn't find her anywhere. His gaze crossed the room, skimming over the pungent prosecutor. The sock skunk sat at the desk next to him, skimming over a pile of notes.

Lefty followed his gaze to her and waved. "Good luck, Ms. Dress Socks!"

The skunk glanced up and over the tops of her violet glasses. She gave Lefty a minor acknowledgement before focusing back at her notes. While Lefty smiled, Row felt all the more nauseous. In front of him the judge was quiet, looking over her own notes on the case.

"Is the jury ready?" she asked.

"Whenever you are, Your Honour," a pink ferret announced.

"Send them in."

With that a dozen or so socks filed inside. They moved in a more organized fashion than usual, filing onto a tiny bench. As Lefty had suggested earlier, most appeared to be ferrets, with the occasional mink and rat sprinkled in. As they settled, they looked to the judge.

"Now," Pillow Bear began, "if there is any reason you feel that you'll be biased in your assessment of this case, please raise your paw."

Every single one of the jurors raised their paw — aside from a kitten that couldn't figure out what the word "biased" meant. After the ferret beside her explained it, she joined them.

Pillow Bear sighed, looking amongst them. "I'll allow it."

Row flinched back in his seat. His lawyer didn't make any objections. She was jittering in place in an attempt to stop her bouncing.

"The prosecution may proceed with their opening statement."

The skunk nodded to herself before climbing on top of the table so all could see her. She pushed up her glasses and cleared her throat. "On the morning of November nineteenth, 2007, something changed for many socks, people and craft creatures alike. A little hedgehog named Oxnard woke up ready for breakfast — honey on toast. That's what every morning for him was, honey, toast, and his best friend Rosie."

Row looked away, hoping they hadn't managed to bring Oxnard as a witness.

"But November the nineteenth wasn't a normal morning for him. You see, when Oxnard came down for breakfast, he didn't find Rosie. She wasn't out in the garden. She wasn't sleeping in. No, Rosie Gareau was somewhere else entirely different, far, far away. No message. No note. Was she dead? In trouble? No. As you can clearly see, he stands as our defendant today. A bad friend."

The crowd made cautious looks at him, trying to remain quiet and cordial.

"What's more, it was not Oxnard's heart alone that was damaged that day. As we will see throughout the course of this trial, there were many which Rosie Gareau chose to abandon. And I would review each individual case, but you see that would require bringing everyone on this island to the stand — and who has time for that?

"Instead, we will see only a fraction of the hurt he caused. I will show you how he has forgotten the names of his once dear friends. You will learn of the damages he bestowed upon even the toughest ferrets we know.

"And finally! Yes, finally, we will feast our eyes upon the most sickening of evidence. We will learn of how this defendant stooped to a level even the most dastardly of criminals never stooped to. We will see how Rosie Gareau abandoned his very own mother."

Chapter Fourteen

Persnickety, Pungent Prosecution
With a Side of Pancakes

For most of Claire's childhood, Sundew had been in the shadows. She'd noticed her on occasion, usually when she was playing with Row. But otherwise she ignored her. It was what people did.

When Claire first noticed Sundew, it was during her Nietzschean phase. She was fifteen and thought she was brilliant after picking up a copy of *Slaughterhouse-5*. Once again, her girlfriend, Row, had stumbled across a book with a cover she liked. And Claire, being Claire, read the whole thing on her spare.

She sat beneath one of the school yard elms, the grooves of bark becoming imprinted on her back. Her eyes shut as she imagined herself becoming unstuck. If time was what she became unstuck from, she'd take it. But if she was being honest with herself, she mostly wanted to unstick herself from Cherrywood. If towns were craft supplies, Cherrywood was glue. Really sticky glue.

She opened her eyes. And while she didn't realize it, she saw into another world. In this world, things weren't dictated by Cherrywood's stories. Things were quiet and alone. Claire noticed Sundew sitting against a nearby tree. She was trying to feed the birds. But few even noticed her seeds, some actively avoiding where she threw them. An obvious anger passed through her, culminating in a fist that tightened around her seed pouch.

"Is everything okay, Sundew?" Claire asked as she stood from her spot.

The girl paled, as if Claire were a ghost.

"Sundew?"

"You're talking to me," Sundew uttered.

"Well… yeah." Claire shrugged. "We're the only ones out here."

"But…" Sundew shook her head. "You must be looking for Rosie, she's in class still."

Claire backed up a step, hoping to calm her slightly. "I know that, don't worry. I finished my book and — you know what? Never mind. I'll stop bugging you."

"Wait! Don't!" Sundew stood from her spot. "We can talk. I don't hate talking."

"You don't?" Claire furrowed her brow. "I always figured you did. You're the shyest person I've ever met."

"I'm not shy." Her cheeks became pink. "What do you want to talk about? I can talk about anything."

Claire glanced to her book. "You like to read books?"

"Yeah, of course I like books."

It was like waking up in a dream. Claire draped her legs off the side of Rose's bed. As she touched her toes to the ground, she felt the throb of her ankle. *So it all was real,* she thought — *that or I found some wicked pain meds.* She wiped her eyes and groaned. It was all too tangible to be a hallucination, it fit too well with everything she knew.

Rose *was* magical.

Claire had always felt it, believing it didn't take much more of a stretch. But that didn't make deciding what to do about Sundew any easier. Claire leaned into her palms, the answer still hazy even after a night's rest. She jostled at a knock on her door, straightening out and staring in its direction.

"Is that you, Sundew?" Claire asked.

"Yes." The tone she used was her usual, vile and demanding. "I was wondering if you'd like to come downstairs and have breakfast with me."

"Breakfast?" Claire frowned, though her stomach growled. It'd been too long since her last meal.

"I made breakfast, okay?" She scoffed. "I'll help you downstairs and then we can talk about last night."

"Fine." Claire's response was cold. "We've got a lot to discuss."

She met Sundew in the doorway after the arduous trek on the tips of her toes. While she'd allow Sundew to help her down the stairs, she wasn't about to relinquish herself entirely. On the other side of the doorway, Sundew was sullen. Her lips were curled into a disgusted frown, the rest of her body sagging with weariness. Her hand was bandaged and there was flour on the ends of her hair.

With the bitter stiffness expected, Sundew took Claire's arm and guided her down the steps. She was more rigid than a pair of crutches. Their awkward walk downstairs ended when they turned to the kitchen. Inside, there was a mess of dishes. Pancake batter dripped from the counter. Streaks of it lined the cupboards, spilling over off of spatulas and a large mixing bowl. On the other side of the room, the dining table was pristine. A stack of fluffy beige pancakes rested in the centre of the table. Two empty plates were set on the opposite ends.

Sundew placed Claire in the seat closest to the syrup. Meanwhile, she took the one closer to a vase of white flowers tied with a pink ribbon.

"So." Sundew took two pancakes from the pile like she was a robot.

"So," Claire repeated. "You trying to butter me up so I remain your word slave?"

"That phrasing is a little harsh."

"Is it?" Claire cocked a brow as Sundew grabbed the syrup, drenching her pancakes in sugar. She only stopped when they were swimming in a pool. "I mean, Sundew, I'm here against my will. I'm not even being paid."

"Do you want to be paid?"

Claire scowled.

"Have you at least considered what I've told you?"

Claire crossed her arms before nodding to herself. "Of course I've been thinking about it. And I've got a lot of questions still."

"Such as?"

"Is there a reason you want me to stay here? I don't want to be stuck in this house all the time, I need to get out and see family and friends."

Sundew scoffed. "And you'd come back?"

"If it's what's needed? Yes."

"I don't believe you."

Claire grimaced. "Well, that's the only way I'm going to write you any stories— Oh! And one more thing, I'm not being an accessory to whatever it is you're trying to do to Row."

Sundew sighed.

"Go ahead and hate him, but I want nothing to do with it." She gave Sundew a pointed look. "I'm not his biggest fan after he ditched me for the city, but I can't hold it against him if I'm stuck here."

Sundew raised a brow. "I mean, you still can. If Rosie sucked it up and took the house, the stories would be in her control and you wouldn't be here."

"Why do you have to say it like that?"

"What?"

"*Her* control?" Claire glared. "With people acting the way they do about him, I really don't see why anyone expected him to stay around." Claire shook her head in dismay. "I mean, I *am* a girl and the fact everyone expects *me* to be *my* mother horrifies me."

Sundew twitched, attempting to stop her eyes from rolling.

"Why do you hate him?"

She shrugged.

"Oh, please." Claire rolled her eyes. "You don't try to kill someone over something shrug-worthy."

"It's complicated — and I'm not trying to kill him."

"You aren't?"

Sundew shook her head. "I want him to know what it's like to be me, to maybe understand for a moment what he's done to me."

"What *has* he done to you?"

She set down her knife, looking to Claire as she allowed her words to steep. "I've lived in Rosie's shadow since the day I was born. She gave me the ability to suffer, made me aware of my painful life... and then left me to wallow in it. As long as she's still walking around freely, I can't."

Claire didn't know what to say. "But don't you write the stories now?"

She shrugged once again.

"Fine." Claire finally grabbed her own plate. Her nerves had died — or, at the very least, her hunger had won. She gave herself only a tablespoon of syrup before cutting into the pancakes. They were lumpy, with an uneven flavour of baking soda throughout. But they were still food.

Sundew went quiet, grabbing the syrup once it was set back down.

"Sundew." Claire glanced up between a bite. "I do have another question, maybe the last for now."

"Hm?"

"Dan brought something up back at the memorial, I wanted to know if it was true." Claire sighed deeply. "Did Rose really spend her last months alone? I mean, aside from myself."

Sundew stared into her syrup swamp. "People stopped coming the day I — for as long as I've been around."

"Sundew…" Claire felt a sadness tug at her as she looked at her face.

Sundew hid behind her locks. The image of her sullen face lined with tears showed through the dense tangle. "I'm a monster, Claire." She sniffled and wiped her eyes.

Her hair grew longer, stretching out like shadows and twisted around the legs of her chair. Between the fine strands of hair, barbed and sticky vines grew. Claire jerked her gaze from the hypnotic magic. "You write the stories now, Sundew. You can be whoever you want."

She shook her head. "I can't make the pen glow. I will only ever be a shadow in this house."

"With that attitude, sure." Claire grimaced. "But you can choose to act better, stop attempting to drown your brother and stop kidnapping people. If you turn around, I'd certainly visit more. I don't care what sort of magic or whatever is going on, I'm willing to see past it."

"I'll consider it," Sundew muttered.

"Hi everybody! I'm Lefty Grey Sock Fox and this is… um… my opening statement."

Row hid his head in his hands as his attorney bounced across their desk. The second she was called to speak, her jittering overtook her. She was as eloquent as an elementary schooler's book report.

"I'm going to create some reasonable doubt." She looked at Pillow Bear to confirm she'd used the right word.

Pillow Bear nodded.

"Yeah, I'm going to have witnesses and stuff that like our defendant, Mr. Gareau. And then all of you will be like, 'Wow! He really has changed!' and then maybe get rid of his sentence." She then bowed for some reason. "Thank you, jury."

Row sank into his chair.

Lefty bounced back into her spot with a wild grin. "Did you see that!" she whispered. "Everyone's smiling! I think we've got a strong case."

"They're laughing at you, Lefty."

Lefty stilled, glancing back to the jury as they failed to suppress their snickers. She deflated in her seat, ears falling flat behind her head. "But... that was my best opening statement yet. I only did one um."

Row sank further into his chair. Maybe if he kept sliding down, he could escape his trial. His eyes met with the prosecutor, Ms. Dress Socks. She glanced at him sidelong as she straightened out her notes. She waited as her witness, a large ferret, swore in at the stand before climbing into his stool. He was made of white socks with rainbow stripes scribbled all over him. Pink threads sealed many holes in his fabric.

The ferret didn't ring any bells for Row, it was another nonsense creation his mother had brought to life. He'd made countless sock animals for her when she'd been in the hospital. The idea came to him after reading *The Wonderful Pigs of Jillian Jiggs*. Though, it got out of control faster than he'd expected. His dad had left so many socks at their house, and he hated seeing the lonely bundles spilling from the drawers.

Row struggled to remember if he'd ever known every single one of their names, or if he forcefully shoved them from his memory. It was probably a bit of both.

Ms. Dress Socks stood up on her desk and spoke to the witness. "Would you mind introducing yourself?"

"Not at all," the ferret said. "I'm Righty Rainbow Scribble Ferret, but most people call me Scribble."

"And Mr. Scribble, how long have you been a lost sock?"

"Well, I became a lost sock back in 1996. Not sure where my lefty went." Mr. Scribble said wistfully. "But Rose brought me to life a year or two after that."

"Who are you referring to when you say Rose?"

Mr. Scribble pointed to Row. "The defendant, Rose Gareau Jr."

Lefty gasped. But Row crinkled his brow, it was hardly fair to say he was responsible for it. His mother had been the one in control of the magic.

"Are you certain that it was him?" Ms. Dress Socks asked.

"I've got an excellent sniffer and you don't forget the smell of a friend."

The skunk nodded to herself. "Very true, Mr. Scribble. But what makes you so certain that you and the defendant were friends?"

Mr. Scribble put his paw to his mouth as he pondered. "Well, he used to play hide and seek with me and my other sock friends. And he always came back to find us. We had endless fun at Honey Walls together."

"And tell me, do you recall the events of November nineteenth, 2007?"

Mr. Scribble nodded. "Um… yes… that was the most horrible day of my life. I don't know how I could forget it. The day before, I'd been trying to play hide and seek like usual, but when I hid, Rosie didn't come to find me. I hid in the cupboard so long I missed lunch and dinner. The next morning, the nineteenth, I came downstairs to find that big confused mess."

"Confused mess? Could you elaborate?"

"Well…" He slumped. "I went downstairs and all the craft animals were in a panic because Rosie had disappeared. I heard them say that he missed breakfast with Oxnard — which never happened before. Ever. We thought something horrible had happened."

"When did you change your mind about it being something horrible?"

"We didn't change our mind until we talked to Mrs. Gareau — Rosie's mom. She told us that Rosie wouldn't be coming back, but she didn't explain why."

The skunk nodded more. "And during this absence did you ever receive a letter from the defendant?"

"No."

"Postcard?"

"No."

"Note, message in a bottle, or phone call?"

"No, no, and no. I've had zero contact with the defendant."

"Thank you, I have no further questions." Ms. Dress Socks climbed down from her table and took a seat on her stool.

Row attempted to speak with Lefty about her cross-examination, but the second Ms. Dress Socks was in her seat Lefty sprang to life. She threw herself to the witness stand, landing on the floor in front of it. Then she began to bound in circles in a way which was out of her control. Mr. Scribble giggled.

"Morning, Mr. Scribble!" she barked.

"Morning, Lefty Grey," he snickered back.

"I don't really have a lot of questions for you, but I hope to do my best."

He nodded. "It's okay, no one's mad at you for taking the case."

"I don't think they should be, I think we need to give Row—"

"Objection, Your Honour." Ms. Dress Socks interjected. "I don't see what any of this has to do with the trial."

Pillow Bear looked over her stand at Lefty. "Ms. Dress Socks is correct, you need to focus on the trial, Lefty."

"Oh!" Lefty bounced. "I'm sorry, Your Honour." She turned back to Mr. Scribble at the witness stand. "Um… alright, Mr. Scribble, are you sure that Row was gone for no good reason?"

"That's what Mrs. Gareau suggested."

Lefty put her paws on her hips. "But you admit that you don't know for sure why Row left?"

"I guess… I don't know for sure, but the implication is strong."

"Well, I rest my case then!" Lefty grinned and wiped the case away with her paws.

By the time Lefty came back to her seat, Row felt like he'd become a puddle on the floor. The judge cast a glance in his direction and he straightened. All that had been said of Lefty's skills was correct. She bounded into the seat next to him with her usual grin.

Row didn't smile back.

He wanted to stand up and make his case, but eyes on all sides pressed on him. He'd have to wait for his turn at the stand before they'd listen to anything. And maybe before then he could finally see Chrys.

The deliberation was tedious. As Mr. Scribble left, another witness was brought to the stand. The new sock looked a little like a pirate. He was a red and white striped otter with a patch for an eye. With his good eye he glared at Row before focusing in on the prosecution. Once again, Ms. Dress Sock stood on her desk.

"Please introduce yourself for the record," she said.

"Ar! I be Otter."

"And Otter, how would you describe your relationship with Oxnard?"

"Oxnard?" He grinned. "That little matey and I sailed the ocean together. Loved his tales."

"Oh? And what sort of tales would he tell?" She raised her brow.

"All sorts, but he loved talking about his good friend Rosie." His shoulder slumped. "Two of them sounded like they be once good friends. Better than good, they seemed to be like matching socks the two of them be."

The crowd stifled their gasps, but soft puffs could be heard. Low whispers echoed, "Like matches?" It was clearly a sacred sort of sock friendship.

"Tell me," Ms. Dress Socks continued. "When you were travelling with Oxnard, did he ever relay the events of the nineteenth to you?"

"Aye, he did many a time," Otter said. "He told me all about the toast, how he'd go down and eat it every morning, the fear he felt when his friend Rosie didn't show up. What kind of friend could do a thing like that?"

Row felt a pang in his chest as Otter met eyes with him. He ducked his gaze in response, pushing away the memories. He was too old for fiction. It wasn't real. It should never have been made real. He shut his eyes and shut out the courtroom.

"Tell me, did Oxnard ever relay to you the feeling that he felt."

"Aye. I be there when he finally realized he be abandoned." Otter sounded weary. "I've never saw a stuffed animal so sad — no, heartbroken. He stopped adventuring. Didn't see the point no more."

"How did Oxnard feel about adventure before?"

"Before he found out? Ar, it be his life."

"And his distress, all of that is because he learned that his friend abandoned him knowingly and purposely?"

"Aye."

Ms. Dress Socks huffed. "Thank you, Otter, I won't make you bear the memories any longer."

Row glanced at Lefty. She was stilled. She stared at the witness and sniffled a bit. When she processed what she'd heard, she climbed down to the stand and approached the witness.

"Do you really think Oxnard stopped adventuring because of Row?" she asked softly.

"Aye, Little Matey." He sighed. "It be the reason he never came back with me."

Lefty's ears flattened. "Why in the world would Row be mean to Oxnard? Don't you think there could be a good reason?"

Otter shrugged. "Not sure, thar be a chance, but that's for you to prove, Lefty."

She nodded to herself before walking back to Row. "Thank you, Otter," she said softly as she wandered back.

When she came back to the stand, she glanced at Row but didn't talk to him. The next few witnesses followed in a blur. One after the other, socks testified against Row. Lefty made no strong rebuttal (mostly kept chatting with the witnesses). She looked to deflate more and more, her energy and excitement sapped by each new story of sad, abandoned socks.

When Row thought he could take no more, the final witness was brought to the stand—yet another ferret he didn't recognize. The ferret wobbled to the top of his seat, beginning to shiver as many eyes looked upon him.

Ms. Dress Socks began to question him like all the socks before. The tiny ferret went by the name Yellow because he was yellow. Like the rest, he remembered Row and remembered being abandoned. He remembered him and Row playing puzzles a lot, and was left alone in the puzzle room the day before he disappeared. It was all mundane at this point, so much so Row could almost fall asleep, at least until Ms. Dress Socks held up Exhibit A.

The evidence was in a small plastic bag, a crumpled paper inside. Row recognized the paper and gripped his pocket. The letter from his mother was gone. He felt dizzy a moment as he watched Ms. Dress Socks slide the letter into the witness's paws.

"Yellow, would you be so kind as to explain to me what this is?"

Yellow nodded. "I-it's um… a letter I-I found it in R-Rosie's p-pocket." He ducked down as he spoke.

"And could you explain the contents of it?" she prompted, seemingly irritated.

"W-well, it's a l-letter signed by Mrs. G-Gareau."

"Yes, could you explain the contents of the letter."

"I-it is for R-Rosie. M-Mrs. Gareau says that she really misses Rosie. And u-um… she's passed away."

Lefty interrupted. "What does that mean?"

Ms. Dress Socks scowled, rage shaking her paws. "It means Mrs. Gareau died, Lefty. You're defending a man that let his mother die alone and heartbroken!"

Lefty shrunk back in her stool.

Pillow Bear cleared her throat. "Ms. Dress Socks, I will not have any bullying in my court."

Ms. Dress Socks nodded through some sniffles. "I-I'm sorry, Your Honour."

"The evidence still stands." Pillow Bear glared at Row. "But we will continue the trial as planned. Lefty, you can cross examine the witness if you like."

Lefty sank, looking between Row and Pillow Bear. "I'd actually like a bit of a break, please."

There was a short recess before Lefty brought her witnesses to the stand. However, Row didn't get much freedom during it. His hands were still cuffed and every movement was monitored by one ferret or another. He stretched his neck searching for Chrys from one side of the room to the other. If anything could save him, it would be her.

He stood out in the hallway for a bit, stretching out his legs. After her short lap around the courthouse, Lefty bounced over to Row with less pomp than previous. She made a sad little puff as she looked up at him. "Row, I think that me and you actually need to talk a bit about this case."

"Yeah." Row looked down at her. "I think that'd be a good idea."

"I don't understand how you could do something to Mrs. Gareau." She sniffled. "How could you leave her alone like that?"

Row scowled. "Lefty, it's not that simple. She wasn't alone. My sister stayed with her."

"Sundew? That's worse than being alone!"

He rolled his eyes, but knew that Lefty was right.

"But why did you leave her in the first place? What possible reason could you have for leaving your mother?"

He felt sick to his stomach as he attempted to keep the memory from surfacing. In Row's opinion, memories were too much like loose thread; pull at one and you might unravel them all. It was something best left alone. "It's personal."

"W-was Mrs. Gareau mean to you?" she asked tentatively.

"What?" Row blinked. "Of course not. Mom was perfectly fine. If anything, she was too nice to me. I had to get away from things for a bit. That's it."

"Were you ever planning on coming back?"

Row slumped. "Well… no."

"Mr. Gareau!" She gasped.

"I grew up, Lefty. I changed. I've become an entirely different person." He leaned against the wall. "I never wanted to come back. And if I did, how could I? Rosie doesn't exist anymore. Who knows if she ever did?"

"What are you talking about?" Lefty scratched the ground at his feet.

Row slid his back down the wall until he was sat in front of her. "I don't know why I ran away in the first place, but at some point it becomes too hard to turn back. What was I supposed to do? Come back and tell her that her daughter's gone? If heartbreak is really that big of a deal, coming back would have been worse."

Lefty put a paw on his foot. "I don't think you would have broke her heart, Mr. Gareau."

"We'll never know now." He draped his arms over his knees, trying once again to turn off the world around him. Thinking about these sorts of things was about as productive as talking to socks. He focused on his aching chest, trying to still the pain. He wondered if somewhere deep inside of him there were still emotions — *no, that would be ridiculous.*

When he opened his eyes, Lefty climbed onto his feet. She curled up on his shoes like a little kitten. Her nose tipped up, and she watched him. "I'm sorry about your mother, Mr. Gareau," she said softly. "I'd be a pretty bad friend to think that you wouldn't miss her too."

"It's okay," he said. She was right though. He didn't miss her.

144

"I'm really sorry. I'll make sure to stay on your side, sir." She nodded to herself. "Alright. Here's the deal, Mr. Gareau, I've got three witnesses before you take the stand. I want you to be yourself, and before you know it you'll be out of here."

"When's Chrys coming up?" he asked.

"She's last, right before you."

"Alright." He took a deep breath.

Chapter Fifteen

The Urge to Run and Remain

Chester sat at the witness stand in a pair of tiny handcuffs. He was remarkably cool, slumped back in the stool like a gangster from the movies. He looked down at Lefty as she bounded about in front of him. After her talk with Row, she'd pepped up a little bit, but still wasn't as excitable as when they'd first met.

"Afternoon, Chester!" She smiled up at him. "Hope you're doing well."

"Doing well given the circumstances." He smirked. "But you probs should stay on topic, don't you think?"

"Oh! Right!" She hopped. "I was hoping you could tell the jury a bit about your relationship with the defendant."

"Relationship?" He thought it out. "I'd say we got a bit of a bond between thieves thing going. I don't really remember playing with him back in the day — wasn't cool enough for me. But meeting him again in the cell a few hours ago, seems alright."

"And does he seem like the type to abandon a friend still?"

Chester shrugged. "Don't really know him well enough."

"Oh." Lefty's ears flattened. "But he hasn't abandoned you yet, right?"

"Guess that's true." The ferret yawned.

"Then I suppose that's that." Lefty smiled up to Pillow Bear. "I'm done my questions now."

Row groaned into his hands. Even after the small deliberation, Lefty was still Lefty… and Lefty was a terrible lawyer. No witness would have been better than bringing Chester to the stand. As Lefty left, Ms. Dress Socks was eager to climb atop her desk and begin the cross-examination.

Ms. Dress Socks cleared her throat. "Mr. Argyle," she began. "Could you inform me on how long you've shared a 'bond among thieves' with Rosie?"

"Um…" He tapped a paw to his chin. "Couple hours at most? Met him in prison, so, guess since he went there?"

"Really? And do you think that is a reasonable amount of time to make a value judgement on a person."

"Nah."

A smile nearly took hold of Ms. Dress Socks's face, but she managed to suppress it.

"Thing is, isn't that the whole point of the trial?" Chester caught the prosecution off guard. "You're judging him based on about an hour of knowing him. No offence to Lefty, but you read Exhibit A. The letter says that foxes don't know a lick about jurisprudence. How's this at all fair?"

"None of this has anything to do with my question, Mr. Argyle. Let's move on."

"Yeah! Let's, because I've got a thing or two to say about unfair trials! Sure I may have been caught gambling with the bailiff, but he wasn't a child so I really don't—"

"Objection. The witness is being non-responsive."

Pillow Bear gave Chester a look.

He slumped down in his seat. "Fiiine, what's your next question?"

"Yes or no, is it true that you are well known for hiding your feelings with sarcasm?" She glared at him. "And I will remind you that you are under oath."

Chester side-eyed the jury. "Yeah, it's true."

"And yes or no, were you abandoned by Rose Gareau Jr. on the morning of November nineteenth, 2007?"

"Yes," he grumbled.

"And is it true that you were friends before he disappeared?"

"Yes."

"Good." Ms. Dress Socks said. "No further questions."

As he was guided from the witness stand, Chester directed a shrug at Row. The cool ferret had tried his best. Row supposed it wasn't his fault that his lawyer didn't know how to pick a witness. Though none of that made anything actually better. At least there was only one more witness he'd need to bear through before he could be with Chrys again. Even if being with her just meant sitting in the same room, he'd take it.

Lefty climbed from her stool before the witness was brought out. A few seconds after, Lefty climbed onto the witness stand. She sat at the stand. She swore she'd tell the truth. She waved at Row.

No. He shook his head, *She couldn't possibly be…*

"Afternoon, Lefty." Lefty hopped onto the desk and spoke to her empty spot.

"Afternoon, Ms. Grey Sock," she said as soon as she hopped back to her spot.

She was. Row buried his head in his hands. She was going to be her own witness. He looked to the prosecution hoping that Ms. Dress Socks would want to object… but she didn't. Row swallowed a lump in his throat. Of course she didn't. Having no witness would be better than having Lefty.

"Objection," Row spoke up. "I don't think it's permissible in court to be your own witness."

Every sock in the courtroom gasped upon hearing him speak for the first time. There was an unanticipated buzz of excitement that passed through the room. Socks bounded over top of one another, making loud gossiping whispers. All the chaos was followed by the pounding of Pillow Bear's gavel (well, her plastic hammer).

"Order! Order!" she shouted, all the while glaring at Row. "I'll have the lot of you sent out of the courtroom."

The socks quieted.

"Thank you." She looked to Lefty. "You're doing a fine job, Lefty, please continue. And I want no more interruptions from you, Mr. Gareau."

Row flinched under the judgemental eyes of Pillow Bear. He adjusted in his seat, making himself less of a presence in the courtroom. But however much he tried to do so, he could still hear the whispers of socks behind him.

Lefty sank in her seat in much the same way. "You know what? I don't think I have any questions for myself. I think Row might actually just be a bad friend…"

"There, there," cooed Ms. Dress Socks. "I think you're an excellent witness, I'm so sorry that your client objected."

Lefty sniffled and wiped her eyes. "You think I am?"

"Of course, would you like to continue with cross-examination?"

Lefty nodded. "I mean, if you think I'd do a good job."

"You'll do excellent," she said softly. "Now Lefty, would you agree with your previous statement about Rosie, where you said he, 'actually just might be a bad friend?'"

"Well… um…"

"A simple yes or no would suffice."

She looked at Row then to Ms. Dress Socks. She then nodded. "Yes… I mean, sort of. He hurt my feelings with the objection."

"I'm very sorry he hurt your feelings. Is this the first time he hurt your feelings?"

"No." She shook her head.

"And tell me, do you also remember being abandoned on the morning in question?"

She nodded slightly. "I thought there might have been a good reason."

"I'm very sorry, Lefty." Ms. Dress Socks shook her head in dismay. "How about we end this trial here? I know this is hardly proper court procedure. But let's be honest with ourselves, the evidence is staggering. May I make a motion to sentence the defendant now without further trial, Your Honour?"

Pillow Bear didn't respond immediately in either direction. She looked to the jury, to the attorneys, and last to Row. A long and bewildered breath escaped her as she stared at him. He had a faint memory of making the bear because he wanted someone to snuggle at night. With his mom and dad gone, the bear was the only decent substitute.

"I'm nearly decided," she said at last. "But I do wish to at least speak to our defendant. At the very least, I want to understand his reasoning."

Row froze as the bear stared at him. After the reaction over his last words, he felt tentative about speaking. "What about the other witness?" he asked respectfully.

"She's unneeded," Pillow Bear said after a quick glance at her notes. "Why did you leave us, Rosie?"

Row felt the weight of each button eye press down on him. The courthouse was deathly quiet, as they all waited on the answer which would change the course of everything. The answer they'd been waiting on for nearly a decade. He turned his focus to the woodgrain of his desk, though even it looked a little too close to a pair of eyes.

"I…" He shook his head to keep memories from forming. "I wanted nothing to do with any of you."

Not long after breakfast, Claire found herself lying on the dusted pink couch. A baggie of melting ice rested on her ankle, while crashes and the clatter of dishes tickled her ears. Sundew's songlike mutters could be discerned beneath the cacophony.

"Is everything alright in there?" Claire called to her.

There was yet another crash followed by a string of grunts from Sundew's mouth. The sounds belonged to no known language.

Claire rolled her eyes, adjusting herself for further comfort on the couch. The two had struck up a deal, that Sundew would take Claire back to the bookshop to visit her family. They'd do so a little while after Sundew put away dishes (a task that seemed less and less achievable with each outburst).

"The dishes aren't out to get you, Sundew! Just calm down." Claire smirked.

The clatter stopped for a moment, allowing Sundew to be heard as she stomped towards the doorframe. "If it's so easy, I'd like to see you try!" she shouted when she surfaced.

"I'd help but I can hardly stand." Claire rolled her eyes for effect. "But maybe it'd be a good idea if you stopped overreacting to things? They'll get clean if you chill out and let them soak."

"Chill out?" Her eyebrow twitched. "That's easy to say while you're lounging on the couch."

"Yeah, I'm chilling out. Running around isn't going to fix my foot." She rested her head back. "And freaking out isn't going to get you any closer to any of your goals — dishes included."

Sundew scowled. "I thought you wanted out as soon as possible."

Claire shrugged. "I mean, sure, but if we're planning to continue writing these stories that means we'll be seeing each other often. I'd prefer it if you could… I don't know, soften some of those edges."

"Edges?" She glared back.

Her hair and the vines which tangled inside it continued to grow outward. It piled over itself spreading back into the kitchen. It formed rolling waves of burgundy, curling out and onto the counters. The strange sight was enough to jostle Claire.

"What?" Sundew continued to scowl.

"Never mind, we'll worry about edges later." Claire stared at Sundew's hair as it navigated the carpet. "I've been meaning to ask, but what is going on with your hair?"

"My hair?" She crinkled her nose as she looked down a bit. It continued to grow outward, wrapping around the vases of funeral roses. It rattled the pots and crushed the flowers. "I don't know." Sundew scowled. "Another mystery of Mother's magic, I suppose."

Claire nodded slightly. "Has it been like this before?"

"Not this long, but I've always found it to grow quickly." She shrugged. "If anything, it grew from spite. Rosie always wanted our hair to be so short. She took safety scissors to it in kindergarten." Sundew groaned. "What an embarrassment…"

"Wait? To both of your hair? Or just his?"

"Both." Sundew huffed, washing away the beginning of a blush. "I can't believe we had to go to school like that. I spent half the day crying… what a mess."

"But why would he?" Claire shook her head. Row didn't seem like the type to do something like that. "You aren't making things up, are you?"

"Why would I make up something so trivial?" She scowled. "For the longest time we were practically the same person. If Rosie cut her hair, so did I."

"Huh, I would have never pegged you two as the type to do that. You've always seemed so different."

"Not back then." She stiffened. Her hands formed into fists as her hair quickened its coiling. "Back then, Rosie picked everything for us. She was the one that got to decide when we got to be our own people."

"And that's when you were left in the shadows?"

Sundew nodded. "I went from being a reflection to a shadow. I can't decide what's worse—"

"A reflection." Claire said on impulse. "I mean, I would rather be forgotten as myself than be forced to live a life that wasn't mine."

"That's easy for you to say." Sundew scowled. "You're beautiful, fun, and everyone is better when in your company. Being Claire is far easier than being me."

"Excuse me?" Claire snorted. "My only real friend is a giraffe with a dinosaur collection. I mean, if we're talking about people that know the real me, that's it. I'd love to go be myself, but I'd be just as lucky doing that as you would be."

Sundew scoffed, turning back to the kitchen.

"Oh please, what? It's true." Claire scowled. "If I don't leave this town, I'm going to live and die a miserable book keeper. I'm a weirdo lesbian, if you think that's easy, go try it. But as far as I'm concerned, we're starting from the same square."

Sundew stopped, turning back to face Claire with a confused look. "From the weirdo lesbian square?"

"What? No!" She raised her hands. "I'm not calling you a lesbian. I'm just saying, I and everybody in this town is afraid of betraying their reflection a little bit. You, me… everybody."

"Right…" Sundew turned back toward the kitchen. As she walked forward, the vases were dragged with her. "Do you think the dishes have soaked enough?"

"Yeah." Claire stretched out her good foot. "I think you'll have no troubles now."

The thought returned to Dan suddenly while on a delivery. As he set the basket of sugar cookies into Mr. Applegate's hands, it hit him like waves of a somewhat invisible ocean. He tried to act normal, returning a strange smile to Mr. Applegate before jogging back to his delivery truck.

What am I doing? How did I forget Claire was kidnapped?

He sat down in the driver seat, gripping the steering wheel for support. He'd been released by Sundew the day before, yet somehow the memory settled in the furthest reaches of his mind. It was as if there'd been a wall placed between him and the thought. And then, magically, it was gone.

He pressed back in his seat, trying to discern if it were just some dream. Elements of it were... strange. Stranger than Sundew. As she'd forced him from the writing closet and out the doors of Honey Walls, there was more off about everything than the kidnapping. From the edges of the ditch, barbed burgundy leaves grew. They swelled out from between the spaces in the trees, curling like grubs atop one another. As he'd been dragged forward through the forest by the tangle, the kidnapping thing nearly felt completely normal.

Then as he'd stumbled out of the woods, he forgot everything. It was as if the memories were stuck in the branches.

He tapped his fingers on the steering wheel, staring out past Main Street. The branches were barren now, the piles of forgotten leaves stiff with frost. Snowflakes made their listless fall to the ground in the still air. Reaching to the back of the truck, Dan found a delivery for the Waters. He slid it into the passenger seat, placing it atop his notebook. Then he started the car and headed for the bookstore.

His van crawled down the block as he continued to make eyes at the forest beyond. A grey winter was beginning, emanating from the hill, the trees, and Honey Walls. He pulled up on the street beside the bookstore. Climbing out of the truck, he carried the delivery close to his chest, his notebook balanced on the top.

The bookstore was cramped tightly, wall to wall, ceiling to floor. The first aisles of books were so close together Dan could barely shimmy through. When he did make it through, things did appear more spacious. Or perhaps his mind was playing tricks with him — after all, he had to live there now. There was no way he could see himself squishing back through the cramped aisle.

Mr. Waters sat at the front counter, a sleepy expression on his face as he skimmed a novel. He yawned and glanced up at Dan. Mr. Waters was a slow sort of man. His glasses weren't properly fitted, continually sliding down his nose. He was bundled in a sweater, one of the many hocked by the local knitting groups. Dan glanced down, checking to see if they were wearing a match.

"Is everything alright, Dandy?" Mr. Waters asked.

Dan looked away from his sweater. "Um... yeah. Kinda. Do you know if Claire is here?"

Mr. Waters placed a bookmark in his book, staring absently as his cogs turned. "You know what? I'm not sure."

"Oh." Dan took a step back to the tunnel of books. "Mr. Waters, have I asked you about Rose at all?"

He shook his head. "No, what about her?"

Dan set down the box of croissants on the front desk, allowing himself to grab his notes. "I was working on a memorial piece about her, and actually, I was wondering if you know anything about Sundew."

"Sundew?" He furrowed his brow.

"Just… um… You used to babysit her, right? You didn't notice anything strange about her, did you?" He paced as he spoke. It all had felt so real.

Mr. Waters stared at him, pushing up his glasses to get a clearer look. "Is there something wrong, Dan?"

"Maybe? I don't know." He took a seat on one of the many stacks of books. His head fell into his hands, the cold of his notebook scratching at his cheek. "Maybe I'm tired, but I was doing my deliveries when the strangest thought popped in my head."

"What sort of thought?"

"I just…" He shook his head. "It's so strange, but I think Sundew tried to keep me in her cupboard yesterday."

Mr. Waters tilted his head, brow tightening further. "She what?"

"You know what? I don't know if she did." Dan rubbed at his face. "It doesn't make sense that she would, but it's all so clear in my head. But there was more to it… magical stuff. It must have been a dream."

"Magical? What do you mean by that?"

"Never mind." Dan shook his head. "I sound off my rocker. I bet this is just stress about this piece."

"You do sound pretty stressed, Dandy. You'd probably do well with a break."

"I would, but this obituary isn't about to write itself," he said. "I sent Claire off to talk to Sundew about it, I think. But I've come across something weird — not off my rocker weird, but doesn't make sense weird."

"What's that?"

Dan glanced up to Mr. Waters. "You and Rose were friends, right?"

He nodded, a somber undertone painting his expression. "We were a lot like you and Claire."

"But when was the last time you saw her?"

His face paled, straining for the memory.

"See? It's weird, no one's got memories of her aside from Claire." He shook his head more, still not making any more sense of it. "No one visited her for years."

Mr. Waters sighed. "This is what's stressing you out? Dandy, what does it matter? I'm sure you can write a compelling piece about her with what's been said in the past."

"You don't think it's strange at all?"

He shook his head. "Of course it's strange. That's Rose."

"What do you mean?"

"She got sick back in '94." He pinched his brow as he took a deep breath. "Though maybe it's been going on longer, I'm not sure. She never liked it. Not just the being sick part, the being a sick person. She died — no, sorry, she was supposed to die years ago."

"What?" Dan clicked his pen.

"I'm not being clear, am I? It's such an old memory," he said. "Before she got sick, she was my best friend. She was fun, adventurous, but always came back down to earth. But when the cancer came on, she became a different person. It was a slow thing. No one ever expected her to make it through. I helped watch Rosie, took her back and forth from the hospital… and then this one awful night, we thought it all was over. I said goodbye."

"But she didn't die…" Dan uttered.

"Exactly. It was a miraculous recovery." He laughed slightly. "I swear, it had to be some sort of magic that did it. If anyone had magic on her side, it'd be Rose Gareau."

Dan smiled back, before he felt a bit sick. "You're starting to sound a little bit off your own rocker, Mr. Waters."

"Maybe it's those Gareaus that'll do it to you," he said. "I do wonder why I never went to see her, but I guess it's strange to go back after you've already said goodbye."

While the socks deliberated, Row waited in his cell. The lamps which once lit the prison at the end of the hall were now out. He sat with his back to the dirt wall, shivering as his sweater failed to stifle the cold. He tried not to recall the time he'd run away. He refused to remember that autumn night, that same cold wrapping him as he navigated that big road down to the bus stop.

No. He forced the thought back down. If he was going to think about anything, it wasn't going to be because of a sock guilt trip. Besides, who knew if he was even capable of feeling guilty. It sounded very much like a feeling meant for people with hearts. And Row, now faced with every ounce of ridiculousness, knew he didn't have one of those.

If he did, it would have been aching. It would have been yearning for Chrys, her warm body close to his. A light in the dark. He shut his eyes, taking control of the moment. When he'd run away those many years ago, he'd thought that it all would be behind him. No more socks. No more Honey Walls. No more Mom.

He knocked his head against the wall, the dirt crumbling on his back.

How long can you run before it all catches up? a voice whispered in his head.

Chapter Sixteen

Oxnard and the Sky World
by Rose Gareau

Wherein Oxnard Braves a Bear's Den

Oxnard was really starting to embrace the pirate spirit. He loved rowing! He loved sea air! He loved never looking back! He and Otter kicked up into yet another shanty. It was by far the best way to pass the time — that is, if time needed to be passed at all. You see, Oxnard learned a while back that adventure was what mattered more than treasure, and being a pirate was always an adventure.

"Are we there yet?" Weasel groaned. He was hanging his head over the side of the boat in case he might be sick. The more they pirated, the more he hated being a pirate. He hated waves. He hated tiny boats. He wanted to go home.

"Ar!" Otter hissed as his song was interrupted. "What ye be going on about, Weasel?"

Weasel bared his teeth. "I said, are we close to the Sky World?"

"Ain't any way that we can tell. Isn't that right, Oxnard?"

"Yeah… sorry, Weasel." Oxnard reviewed his notes. "We need to keep following the sun until we reach where it touches the horizon."

"You sure those are real directions?" Weasel scowled.

"Of course, I got them from a trusted friend back home." Oxnard smiled. "Ms. Crow is a brilliant bird, she knows everything — though she's a little too capitalistic with her advice."

"Suppose, I'd have to ask her myself to figure out what the heck you just said," replied Weasel (except he didn't say 'heck,' and would have certainly gotten a time out if he wasn't a pirate alone at sea).

"Oh, Weasel," Oxnard spoke. "Are you still feeling sick? Is that why you're so grumpy?"

"Grumpy?" he grumbled.

"It's okay, Weasel." Oxnard offered a smile. "When I was back home, Ms. Gareau taught me the best cure for tummy aches." He paused, beginning to feel a tummy ache of his own.

"What is it?"

"Oh… um…" He felt a little balled up even though he was standing straight. "It's ginger tea and honey, but I guess we didn't bring that out here."

Weasel scowled back at him before hanging his head back over the side of the boat.

Oxnard let out a little hedgehog sigh (which I suppose is exactly like a normal sigh), then turned to face Otter. His tummy still felt a bit seasick and he still felt a bit balled. "Otter," he began, "do you ever think about home when you're off at sea?"

"Of course, I think about home all the time." He grinned back with his sharp-toothed smile. "What do ye expect a lost sock to do?"

"Does it ever just suddenly make you sad?"

Otter shrugged. "Matey, life be the ocean blue. You sail along at her whim, and you're bound to be sad from time to time."

"But um… particularly about missing home? Does that make you sad?"

He shrugged more.

"I've been wondering because of something Mrs. Gareau said. She doesn't think that this adventure is the same as other adventures, and I'm worrying that she might be right, but I also don't know how she could be."

Otter tilted his head. "What has ye thinking that?"

"It's strange, but every time I think about all the fun I've had back home with my old friends… it makes me really sad. Something in my tummy says that I'm never going to go back, even though I know I can turn the boat around. But maybe it is true, because once I make it to the Sky World, those adventures will be nothing but tiny things."

"That's a big thought for a wee little head."

Oxnard nodded. "Do you think Rosie ever thought the same thing on her adventure?"

"I'd imagine she might've."

"Do you think that when we meet, we'll be the same enough to still be friends?"

"Of course!" Otter gave a hearty laugh, patting Oxnard on the back. "The two of you are matching socks, matching socks don't be split apart!"

Oxnard smiled back as Otter unstuck his paw from the quills he'd patted. He started up a brand new shanty and Oxnard did his best to sing along. They rowed the boat toward the sun, carried by their songs and Weasel's musical grumbles. But deep inside, Oxnard's heart began to ball. Never in all his years had he expected to feel so strange about seeing his friend again.

Sundew's hair was out of control. It grew out of the kitchen and along the walls. It tangled in the furniture, causing everything to creak and shake when she walked. From her spot on the couch, Claire searched for a pair of scissors. Being so close to the writing closet, she assumed there might be some nearby. She swung her legs off the side of the couch and wobbled onto her feet.

She braced herself against the wall as she crossed the carpet. While the pain in her ankle had decreased, it felt far from gone entirely. The minimal amount of weight put on it caused her body to cave in protest. She made do with hugging the wall, sidling slowly until she could rest on Rose's writing stool.

Goosebumps ran up her arms. The experience of sitting in Rose's chair felt sacred. The last time she was in the writing closet, the vibe was different. While writing her mermaid story, there hadn't been time to respect the space, the walls of intricate notes. She pawed through them, seeming to forget she was searching for scissors.

The hair is clearly a magic problem, why not write a story? a part of her thought.

She flitted her gaze to Rose's pen. The pen with its delicate stem. *Where in the world had such a magical item come from?* She picked it up, shifting it to fit in her hand. For a moment, she could pretend she were a real writer, but then she hesitated. A story commissioned for Sundew was one thing, but creating her own… No. She couldn't mess with that. She pulled open a nearby cabinet and found a pair of scissors with a plastic pink handle.

Pushing Rose's chair aside, she returned to the living room. She wielded her scissors, approaching the nearest strands of hair. Leaned against the wall, she gripped a handful of hair and *snip!* She cut it at the base. But as the hair fell to the ground it continued to grow. Faster. Like a hydra it multiplied, climbing back up the wall.

The loose strands in her hand became invigorated with the same life. They wrapped around her, coiling her fingers and swirling up her arm. She thrashed in response. With some force, the hair fell to the ground. It broke into clumps which melted into the carpet and congealed into leaves. The sticky plants then began to grow and grow.

"Sundew! I think we need to talk about your hair again!"

There was no response.

Claire leaned against the wall, beginning towards the kitchen. After things had gone quiet, she'd assumed that Sundew had taken her advice. Just let it soak. Claire slid her shoulder along the wall, stopping at the doorframe. She rested against the shifting locks, before peering into the kitchen.

The trails of burgundy hair ran across the floor like dark rivers carved into the kitchen tile. At their end was Sundew. She was balled up on the floor with her back pressed to the fridge. Her body shivered as soft whimpers escaped.

"Sundew…" Claire neared.

The dishes were still covering the counters. Some of the larger bowls sat in the basins in deep pools. The suds greyed at the surface, clinging to the edges of partially submerged plates. Claire wobbled along with a hand to the counter for support.

"What's the matter?" Claire asked as she neared. She brought herself down to Sundew's level, taking a seat beside her.

Sundew remained quiet, curled up and hiding in her hair. She quivered as the sounds of sniffles resonated. "It's nothing," she muttered.

"Nothing? Sure thing." Claire reached out to her, setting a hand down on her back. "You just been sitting here the whole time?"

Sundew shivered at the touch. "Yeah."

"How come?"

"I can't do things anymore. All I seem to feel is sad or angry." She planted her hands down onto the ground. As she pushed herself up she remained small, glancing at Claire before retreating back to her tears. "I wish I didn't have to feel pain."

Claire rubbed her back, feeling her own heart begin to ache. "It's okay."

"No. It's not. Why do I have to feel things?" She shook her head. "She never gave me an ounce of her love, why does she get to take my heart?"

"No one can take anyone's heart." Claire kept her hand pressed to Sundew's back.

Sundew scoffed. "I can assure you that they can."

"I—"

"They can," she stated. "You don't understand what I'm feeling."

"Sorry... You're right" Claire said. "I'm sorry that you didn't get to have her. I can't really imagine what you're feeling."

"Alone... But I always feel that."

Claire nodded slightly.

Sundew pressed her back to the fridge. Her face could be seen clearly now, streaked with the translucent streams of tears. "Maybe it really isn't that different now that she's gone." She wiped her eyes. "Maybe the only thing that died was a chance to have what Rosie did."

New locks grew, weaving between their legs. Claire watched them without making a move. "I bet somewhere deep down she loved you, even if you feel like you're a monster. It's just, Rose didn't believe that monsters are evil. Like in her book Oxnard and the Bog Witch—"

Sundew glared at her.

"S-sorry. You're right, that probably doesn't help."

The tenseness of Sundew's expression softened. "It does and it doesn't."

"Yeah?"

"Yeah. I don't know what Mom thought of me. I wasn't her daughter like Rosie was. When she held me... she wasn't. I was a placeholder." She sighed. "Once, a while after Rosie ran away, she gave me a hug. It was the best thing that ever happened, and seconds later it was the worst. '*Rosie.*' That's what she called me."

"Oh god… that's shitty."

Sundew nodded. "I get it, though."

"Doesn't make it less shit."

Shock paled her complexion, her eyes widening in Claire's direction. The beginnings of a smile toyed with her lips but didn't form. "Thanks. But if she could even love a monster… It makes it worse that she couldn't love me."

"I could see that," Claire said.

"It's not her fault, though, so I can't hate her. I want to forget her, but she doesn't deserve that. I want to make someone pay for this. I want to *do* something, stop crying and fix things. But I can't, because it's over. It's the end."

"It's not the end."

"It is." Sundew scowled. "We're living past the ending of her stories right now, struggling on without a plot to guide us anymore. What do we do?"

"No clue." Claire shrugged. "Want to stay home?"

"You don't want to go out and see your family?"

"Foot's killing me."

"Oh." The tangles of her hair appeared to become limp, giving space for them to move their legs. The growth was as endless as her tears, spilling out from her heart. "I guess we could stay here."

"Rose Gareau Jr., you have been found guilty of abandoning your match and on all counts of being a bad friend," Pillow Bear read from the verdict. "As such, you are sentenced to ten years in laundry prison following a sincere apology."

Row gripped either side of the podium. He stood at centre stage with his back to the internal cheers of sock ferrets. He looked to Lefty but she gave him no support, then he turned back to Pillow Bear. "Your Honour, I don't have ten years to spare. My girlfriend still needs my help."

"Your girlfriend?" Pillow Bear scowled.

Row nodded. "She was supposed to be a witness in all of this, but I guess that doesn't matter. My sister turned her into a mermaid and I'm looking for my heart so I can turn her back."

"Your heart?" Lefty gasped from the defence table.

Row slumped, bringing a hand to his chest. He could almost feel the void. "I don't have a heart. My sister ate it forever ago."

"I see." Pillow Bear hummed to herself. "But having no heart doesn't excuse your crimes, and our sentencing is all very final. How were you planning on finding your heart?"

"Well… um, I guess we were going to talk to my sister." He scratched at his beard. "I didn't think it out too much, but maybe she could throw it up? Seems about as logical as the rest of all this."

Pillow Bear looked away from Row, skimming and shuffling through her papers. "You know what, Rosie?" She set the paper aside. "If you really are without a heart, then I suppose a sincere apology is off of the table. So, this would no doubt be a life sentence if you aren't given a chance to search for it."

He nodded along slowly.

"However, with your history of running away, it would be unwise to have you leave without consequence," she said. "So, Chrys will be staying with us."

"What?" Row winced as a fire flared inside him. "I can't leave her here."

"If she goes with you, it's doubtful that you'd ever return," Pillow Bear said. "And given the record, even if you leave her here, it's still doubtful you'll come back."

He scowled in response. "I wouldn't leave Chrys here."

"I'm merely pointing out the record, Rosie."

He looked over to the record laid in front of her. *Maybe she's right. You've already abandoned her before.*

"Lefty Grey." Pillow Bear broke focus from Row.

"Yes, Pillow Bear?" Lefty bounded onto the table.

"Would you be able to go with Rosie on this adventure to make sure that she stays on track?"

"I think I could do a really good job at that." Lefty paused, looking over at Row. "Will we be going back to Honey Walls?"

"No." Pillow Bear crossed her paws over her chest. "I have a much better idea. You will go to the Sky World. The stars will heal your heart far faster than reasoning with Sundew."

"The Sky World," Row uttered.

It'd been a long time since Row had heard the name. He'd made the Sky

World one day when his dad came home with a load of boxes. They filled them up with all his dad's things, and then stacked them into tall towers. Row painted them during the day and at night he lay at their feet.

The night before they were packed in the truck, he and his dad lay on the floor together. They filled the ceiling with flashlight stars. His dad tried to point out constellations but Row had trouble seeing them because tears kept getting in his eyes.

"I promise I'll be back soon," his dad had said.

But those were the last words Row ever heard him speak. The Sky World disappeared with his father.

"You mean where Oxnard went?" Lefty bounced and barked. "You mean we'll actually get to see Oxnard?"

"I don't know about that," Pillow Bear said. "But there certainly is a chance. The Sky World is a magical place where stars can be trapped and wishes can be answered."

"But it's impossible to get to," Row interjected.

Pillow Bear tapped her puffy paw to her chin. "Oxnard may have never shared the directions but that doesn't mean they aren't out there. I believe the Craft Feather Crow would be able to direct you."

Row grimaced. "I think she's back in Honey Walls, last I saw her."

"She's grown closer to Sundew from what I've heard." Pillow Bear looked to Lefty. "If you take a look through the glass, I'm sure that you'll be able to find her."

Row swallowed a dry lump in his throat. Anything remotely having to do with Sundew didn't sound pleasant. Unfortunately, Lefty was as world weary as she was lawyerly. She bounced at the prospect of meeting Craft Feather Crow.

"Judge Pillow Bear," Row began. "Before I go anywhere, would I be allowed to speak with Chrys?"

"You may, but under tight watch. We won't be losing you again, Rosie."

"It's Row," he said. At last he found it was safe to speak. "Or Mr. Gareau if you would prefer."

"Alright." She lifted her head up so that Row was looking down her nostrils. "Have the detainee brought to his cell. From there he may speak with Chrys before his temporary release."

With that, the courtroom sprang to life. From all sides, socks bounded to him. They nipped and scratched and dragged him along. As he passed the many snapping faces, he caught eyes with Ms. Dress Socks. Ferrets were hoisting her in the air and cheering. As she looked to Row, she sneered like Sundew. Then Row stumbled back into the dark caves.

The tunnels were no warmer or brighter upon Row's return, but they certainly were louder. The pitter patter of ferret feet echoed from every direction. There was nary a spot in the cave that wasn't accented by some whisper, dance, or mutter about the successful trial. Further down the hall, Row could hear the cheers and jeers. However, up close they remained professional.

At least, they remained so until they pushed him into the cell. When the plastic gate was slammed shut, they roared into applause. He fell backwards, landing hard on his rear. The wall isolated him, his cold, lonely cell divided from the beginnings of a party.

All of it reminded him a little of the funeral. That is, if the funeral home were filled with a zillion dancing ferrets instead of grumpy old ladies (okay, maybe not so similar upon further scrutiny). They took turns making faces at him, snapping at him, and saying things like, "Pillow Bear should have locked you away forever, Bad Friend."

Bad Friend. The words sank inside of him.

From the end of the tunnel, something caught his eye. Sailing down a sea of ferrets was a red wheelbarrow. Chrys sat inside of it, her tail draped over its edge. The other half of it rested in what little water the wheelbarrow could carry. Sock otters climbed over her and splashed the water in every direction. But Chrys didn't mind. She was smiling.

"Chrys." Row stood up, but didn't get too close to the bars and the snapping teeth. "I'm in here."

"Row? I've been having such a lovely—" Her smile stopped as she spotted him. "What are you doing in there?"

"They didn't tell you?" He rolled his eyes. "It's all very ridiculous, but I've been sentenced to ten years in prison."

"What?" She braced herself as the wheelbarrow came to a stop.

She was several feet away from the gate, and it made him feel a little sick. Her warmth was already distant enough since she'd changed, but those few feet between them was enough to seal it away entirely.

Row shivered. "I'm allowed out to go find my heart, but after that I'm back in here. Maybe I can bring my laptop and get work done. It wouldn't be so different."

"Row." She gripped the sides of the wheelbarrow. "Don't be silly."

"Don't be silly?" He scowled. "Look around you, Chrys! How in the world am I supposed to keep from being silly?"

Chrys looked around at the ferrets as they continued to party between them. Absently she scratched the ears of an otter in her lap. "I don't know, Sweet Heart. It's not all silly. Could you get an appeal?"

"An appeal." He scoffed at the very notion of a second day in court. "These lousy socks want an excuse to put me in here."

"Row," she soothed. "What are your charges? I'm sure it's just a misunderstanding."

"Misunderstand—" He stopped himself. "No, it isn't. I was sentenced for running away and being a bad friend. And guess what, I was telling the truth. I'm a bad friend, I ran away. And I had good reason to do it. I wanted nothing to do with ridiculous ferrets and everything that comes with them."

The levity drained from Chrys's face. "Why?"

"What do you mean why?"

"I mean exactly what you think I do." She scowled. "Your mother is magic. I'm a medium. What's the point in denying it? Why run away?"

"I—" He sputtered and shook his head. "Because it's ridiculous."

"I'm ridiculous. Would you run away from me?"

"What?" He furrowed his brow. "You are not. You're normal."

She shook her head, unable to respond. It was like every time her mediumship had come up before. That same circular fight. "I'm not normal. We're not normal."

He rolled his eyes. "Not now, but—"

"No, never." The socks quieted so that they could listen to her speak. "You told me that your mother is a wizard. I've been a medium since the day I was born. We aren't normal. You lived with these socks since you were little, so why did you run away?"

Row felt the weight of every eye press down on him once more. "I already told you…"

Chrys's shoulders slumped. "Fine."

"I need to get going, actually," he said, brushing his pants and looking away.

"Row… don't… I didn't mean…"

"No, it's fine." He waved her away. "I'll see you when I get that heart."

Chapter Seventeen

Behind the Silver Wall

The exit of the sock den led out into the woods. The ferrets watched Row from the safety of their home, while Lefty followed at his heel. It was bright outside, the brush thinning above as winter neared. The leaves littered the ground. The air smelled of earth as willow leaves danced through the breeze. Yet he could also smell the cold of frost.

Row crossed his arms as he weathered the icy beginnings. They were headed in the direction of "glass" or whatever Pillow Bear had meant. Row, however, had no direction planned, and no answer when Lefty asked. He wanted to walk into the cold, and maybe disappear for a while.

The wind picked up. One snowflake caught in the breeze and soon more fell with the leaves. The further Row and Lefty walked, the more snow fell. Row tucked his hands to his sides, protecting them from the cold sting.

Snow blustered and blurred the sky. Like the rain storm, it picked up quickly, blinding the way ahead. *Perhaps it's one of Sundew's stories,* he thought. But snow wasn't her style. It piled around Row's feet, blanketing on the farther reaches of the island. Row vaguely remembered a few terrible snowstorms back at Honey Walls, though the memories were mostly fond ones. Whenever he wanted there to be a snow day, the weather responded.

Without warning the trees thinned. Row stood alone, Lefty lost to the storm. The sky was a sheet of falling snow. He stepped forward. The ground was uneven. The moment was silent. And then the wind rolled on, clearing the slick ground beneath him. He stood in the middle of a frozen lake, his icy reflection staring at him from the dark water.

Crack. He stared at Sundew as lines appeared across the surface.

He stilled. His body shivered, his nerves buzzing, and the ground silenced.

Just don't move.

The silence broke with the ice. Row fell into the water, scrambling and grabbing at the ice. He thrashed about but couldn't resist shivering and closing in on himself. As he struggled against a current pulling him down… he felt warmer.

Whenever Row went beneath the water, it was the same. Whether Sundew led him to the tub, or pushed him in the river, it was always the same. Beneath the water, the surface above was silver, like a mirror without a reflection. This time was no different. He stretched for it but the current held him.

As Row fell deeper and deeper under the water it felt warmer and warmer. And then, he breathed. It felt like air. He closed his eyes a moment, feeling a distant world.

Ms. Crow… I need some directions, he said into the current.

Row gasped for air, and stumbled out of the water. Lefty Grey Sock Fox's teeth clamped to the arm of his sweater and Chester tugged its opposite. They dragged and pulled at it with a lot a spirit, but weren't getting far.

"Wake up! You idiot." Ms. Crow cawed as she pecked Row's face.

He sat up slowly. Around him the snow had melted. The ice of the pond was now thawed, streaming into the ocean. The rest of the snow had gone with it.

"I thought you were going to drown!" Lefty bounced into his lap as he sat up.

"Me too," he muttered and flicked the water off.

"I ran to get help! But only this felon wanted anything to do with you." She motioned to Chester.

Chester waved. "It was no problem, dug out while all them other socks were dancing and distracted."

"Ah." Row nodded. As he did so, he felt Ms. Crow shift her grip on his head. "And what about you, where'd you come from?"

The crow craned her neck until she was beak to nose with Row. She gripped tight onto his hair, scratching his head with her pipe cleaners. "You asked for my help, didn't you?"

"Oh… right." Row had nearly forgotten. He'd slipped into the shadows of the water for a bit, forgetting all in the numb moment. A shiver ran through him as he thought of Chrys. "I was looking for directions to the Sky World to find a wishing star."

"What a big request. That'll need a big payment."

Row reached into his pocket, pulling out all that he could find. Amongst his keys were the many gifts Zelda had given him. There was the remaining stem of the four-leaf clover, the tiny specs of rose seeds, and the baggie of healing crystals. "What about these?" He hoisted up the bag for the crow.

She snatched it from his hands, launching off as she did so. From the boughs of a nearby tree, she inspected the contents. She shifted through the jewels with her beak before looking back up at Row. "This certainly is a fine payment. These are high quality shinies."

"So you'll give me directions?"

"I'll do you one better. I'll lead you there." She rubbed her beak on her crystals, taken by the beauty of their sparkles. "I've been meaning to go back to the Sky World anyways. It's my kind of place."

"It is?" Lefty bounced about on Row's lap. "Is it true that Oxnard is there? Can you take us to meet him!?"

"Lefty Grey." Crow ruffled her feathers. "These were Row's gifts, not yours."

"Oh!" Her ears flattened. "I'm sorry, Mr. Gareau."

"But I suppose it would be no great secret if I told you. If you are looking for a falling star, you will start by following the sun. The Sky World exists in a space where its light touches the horizon. You'll know you've found it when you see towers like fingers that reach desperate for the stars."

"Like skyscrapers?" Row asked.

"Yes, in the tallest tower you will find what you seek. And yes, Oxnard will be there."

As Row felt a knot inside him, Lefty began jumping with joy. "Mr. Gareau!

This could be your star witness!"

Row tried his best to ignore Lefty. "So he lives in an apartment? Or a condo?"

"Yes, that's the human word for it. The city. Where else would he go? That's where he thought you'd be."

"Oh…" Row looked into the barren branches. "Does he live alone?"

"Hedgehogs don't own credit cards." The crow scoffed.

"So no?"

"Yes, he's living with Aster on the top floor."

Row felt weightless. "Aster… do you mean?"

"Yes. Your father," she said. "The two of them have been getting along well, if that's what you're about to ask next."

"I wasn't."

"Oh." She fluffed her feathers. "Well, I can't always be right."

He certainly had a lot of questions, but none for the bird. The questions had sat inside of him for so long he wasn't even sure if they were for his father either. They existed inside, welled up in that dark and empty space. "Do we have to go to his condo in particular?"

"It's the tallest you'll be getting into."

"Right." Row pushed himself onto his feet. "Let's get this over with then."

Lefty hopped and skipped, weaving between his feet. "Let's go! Let's go! Let's go!" She kept darting as he walked to the ocean. By the time they reached the shore, she must have walked the same distance ten times over.

Their boat rested on the shore where they'd left it, rocking against the longer waves. Lefty hopped ahead of Chester and inspected the little brown row boat. She sniffed its sides and jumped away when it moved. She scrambled into the boat, poking her nose off the side when her curiosity got the better of her.

The sun set over on the edge of the distant blue water. In his mind, Row called out for Chrys, but her beautiful voice never called back. *You really like to ruin things, don't you?* He climbed into the boat, burying his face in his fingers. He rubbed at his eyes, hoping that there were tears to clean, but they were dry.

Chester crawled inside after, followed by Ms. Crow. She flew off into the silent night. The glitter of her purple wings was Row's only guidepost as he pushed the boat forward. Lefty squished herself under his arm and into his lap. The island night brought the cold back. Bundled in his wet sweater, Row attempted to maintain his warmth out into the icy sea.

There was no time for stories or dishes. Claire and Sundew sat on the couch eating apples instead. Neither of them were up for cooking or cleaning, so they'd opted to sit around and eat fruit. They stacked a pile of cores onto an empty plate on the coffee table, kicking their feet up beside it. It was all blasé in a way which sent Claire back in time. It was like she were a teenager again.

As her current self, she wouldn't have scuffed Rose's coffee table, but back in the day, would she have cared? Of course not. Back when Claire was a teenager, she would have burned Cherrywood to the ground if it meant she could escape. She'd ripped free of tradition at every turn. She and Row were going to escape together.

"When did I become such a loser?" she asked Sundew as she tossed a core to the plate. It missed, rolling off the table and onto the floor.

"Huh?" Sundew looked at her.

"Sorry." Claire picked it up from the carpet. "I'm off on some other planet apparently."

"Same."

"Where you at?" Claire asked.

"Still thinking about Mom."

"Ah... makes sense." Claire reached out and patted her knee. "Would it be rude to ask you to humour my thing for a bit? I mean, if you want to get your mind off of it."

"Honestly, I'd love to get my mind off of all this." She rested her head in her hands. "So go ahead, what planet are you on?"

Claire smiled back at her. "Okay, thanks, because I'm on like a planet made of déjà vu." She pressed her back harder against the couch. "It feels like I'm back in time, visiting for something other than Rose."

"Because of Row?" She grabbed another apple and took an angry bite.

"Not gonna lie. It reminds me tons of exactly that." She stared at the coiling hair which climbed the walls and caged them in. "Row and I used to do stuff like this."

"Like eat apples?"

She shrugged. "I don't remember that specifically. But we'd sit in rebellion and maybe make out on the couch a little."

"Oh. That." Sundew scowled, though her cheeks reddened. "I'm sure you thought you two were entirely sneaky and not an ounce gross."

"It was an objective fact." Claire smirked.

"That you were gross idiots?"

"What?" Claire tried to scowl but couldn't fight off a laugh.

"No longer having to see you two on the couch almost made Rosie's disappearance worth it."

"Almost?" Claire tilted her head. "Meaning to say you didn't want him gone?"

"I wouldn't go that far, but it was hard to see how Mom took it." She gave Claire a quick glance. "And you too."

"Me?" Claire felt her cheeks flush.

"He didn't tell you, right?" Sundew took another bite, swallowing the chunk of apple before speaking again. "What kind of idiot leaves a girl like you?"

"Oh, I don't know about that." Claire's face continued to feel hotter. "Row and I weren't really meant to be anyways."

Sundew crinkled her nose. "And what, that makes it okay to disappear on you? I at least had the means to know that he was alive — unfortunately. You were miserable, it was depressing."

"All break ups are a little like that." Claire smiled slightly, trying to dull the pain of the memory. "Besides, he was going off to be a man. So, not exactly my type... and it's not like I'd want to hold him back. I mean, there's a lot to miss about him, but there's always been something so flat about him too. Like, I never knew what was going on in that head of his."

"That's because he doesn't have a heart."

"Sundew."

"No," she said firmly. "He actually doesn't have one. I took it."

Claire grimaced, keeping an eye on the endless hair stretching out above her. "You... took it?"

She nodded slowly. "Magic and stuff. It was the first thing that I ever did..."

ever. That night, when we both were little, was when I first came to be."

"Right…" Claire's stomach sank. "So before you took his heart, what were you?"

Sundew dragged her feet from the coffee table. She tucked her knees in close so that they pressed to her lips. Her voice became trapped in the space. "I was Rosie's reflection."

Claire stared at Sundew unblinking. The resemblance they'd once shared had always been easily explained with them being identical twins. To believe that they were reflections wasn't a far stretch. They had the same eyes, same burgundy hair, and even the way they moved felt so close.

"One day, I woke up different." She scowled. "He was in his bed crying, and crying, and crying. And I wanted him to shut up."

"What was he crying about?"

She shrugged. "I don't remember."

"Right…" Claire crossed her arms as she thought things out. "What did you do with his heart?"

"Ripped it up and threw it away."

Claire gasped. "Why?"

"It felt like that was the reason I was created, to tear that thing up." She kept shrugging. "Maybe it was one of Mom's stories? Maybe I was a monster come to life."

"If you're a monster from Rose's stories, then you'd have a good reason for doing what you did."

Sundew sighed. "But I don't. I've gotten plenty of reasons for everything else I did after the fact, but it's so long ago, I can't think of it."

"Like how long ago are we talking?" Claire asked.

"We were six or seven, I think."

"Oh…" Claire thought it over. "I still can't imagine forgetting something like that."

"It was an instinctual moment." She gripped her knees tighter. "I was sitting inside that mirror, listening to him cry. Then when I pressed my hands to the glass, I was free."

"So before then you lived inside the mirror?"

"Not always a mirror, but behind this silver wall." She looked up in awe at her imagined wall. "I lived alone in that space, waiting for small moments when I could see into the real world and pretend to be Rosie. Even when I was tired or sad I always had to copy her, be her. I didn't have my own life until that crying. Oh god, I can still remember that crying."

"And then, when I finally escaped from that prison, it isn't any better. I'm still alone… I still get to be nothing more than a copy."

"Sundew…" Claire pressed a hand to hers. "You're way better than any copy. Give yourself a little credit."

She shook her head, the tears brimming in her eyes. "I'm not. Anything you hate about Rosie is my fault. Anything different is a mistake."

"Don't be like that," Claire scowled at her. "So what if you started off from the same point, you're plenty different now, and maybe you've always been. I'm having fun eating apples with you, way more fun than I ever had with Row."

"Because I have a heart?"

"Because you're honest." Claire looked into Sundew's eyes. "Row was always ten seconds from running away, but you're right here. You're telling me how you feel. And you know what? Even though it's weird as hell and I'm probably tripping out or something, it means a lot. It means a hell of a lot."

"It does?"

Claire nodded. "For a few seconds, when we're chilling, I sometimes feel like I don't need escape, I don't need to fight my way out of this world. You're cool, Sundew."

The deliveries happened slow under the shadow of the greying forest. Dan stopped at its edge when his truck was empty. Throughout his entire day the thoughts had nagged at him. *Claire had to be trapped there.* He grimaced, staring back at the surrounding forest.

The grey haze clouded everything, from the roots of the trees to the stars above. It was like there were a dusted pane of glass between him and them. The starlight which fell through was bathed in silver. Dan stepped into its glow as he opened his door. He made careful steps from his truck towards the path to Honey Walls.

The path along the road was usually dense with brush, but it looked worse than normal. Vines of sticky barbed plants grew between the tree trunks and branches. They knitted themselves together into a near impossible wall. Dan bit his lip, examining the wall for a possible entrance.

What is going on? He found a small space which was uncovered. He ducked beneath it the best he could. The branches snagged onto his sweater as he crawled into the darkness. The forest closed around him with the distant howl of wolves.

Chapter Eighteen

Oxnard and the Sky World
by Rose Gareau

Wherein Oxnard Learns the Truth

Oxnard had made it. He peeked out over the boat's edge and got the best look he could at the tall city. They'd made it by nighttime, the perfect hour for star watching. The sky was a deep and dark blue like the ocean. Everything in the city was a reflection of itself — the sky, the ocean. The buildings stretched up to the stars, while their reflections grasped at the reflected light which tangled in the ocean depths.

Otter and Weasel climbed on top of Oxnard. Then they climbed over top of one another to make a little totem pole to get the best view. "Guys! Haven't we learned our lesson from the last time we tipped the boat?" Oxnard squeaked and the socks tumbled back to redistribute the weight around.

"Ar! I be not afraid of the water," Otter said with a haughty satisfaction.

"Well, I be," Oxnard said back. They would have argued more, but they were all too excited to have made it to the Sky World. They crawled about their ship, looking the city over from every angle the could. And each angle they looked at was better than the last.

Oxnard bunched up his directions as he looked up at the towers. Everything about the Sky World felt bigger and bigger the more he looked. He felt doubt begin inside of him as he tried to imagine all the spots that Rosie could hide. *How will I ever find her?*

"Ar, so we be headed to the tallest tower, right?" Otter prodded a paw to Oxnard's shoulder.

"I think so. That's where the stars are, and where my friend said she'd be."

"And maybe a whole load of treasure!" Weasel cheered. "I mean, every great pirate adventure ends with treasure!"

With a big laugh, Otter dipped into the water and pulled their boat through the city's flooded streets. Oxnard braced himself, looking up like he had many nights before. The sky was at last in his grasp, he was so close to finding his friend. At least, that's what he'd assumed when he left. Now, after such a long adventure, he wasn't so sure about anything.

They headed for the city's centre, the tallest tower that scraped the sky. Weasel and Otter were just as antsy, but for completely different (and much more fun) reasons. After years on the Island of Lost Socks, it was always wonderful when they found a new place. And by their reckoning, the Sky World was particularly fascinating. With each minute they got closer to the centre, the more nervous Oxnard got. He was full of butterflies.

Like with most of their travels, they moved at a slow pace. Otter was a good paddler but not so good at pushing a ship at the same time. Nerves aside, they didn't mind. They waited under the stars, letting the beams dance down on them. It was sort of relaxing and sort of nerve-wracking all at the same time.

The boat crashed into the wall of the tallest building because Otter misjudged the distance. Oxnard balled on instinct, rolling around the boat as it rocked and shook. Thankfully, no one fell out. Weasel and Otter burst into good long laughs, and Oxnard breathed a sigh of relief. Their boat was pressed to the wall of the tower, a couple feet beneath an opened window.

"What luck!?" Weasel ran up to the side closest to the tower and tried his hand at climbing. His claws slipped and scratched the glass but he couldn't get a grip.

"Move over, Matey!" Otter laughed as he dragged himself out of the water and onto the boat. Then he tried exactly what Weasel had. He scratched and slipped but got no further than Weasel had.

"Well then, I guess we're done with all of this." Weasel looked up at the window. "It was a good trip."

"Aye, a very good trip." Otter nodded in agreement. "Ye think that we should go on a new adventure now?"

"Wait, hold it," Oxnard spoke up. "We're not done this adventure until I find my friend. We can't give up here."

"I mean… we could?" Weasel shrugged.

Otter looked down at his feet and then at Weasel's. Then suddenly, he lifted Weasel into the air!

"What are you doing!?" Weasel flailed from atop Otter's head.

"Reach up for the window, Weasel!"

"Oh!" Weasel stretched up as high as he could on his little tippy toes until he was about a hedgehog length away from the open window. His paws shivered as he tried keep himself still against the glass wall.

"Climb us!" Weasel said in a strained and tired voice. Otter was fairing not much better beneath him (but you see, Reader, they couldn't leave their friend in such a sad way).

Oxnard was moved by the whole ordeal and because of this he left them to suffer a little too long. He climbed up the friend ladder and stretched up into the open window, barely making it inside. Once inside, he turned around and looked down at his friends. "Thank you so much."

"No problem," Weasel said, as he wobbled off Otter's head. He hit the boat hard, causing Otter to fall in the water due to the wobbling.

Otter splashed about, but regained himself pretty quick. "We'll sail around to find a better way inside."

"And food! I'm starving," Weasel added.

"Aye, that too," Otter said. "But we'll make sure to come back. Ye go find that friend of yers!"

"Okay, I will." Oxnard smiled and watched Otter duck beneath the water and paddle them along. But as they disappeared, he frowned.

He sat in the window for a little bit. His toes were quivering, which was making things more difficult than they needed to be. When they quivered less, he took his first steps inside the building. "Okay, Oxnard, this is it."

The building was very large, like it was made for giants. The doors were at least fifty hedgehogs high and that was a rough estimation leaning on the low side. He walked through weird rooms, the kind that he'd only ever seen in Honey Walls. They were people rooms. He'd never thought that there were other people out in the world, but stranger things had happened.

He walked through the large living room until he found an open door that led out into the hallway. The hallway brought its own challenge. To get up there was a staircase — but not a reasonable one, a ridiculous one with steps taller than ten chapter books each. Oxnard sighed. Everything good was worth the work. And so he took to it and climbed each big step one by one. He stopped to catch his breath multiple times.

After about a day and a half (hedgehog reckoning mind you, it was most likely a few hours), he was at the top. At its top was a somewhat open door with shoes thrown out in front of it. His heart fluttered and he ran right inside.

"I made it!" he called out into the dark room. "Rosie! I made it. I found the Sky World too!"

The room around him was deep and dark. He blinked and squinted, searching for his friend, but the tower bore no prize. There were no stars, no friend, not even a treasure like Weasel had suggested. There was nothing and tons of it. It pressed down on him from all sides.

Oxnard's heart deflated, squished down by all the disappointment. He curled up, but not all the prickles in the world could protect him from the nothing. He was alone. There were no prizes. No happy surprises.

You see, Reader, when you're an adult, adventures don't guarantee a prize. In the very real world of adults, I'm sorry to say we don't get to choose happy endings.

A long time ago in the House with Honey Walls, there was a very adult little girl. Her name was Rosie Gareau, and she was the favourite of all that knew her. That is, she was their favourite as long as they ignored her unseemly adultness. You see, when you played house with Rosie, she talked about mortgages. When you played tag, she spoke of the medical costs of broken elbows. And when you tried to snuggle her at night, Rosie would talk about how all magic was fake and how it should never exist.

And when little Rosie Gareau turned sixteen, everything got worse.

It was a Sunday night and all who were supposed to be in bed were sleeping. Rosie was the only exception. After a short nap, she'd woken up, sliding out of her bed carefully so as not to wake Oxnard. She'd picked up a few skills on sneaking out from her friend Claire, but she'd hardly put them to practice.

From beneath her bed she pulled out her backpack. She'd gotten it at the beginning of the school year, but hadn't filled it with school supplies often. Instead, she'd packed it with everything she might need. A blanket, water bottle, soap, some bus tickets, directions, and all other things that had come to her mind. It was tightly packed and a little bit heavy, but it'd get her to the couches she intended to crash on.

She pulled on a sweater, threw the backpack over her shoulders, and then tiptoed out the door. Oxnard was none the wiser, still bundled in blankets and dreaming of breakfast. He never received a goodbye, but Rosie never planned to give him one. You see, Rosie was finished with magic. She didn't want to put a close to it gently, like finishing a book. She wanted it gone, ejected from her thoughts. All her memories could go with it for all that she cared.

She descended the stairs to the living room, stepping down onto the plush cream carpet. The room was dark in a way which Rosie had never seen. She'd always been one to go to bed when expected, so she never saw Honey Walls in the dark. The room was usually bathed in the golden glow of incandescents. Usually it was warm.

Rosie turned her back to the pink couch, the writing closet, and then grasped the doorknob. As she went to turn it, a light illuminated the room. It caressed Rosie's back, enveloping all but the room's corners. "Rosie?" her mother spoke. Her footsteps sounded like the rustles of paper.

Rose Gareau stood at the centre of the room, lit by the single lamp she'd turned on. To Rosie she was inhuman. To Rosie, her mother was a shadow puppet, a magical creature made of construction paper and fasteners. She was faceless, forgotten, and when Rosie tried to remember a time when she was a normal mother… she couldn't. It was something insidious that (like many things) Rosie chose to forget. Chose to run from.

"You're leaving now… aren't you?" her mother asked.

Rosie shrugged, pressing her back to the door.

"I'm not here to stop you," her mother said. "If it's what you want to do, you'll do it."

Rosie looked to where her mother's eyes would be if she had them. That empty paper.

"But Rosie, you can't run away from these stories. They belong to you. I can keep them for a while, but one day they'll find you. One day, running away and pretending won't work anymore."

"You don't know that."

"I do know that. Stories have endings, Rosie." She took a step forward. "You need to learn to say goodbye. You need to let go."

Rosie's hand tightened around the doorknob. "No."

"If you run away, it doesn't end." She took another step towards Rosie. "It only ends when you acknowledge what's right in front of you. I'm not your mother anymore."

She turned the doorknob, unable to bear looking at the paper woman.

"Goodbye, Rosie."

Without a word, Rosie threw open the door.

Row, row, rowed his boat gently across the sea. He'd gotten only slightly better after a few days at sea. Well, he'd at least stopped rowing in circles (though they still weren't getting too far too quick). The ocean was still endless and uninteresting. At night he rested and at day he followed the sun. Row argued with the crow that they were going in circles a lot. However, she remained convinced otherwise.

They neared the end of another evening and Row was past tired. Behind him, Chester was on a tear through the suitcase. He and Lefty had made themselves a nest in the sweaters and shirts. Lefty's favourite spot was in Chrys's sweater. Meanwhile, Chester preferred to root through all of Row's shirts, running around in them like tunnels.

"We're out of crackers," Chester said, poking his head out of the suitcase.

"No, no, *you* are out of crackers, Row and I didn't bet all of ours." Crow tipped her head back and flew up onto Row's head.

"It's true, I've still got plenty of crackers." Row glanced back at Chester.

"Ugh, I'm sorry that I can't sit here and do nothing!" Chester flung himself starboard in a mopey gesture.

"You don't need to gamble. You can play go fish," Row suggested.

Chester lifted his head to give him a mean look.

Lefty poked out of the suitcase. "Are we there yet?"

"No, we'll tell you if we're there yet, Lefty."

Lefty dropped down into the suitcase in a depressed more-cute-than-Chester way. "Are we at least almost there? How many more minutes?"

"I don't know, a long ways still, Lefty." Row sighed, not convinced they'd ever actually get there. "How about you play cards with Chester? He's bored and I'm sure he'd love to play."

"I'm not playing cards for nothing," Chester snarled.

Row rolled his eyes. "I'll give five crackers to whoever wins."

Chester jumped into the suitcase and rummaged for the cards. He was horrible at cards, Craft Feather Crow won every time. Meanwhile, Lefty was too young to play. Gambling made her cry as she didn't understand why everyone wanted to take her crackers. Eventually, they dealt her cards so she could feel like she was playing while leaving her crackers alone.

Chester played go fish with Lefty. He had the most gusto ever seen in a go fish player. If he did end up winning, Row had a cracker set aside for Lefty. She was such a young and easily upset fox. It wasn't worth her crying.

Crow adjusted on Row's head, nesting in his hair. She nestled quietly, not napping, looking out at the scenery. On her right there was water, on the left there was water. Row yawned, and Crow followed suit.

"Do you know how much longer until we get there? Or do I have to pay to find out?" Row looked up at the crow, though he couldn't really see the top of his own head.

"No, I imagine we're very close. Look carefully at the horizon and I will too."

Row watched the horizon. For the next hour, it did nothing interesting. No Sky World… just water. By then, Crow wasn't even looking anymore. The game of cards was on hold because the socks had fallen asleep. It was just Row and the ocean, rowing quiet and alone into the setting sun. The light melted over the edge of the world. The sun melded and then disappeared. The water rippled, the darkness its own form of silence. This was like every night before.

When Row was younger, he'd spent many nights looking at the sky. Back when he had a heart, he and his dad played games in the dark. His dad was a stargazer, always messing with that telescope of his. When the weather was poor, he'd play games inside, make hand and shadow puppets, draw constellations on the ceiling.

Row stared out across the boat. From the dark wall of ocean and sky, Row made out edges. Opaque obelisks raised up into the sky, brushing up against the stars. They became clearer the more he stared. It was a city of skyscrapers, the lights from windows shining like stolen stars. Beneath him were unending streaks of car lights, zipping across the freeway. A dazzling world of stark light and dark.

"I think we've made it," Row said as he jostled Ms. Crow.

The crow yawned. "Hm? Oh, good eye."

Row swallowed, watching the giant buildings. "Which one's theirs?"

"Follow me and I will show you." With a few beats of her wings, she took to the sky.

Row paddled the best he could to keep up. The crow disappeared every so often against the dark patches of the city. She followed along the street, weaving down the occasional turn. Every building was taller than the next, looming over them. It was far different from where he'd settled, and far, far, different than Cherrywood. But it certainly wasn't any less magical. The magic in the city was different, mechanical.

Crow turned down a final street, before landing with a flock of pigeons on the lip of a building. "It's over there." She gestured down the road.

At the centre of the city was a building taller than any other. A real skyscraper. The stars rattled above it, struggling to hold in their spots. Row felt his own body begin to do the same. His chest ached, breaths warbled.

He was going to meet his father again.

Chapter Nineteen

The Tallest Tower in the Sky World

The week was intangible. Claire's ankle felt better slowly as her want to run drained away. She'd grown accustomed to the small, strange life. She sat out in the garden, rereading her favourite stories and scratching the ears of the old grey cat. However, she couldn't entirely put herself at ease, not with Sundew, her grief a fog, her hair a maze.

Claire shut her book, setting it down on her lap. Beyond the backyard porch was the field of wildflowers. All the colour had drained from the flowers, their petals resting on grey foliage. Amongst the leaves grew the vines and hair. It almost didn't phase Claire, she'd grown so accustomed to stepping over the stuff.

But had it really grown outside? She stood up, scrunching her nose as she examined the ring around Honey Walls. She watched as Sundew's hair grew out into the woods. *How far would it grow?*

The bushes rattled and Claire stumbled back. From between the branches, Dan tumbled out. He was like a wild man. Scratches and dirt marked his body, while definite bite marks were chomped on his pants. His sweater was half unravelled, still snagged on the branches behind him.

"Dan?" Claire covered her mouth.

"Cl-Claire?" He stared at her with wide eyes, as if he were seeing a human for the first time in his life. "I made it?"

Claire navigated through the field, finding where Dan waited at the forest's edge. His fingers trembled, but that appeared to be the only way he could move. As Claire reached his side, he managed to turn his head to face her.

"What's going on?" he asked, no less bewildered. He stared down at the curling piles of hair.

"Bit of magic, nothing serious." She smiled slightly, eyes darting to his bloodied legs. "Did the wolves get you?"

He glanced down, then nodded slightly. "Vines got them back."

"That's good." She grabbed onto his hand, pulling him to the house.

But his feet remained locked in place. "Magic?"

"Yeah, it's a long story. Let's just go inside and clean you up first."

"But magic…?"

"Move your feet, Dandy." She tugged him again.

The second time was the charm. He bumbled forward, barely coherent and wobbling on shaking legs. As Claire braced him, she used him a little as a crutch, keeping light on her healing foot. The pair came crashing through the front door, and tracked their muddy steps to the couch.

Dan fell hard onto the cushions, turning over onto his side almost as soon as he was sat. The tiredness hit him like a wall. Claire looked at his legs, getting a closer look at the bites. From a glance, it didn't look too bad. Most of the blood was dried, the cuts more jagged than deep, though at the same time she could imagine a need for stitches.

All their noise and fuss alerted Sundew. The house creaked as she moved from one room to the next. "What's going on down here, Claire?"

Claire looked to the stairs where Sundew was grimacing back at the couch.

"What's this?" Sundew asked.

"He just came out of the woods." Claire frowned. "I'm certain that those wolves of yours got their claws on him."

"My wolves?"

"Sundew." She glared back.

"Sorry… is it bad?" She began towards Claire.

Claire offered a so-so gesture. "He looks pretty rough, might be worth taking him to the hospital. Your wolves aren't diseased, are they?"

"They aren't 'my wolves' and I really doubt they're diseased."

"Either way, I don't think he should stay here," Claire said. "Would it be possible to clear the path long enough for him and I to go back to town?"

"Both of you?" Sundew paled.

"Yes, both of us. He's my friend, I want to know that he'll be okay."

Sundew glanced down at Dan. He'd already fallen asleep, snoring faintly into the throw pillows. "Would you come back?"

"I already said that I would." She smiled. "I mean, we've barely written any stories."

Sundew nodded to herself, letting it turn through her mind. "Fine, I'll see what I can do about the path."

Row's nerves buzzed, sinking in his stomach and burning in his fingers. The time out in the boat had been long and drawn out. Day after day they'd seemed to be moving aimlessly through the sea. It hadn't sunk in that he'd actually be seeing his dad. Before finding the tower, it'd been an impossibility.

As they neared the building, they mounted a slope. The tide shrank away from the building, giving Row his chance to reach it on foot. He tied his boat to a lamppost, packed the socks into his suitcase, and waded out. As his feet touched the ground, he appeared to fade into the real world. The crowds walking the street bumped into him, glanced at him, but none noticed the peculiar boat. It was like old times.

He breathed easy as he wobbled onto land, and escaped the ocean at last. It'd been so long, he hardly remembered how to stand. He stood still for a time, becoming accustomed to the real world once more. It buzzed around him in predictable movements.

But Ms. Crow didn't care to wait long for him. She flew ahead, stopping on the occasional streetlamp when she got too far from sight. Row power walked down the street, following her to the building. After a few blocks they reached the condo. Row stumbled back when he neared it. When he looked up from the base, he couldn't see the top. He couldn't determine whether it were magic or the marvel of engineering.

Lowering his gaze, he was met with a wall of clear glass. Through the panels, he could see the lobby… it looked fancy. It was decorated with cozy but contemporary décor. Angular couches sat back to back while vases of painted twigs and orchids decorated the tops of tables. There was a coldness to the colour, greys and charcoals, darks and lights.

"Do you think they'll even let me in?" Row muttered to Crow.

"Is that an actual question?" the crow cawed.

Row shook his head, making his way for one of the clear doors. He steeled himself, taking a deep breath before he touched it. The glass pane swung open with ease, leaving Row inside and centre stage. He looked and felt homeless, unfit to stand on the pristine tile. His hands shook, chest flaring hotter and hotter. His eyes met with the concierge. Row felt words fizzle out in his throat, and wondered if he even still remembered how to speak to humans.

He hobbled forward, his thoughts draining with the droning sound of suitcase wheels on tile. His voice continued to fight against him as he reached the desk.

"Hello, Sir?" The concierge scrutinized him as he spoke.

"H-hi…" Row managed to force out the single syllable.

He waited a little while for Row to continue. His uniform was pristine, a black suit with a satin grey tie. Behind his desk was a simplistic mosaic, a geometric abstraction of a silver hourglass full of black sand. It was hypnotic, striking a chord deep inside of him. "Can I help you?" the concierge prompted.

"I — Um, yes…" He faltered. "I'm here to visit Aster Gareau."

"And is Mr. Gareau expecting you?"

Row shook his head. "Um… I'm here to talk to him about his wife. I'm from Cherrywood."

"Just wait here a moment, and I'll see if he's available."

Row nodded as the man took up the phone and backed up a bit. He spoke in low tone, making eavesdropping difficult. Part of Row hoped that he'd be turned away. He wasn't prepared for this. Looking behind him, he searched for Craft Feather Crow, but she hadn't followed him inside.

"Sir?" The concierge rattled Row from his thoughts.

"Huh?"

"Mr. Gareau will be down in a moment to meet you."

"He will?" Every nervous shake and tremble stilled in the place of a frozen shock. *You don't feel anything, Row. Stop pretending.*

The seconds which followed were some of the longest in Row's life. And with each that ticked by, he wanted to turn and run. But he couldn't. Not without seeing him first.

He heard the elevator open down the hall. Then he heard the shuffling steps. And then a man stepped around the corner. The man was in purple PJ pants polka dotted with yellow stars, his sweater was a stretched green one which was covered in pills. His hair was more salt than pepper, pulled into a bun. And Row supposed that someone could mistake the two of them if you'd been given only the two descriptors: glasses and beard.

"Evening," Aster said, taking Row's hand in both of his to give it a shake. "You know, I heard that you were from Cherrywood, but you really are, aren't you?"

Row crinkled his brow, unable to imagine what was meant by that.

"Thank you." He smiled to the concierge before waving Row along. "Come with me, we can talk in private."

"Alright…" Row took tentative steps behind him, following his dad to the elevator. He remained at least a foot behind him, not wanting to stir conversation. He still wasn't ready. He wondered if he ever would be. But once they were inside, there was no escape.

Aster tapped his key to the reader and the elevator doors shut. "How are things in Cherrywood?"

"Same as always." Row stared down at their feet. Aster was in his socks.

"Figures… So, I must know you, right? I'm not the best at faces… or names. But I'm sure we could ring some bells."

The elevator bell dinged.

The entrance into the penthouse was lined with bookshelves. This was the man that married Rose Gareau, after all. Row took a step onto the mat next to his closet. Aster had his boots thrown to the side of the closet while inside there was a winter jacket and a set of dress shoes. The interior was far warmer in colour than the lobby, almost a part of Cherrywood. An island of small town charm in the sky.

Row took a deep breath. And then another.

"Feeling lightheaded?" Aster walked in ahead of him, headed in the direction of his kitchen. The layout was open, sprawling and spacious. "I used to get the exact same way. How about you get situated on the couch, I finish making my tea, and then we talk about Rose?"

"Um... sure..." Row pulled off his shoes and arranged them by the closet door with his suitcase. He took a long time with it before he followed into Aster's living room. He took a seat on the couch, perching at its edge without allowing himself to become comfortable. He gaped at the tall ceiling, the stairs which led up into another portion of library. It was the sort of dream home Row had only ever seen on television. It was as if no one lived in it. His gaze flitted to the side table next to him, and it all became grounded again. There were magnolias, a deep magenta arranged with care.

At the foot of the vase there was a picture frame. Aster said something, but Row missed it entirely. The photo was of a woman with dark red hair. It fell in waves down over the floral pattern of her shirt. Her eyes were bright and happy. Her magnolias bloomed behind her, climbing the sides of Honey Walls.

"She looks like Sundew," Row muttered.

"Pardon?"

"Sorry. That's Rose, isn't it?" Row kept staring at her, aligning her with the fragments he could remember. He tried to replace the shadows in his memories with the face, the smile.

"Yep, that's her." He nodded. "Beautiful, isn't she?"

"Yeah." Row gripped his cellphone. "Would it be weird if I took a snapshot?"

"Suppose you could. She must look pretty different now, huh?"

"Yeah... aren't any old pictures of her in Cherrywood." Row took out his phone to take the picture, but found the battery was long dead. "Oh. Never mind, I guess." He shook the thought away. "She's a lot like her daughter... I-I thought I'd show her is all."

"That's too bad." Aster sighed. "Are you friends with Rosie? I imagine you were a lot younger when I last saw you, but you bear a striking resemblance to someone. I bet I can guess, give me a second. Are you a Fletcher?"

Row shook his head.

"What do you do for a living?"

"That's cheating, but I'm an illustrator slash graphic designer."

"Graphic designer? I didn't know there were designers in Cherrywood... Hm... You're not a Waters, they only had the one, right?"

Row nodded.

"Hm... this is tricky. Who from Cherrywood would be a designer, be friends with Rosie, and not hate me? I mean, you don't hate me, right?"

"I'm incapable of hate." Row shrugged. "But Sundew's trying to teach me."

"Sundew?" Aster crinkled his brow. "Who's that?"

"Sundew. You know? Your daughter?"

His head swayed. "You must be thinking about someone else, I only had the one... unless Rose didn't tell me something." He laughed slightly.

"How would she hide it? You two had twins."

"I'm sorry." Aster shrugged. He looked uncomfortable, like he was about to call for security. "I really only had the one daughter, maybe she uses a nickname now or something. People change."

"That's not the point. I knew Rosie, and I knew Sundew. They're twins. There's no way you could forget something like that."

He shrugged more.

Row waived the issue for a moment, trying to regain cool and jump topics. But for some reason he couldn't explain, he ran headlong into the worst topic he could think of, saying, "Mom passed away a couple weeks ago."

"Mom?" Aster furrowed his brow.

"I meant to say Rose." He bit his lip, trying to let it slide. "I didn't know if anyone told you. I don't know what happened exactly, but there was a funeral. Based on what people were saying... I imagine you weren't invited."

"I wasn't," he spoke quietly to himself, nodding slightly.

"I'm sorry for your loss."

He nodded more, his expression airing on the side of perplexed. "How strange... I give up. Who are you? I mean, thank you, but everyone in that town has a bone to pick with me. It's hard to place the exception."

"Family friend?" Row offered, face contorting awkwardly with the half attempt at a lie. Aster didn't buy it, didn't even give it a thought. "I'm Row," Row said, a noncommittal beginning.

Aster waited for more.

"Row Gareau."

"Row Gareau," he repeated for himself, shuffling the words through his thoughts. "We're related? I don't recall having brothers, but apparently I had twins?"

Row tensed, not sure how to explain.

"Do I have a son I didn't know about too?"

"Sort of…" Row thought out the best way to say it… or whether to say it at all. There was no best way, and he figured he'd end up puking on Aster instead. "I'm, um… Sorry, I don't know the best way to put this. I'm Rosie — well, I used to be Rosie."

For the moment he was confused, then the gears shifted in his brain, eventually clicking. "You're Rose." He looked relieved, the elation of answering a riddle. "You're Rosie," he said again, this time without the joy.

"Yeah… Row."

He nodded more and more, slower and slower. "I knew you looked familiar."

"Sorry, I know it's too much to spring on you." Row got off of the couch. "I didn't really think I'd ever see you again, I wasn't going to bother with it at all. It's a confusing mess and Mom's dead so it's really not the time to learn that your daughter is too."

"What? No!" He gasped. "Sorry, it's a bit to process. Are you okay? I mean about your mother."

Row nodded, but wished Chrys were there to call 911 again. This moment was now on the top three list of places he didn't ever want to be.

"Hey, it's alright, Row." He raised his hands, slowly motioning for Row to sit. "Please don't run off. I won't do anything, I just want to talk."

"Yeah?"

"Yeah." He smiled back, though an obvious concern was hidden behind it. "I never got you your drink. I have coffee, tea, soda? I might have a beer or something but I'd have to check."

"Oh, tea'd be fine… whatever you got as long as there's sugar."

"Sugar?" Aster nodded some more. "I've got enough honey for an army."

"That should be enough."

Aster headed back to the kitchen, probably wishing that there was a wall to hide behind. All the while, Row remained frozen in the same spot. He was too rigid to sit back down. After a day in sock court, it was strange to think that this moment was the most surreal in his life. But it was. If only his dad were a normal dad that threw out transgender imposters instead of serving them tea.

He'd have much preferred to be yelled at. If he were yelled at, he could leave.

"So…" Aster returned with a cup of tea. "Did your mother know?"

Row shook his head. "I never got the courage to tell her. I moved out and never said anything."

Aster smiled a bit with only his mouth, and did some more nodding. The distance must have made it easier for him. Row took a seat, feeling slightly more relaxed. *Could you even lose someone you abandoned?* Row leaned back. It was a good question. *Was that why they were both so still?*

But as Row accepted the tea, he saw the artifacts of tears on Aster's face.

He drowned the thought with a sip of the tea. It was a little too bitter, heavier on the cream.

"So, you're a graphic designer?" he asked after some silence. "I thought you'd end up writing like your mother."

"I'm not like Mom, I don't have any stories to tell. Design? It pays the bills."

"Ah." He leaned back, taking a sip of tea. "So Cherrywood is doing well? Last I left it, it was nearly a ghost town."

"Really? I don't live there anymore, but it was doing well when I went down."

"That's good. Your mother loves it there," he said. "When she first got sick, we were about to leave to the city. We couldn't afford the treatment and the mortgage." Aster rubbed his eyes. "That house always meant so much to her, that town. I don't know how much you know, but it was a hard decision to make. Her house meant so much to her, passed down through her family, I believe…

"I had to move out here, make money for her sake. It was understandable enough when I left. I was going to call and visit all that I could." The tea shook in his hands. "I promise I meant to, but when I got here I got tied up in my days — not to mention how they hated me back in Cherrywood." He set the teacup on its saucer, allowing his arms to cross. "At some point I think Mr. Waters said it wasn't worth calling in. Never liked the man."

Row set down his cup. "So, they told you not to call, and you just didn't?"

"Oh no, no, I didn't mean for it to come out like that. I called as often as I could for as long as I could. I honestly don't know what made me stop. I've thought about it from time to time, especially when I look at my Rose."

"I don't remember a single call."

"I did though."

Row shook his head, pressing the memories down as they began unravelling. "I guess you're right. I didn't need you. Mr. Waters was good enough."

"I…" He shook his head. "I've got no excuses. I've been off chasing stars… caught in another of those fairy tales."

Row became rigid, staring at the hourglasses which speckled the book shelves. "…A fairy tale?"

"It was something your mother used to say. Back when we first met, we had this spot in a park downtown. I don't know if it's still there, but it became a study stop for us. Every night she'd bring up these stories about the stars. She really believed with all her heart that they were magical.

"She was especially interested in the falling stars. We made a lot of wishes, most about passing exams. She said that cities were especially good for finding them because of the skyscrapers. It's right in the name, they reach into the sky and knock the stars loose." His dad paused. "Think I told you that too."

Row nodded.

"When she got sick, she was certain that, as far away as I had to be, I'd find the star to save her. I think about her being gone now and wonder, if I find that one star, will I be able to bring her back?"

A dry lump formed in Row's throat.

"I wonder, but it won't stop me. In a way, it feels she died years ago."

Row swallowed the lump and spoke into the silence, "Mom told me stories like that too. Every night before bed."

Aster smiled to him. "Was she good to you? I mean, she wasn't too sick to take care of you?"

"She was always there for me." Row bunched his hand around the loose fabric of his pants. "…Even though I was never that good to her… She just… she deserved better."

Aster didn't say anything, staring at Row again. He looked about ready to cry, then a tear spilled over. His cries were silent. The type of solitary tears Row could have ignored if they weren't alone.

"Dad — er, Aster, I was wondering about one thing." Row gave him a chance to wipe his face. "I've misplaced a hedgehog stuffed animal thing. It's childhood sentimental stuff."

"Oxnard? You and him were inseparable, do you remember that? You once spilled a whole glass of juice on him." He laughed a little. "I told your mother you weren't ready for a big kid cup. It was such a mess. Your poor mother had to put Oxnard in the wash and console you through the entire rinse cycle."

"I don't remember that. I guess you don't have him here?"

"He's out looking for berries for a pie, actually."

"Oh…" Row hesitated. "Do you see the ocean?"

He nodded.

"I think it's a Cherrywood thing."

"I think so too."

Chapter Twenty

Reuniting With Old Friends
at the Worst Times

The gnarled vines twisted over themselves, curling back and revealing a tunnel ahead. Claire led Dan forward, holding his elbow to better support herself. It took a bit to wake him up and get him on his feet, but eventually it worked. He stumbled along next to her, slumped forward and rigid.

"You okay, Dandy?" She nudged him.

He took a deep breath then shook his head.

"Is it the bites?"

"No, not that," he said. "Claire, what the hell is going on?"

"Oh… that." She watched the vines ahead, spotting the occasional strand of unruly hair. "It's not as bad as it looks, it's just some magic and a bit of grief."

"*Just* magic and grief?" He shook his head in disbelief. "That doesn't answer anything!"

"I mean, it's kind of the only answer that makes sense." Claire shrugged. "Sundew's told me a lot about Rose, and well, she was magic. I don't think it's that far of a stretch to say that her daughter is too."

"How is Rose magic?" He pulled his arm from Claire to rub the tired from his face, inadvertently throwing Claire off balance.

"Dan!" She wobbled into him, then gave him a punch for his smooth move.

"Sorry!" He braced her once more. "What happened to your foot anyways?"

"Threw myself from a window — but that's not what we're talking about."

"You threw yoursel—?"

"Not what we're talking about," she repeated. "We'll get to that part, but I was on the topic of Rose and magic. You see, Rose has this magical pen thing that can turn stories into reality, like the glass wolves — and yes, I know they don't look like glass wolves to you. I don't think we have the ability to see the magic."

Dan's mouth hung open, watching the vines move in front of him.

"Okay, maybe some of it, but I think the vines are different. Sundew's hair's been going crazy for days now and I don't know if it has to do with the stories. I think it's her."

"So she's the one that's blocked off Honey Walls?"

"Yeah."

"And you've been trapped here?"

"Not against my will."

Dan glanced down. "And what about your foot?"

"That's from when I first traded spots with you," she clarified. "Sundew locked me up in Rose's room and I threw myself out to escape. But we've talked since, and she's been willing to let me go for days now."

Dan scowled at Claire. "And she's not controlling your mind with some sort of magical spell?"

"Be serious, Dandy."

"Be serious?! Are *you* serious? How can you be sure she's not controlling your mind what with all of this going on?" He groaned. "It's making my head hurt to think about it."

"Rest easy, Baker Boy. Sundew doesn't have mind powers."

He grumbled more, stumbling down the path. "Look, Claire, I can sort of buy that she's magical. I'm coming around to it. After a couple days in an enchanted forest? Well, I'll buy anything. But this is Sundew we're talking about and opinions on her are pretty unanimous."

"What you mean by that?"

"That she kidnapped you — and me! I'm pretty certain she wiped my memory on the topic too, because for the longest time I forgot about what happened to me."

"If that's the case, she must have had a change of heart after our talks."

Dan scowled. "Are you serious?"

"You keep asking that."

"Because I can't believe you're actually being serious! No one just kidnaps someone because of some misunderstanding, Claire."

"Well, she did and she's letting me go free, so maybe you should calm down," Claire huffed back at him.

He rolled his eyes in response. "You should have gotten help."

"I didn't need help." Claire glared back. "I got you out of the cupboard, didn't I?"

"And then you sat around and let everyone worry."

"You could have texted."

"We. Don't. Have. Cellphones."

She quickened her pace, somehow wanting to stomp ahead of him while still using him as a support. They were nearing the end of the forest now, the last vines parting the branches to reveal the country road. She nearly touched its edge before her arm was jerked back.

"I was worried about you, okay?" He was standing still, his feet planted firm to the ground. "I thought something awful had happened to you, is that so wrong? You're my best friend."

She paused, looking him over from head to toe. On the short walk she'd nearly forgotten how battered he was, cuts, scratches and bites. All of it was for the sake of seeing she was okay. Claire probably would have done the same for him. If she were in his place, she would have kicked Sundew in the teeth and then asked questions after. *The Three Musketeers* — Nah, the Two Stooges. Okay, there was definitely a better allusion for pairs but she couldn't think of one.

"I'm sorry, Dan. I should have gone down to see you as soon as I was okay," she said. "But I honestly didn't realize the thing about the woods… and then there's Sundew."

"What about Sundew?"

"She's in a rough spot." Her shoulders slumped. "I couldn't leave her. It wasn't because of magic, or threats, or… anything. She's hurt, Dan—"

"Dan?" A voice from the end of the path cut her off. Mr. Applegate stood on the dirt road. In his hands he held a pair of garden sheers, warily pointing them to the swirling coils of hair. He stared at the vines, barely parting his gaze to look at Claire and Dan. "Move it, you kids." The old man motioned them forward. "It'll get wise to you in a second."

"What…?" Claire faltered as Dan scrambled forward to Mr. Applegate's side and out of the wood.

As they broke free of the forest, Claire was met with a dismal grey. The entirety of Cherrywood was basked in the colour of Sundew's grief. Her hair grew out from the forest and rolled down the hills, wrapping the buildings and flooding the streets.

"Come on you two, your parents have been worried sick."

Row released the socks from the suitcase, much to Chester's chagrin. He didn't take too kindly to being trapped inside the suitcase like a run of the mill foot bag. However, his mood switched quickly upon climbing out. He ran circles in the living room and kitchen, jumping on the cushions and counters. Thankfully, Aster didn't seem to mind, laughing along with the silliness of both Chester and Lefty Grey Sock Fox.

The embarrassing antics were enough to make Row want to hide. Thankfully, Aster gave him an out, offering him the shower while he worked on a quick dinner. Row climbed up to the second storey where a spacious bathroom met him. It looked and felt larger than his bedroom back home, though that likely was a trick of the mirrors. The room was widened by them, made almost endless.

Row tried not to fixate on them. He'd never been a fan of reflections. He hopped straight into the shower, undressing behind the safety of the shower curtain. He rinsed away the grime and aches. The stiffness and sea salt. It drained beneath his feet, leaving him soft and tired. Row dried himself off, then forced himself back into his grimy clothing.

At dinner they talked a little more, keeping topics light. His dad told him a bit about his work, how he didn't understand how it could afford him the lifestyle he lived. It was all very plain, almost normal. That is, if it weren't for the socks on either side of them squabbling over meatballs. Row looked out the window at the Sky World, remembering how far from home he was.

Soon after, he retreated to the guest room (after Aster offered him some pyjamas and to wash his clothes). The guest room had a bed so intoxicatingly soft it could put any who lay on it to sleep forever. At least, that's what Row thought. After he managed to sleep crammed in a small boat next to a snoring ferret and twitching fox, sleep should have been easy... but it wasn't.

Row swaddled in the down comforter and wool blanket. His head rested on pillows with the consistency of marshmallows. He yawned. He turned. And he turned. And he turned. And he turned. He closed his eyes, opened his eyes, closed, opened. But he couldn't stop thinking. He slid out of bed.

Tea might calm my nerves, he thought.

And so he made his way back downstairs, crossed into the kitchen and made another cup of chamomile tea. He took it away from the darkness, and walked outside onto the starlit patio. The patio clashed with the greys and simplicity of the building with an eruption of flowers. Aster clearly had taken a liking to tropical flowers, safe in the warmth of the heated deck and glass greenhouse roof. Despite the exotic tastes, they were still the same magentas and oranges, Rose's favourites.

Further out on the patio was a section exposed to the air. Flowers withered in the grips of frost over black railings. And further than that, Aster's telescope was set up in the middle of the dying winter garden. Alone beneath the clear sky.

Row took a seat on a patio couch, its metal slats barren of cushions. He allowed a shiver to run through him, staring up into the stars. They really were so close. His hand extended upward. If he could only grab one... maybe it really could make things better. He could put it in the place of his heart. Then he could have Chrys back, make up for what he'd said.

Can't I be normal? They were a breath away, just like in the story.

"What are you doing?" squeaked a little voice.

"Stretching," Row said, pretending to move into a stretch.

Oxnard raised a brow. He was no taller than Row's foot was long, and was more ragged than ever. His stuffing was lumped, squishing out at frayed seams. Across his chest was a brand new patch, a swirly silk pattern of leaves. He crossed his paws over it, squishing out an inadvertent squeak.

"I wasn't sure you'd be back tonight. Aster said I could wait till morning."

Oxnard nodded slightly. His too short arms were still tight across his chest.

"Did you get all the berries?"

He nodded, slow, the movements dragging out his thoughts.

"Um… That's good. What kind of pie are you making?"

"Mixed berry."

"Ah… There's no time in this life to be picky with berries."

Oxnard said nothing. His jagged claws picked at a loose string at his side. As he thought, his nose twitched. "I've had a lot of time, actually."

Row let his fingers stand on his teacup's base, burning them slowly.

"I've thought about what I'd say to you my whole adventure."

Row looked into his teacup for an escape.

"But after all this time looking for you, I don't have any words."

Row took a short sip of burning tea, but it brought no comfort. There was no calmness in the flavour. He might as well have been drinking warm water.

Oxnard took a deep breath, causing his quills to ripple. "Do you have any words to say?"

Row said nothing.

A stillness crossed over Oxnard. He latched his claws tight onto the loose thread, hanging onto it like he hung to his last breath. "Nothing?" he said. "You aren't even going to pretend to apologize?"

Still nothing.

"I've travelled all over this world looking for you, you know?" Oxnard threw his paws to his sides. "I've worn my fabric thin, stretched my seams, and said goodbye to friends I never wanted to leave."

Row tried to say he was sorry, but the words got lost. "I can't apologize."

"Why not?" His patience was as worn as the rest of him.

"I don't have a heart."

Oxnard scoffed.

"It's true, Sundew ate it. No matter how hard I try, I can't apologize for leaving, not sincerely."

"That's nonsense." He turned his nose to the stars. Pivoting back on his hind paws, he crossed his arms again. "For as long as I've known you, you've never had a heart. It's a disability, sure, but you used to at least try. For everyone's sake, you tried."

"Maybe I got tired of trying." Row scowled. "No, not trying. Pretending. I got tired of pretending that I was something I'm not. You didn't lose me, Oxnard. I was never your friend."

He balled slightly.

"I'm not capable of friends. I'm not capable of love. Can everyone just realize that and leave me alone?"

"That's a big lie." He teared up. "I think you gave up."

"Pardon?"

"It got too hard, and you gave up." His voice was drowned in sniffles. "You're worse than your sister."

Row's face felt hot like a blush, the emotions bubbling over from his gut.

"You heard me." Oxnard pointed a single accusatory claw. "You're worse than Sundew. You aren't unfeeling. You're selfish and rude. I have half a brain to say you made her take that heart of yours so you'd have an excuse to act the way you do."

"That's not true."

"You left everyone! If you didn't have a heart why would you even care so much about running away?"

"I don't know." Row looked away. "But that doesn't fix anything, Oxnard. I'm still empty. I still know what it's like to be me better than you ever will."

"Not if you're in denial."

"Oxnard. I'm working on things. Why would I be here if I wasn't up to *something?* Not to feed the fire further, but I'd never come out here if there wasn't something on my mind. I'm trying to get my heart back." He sighed. "It isn't easy, but I need it back."

"You want it back...?"

"I need it," Row said. "I don't know if I want it, but I guess it doesn't matter. I can't give anyone an apology. I can't save Chrys... finish my sentence. I need a heart."

"Sentence?"

"Sock trial. I owe them ten years in prison."

"Oh…" Oxnard lowered his head. "You're actually going to serve your time?"

"If I can find my heart." He shrugged. "I came here because I heard that I could get a wishing star and maybe fix things that way."

Oxnard looked up at the stars. "I'm not sure about that. Aster's been trying to catch one for years without any luck. I'm not sure what it takes, but I don't think the tallest tower in the world will cut it."

"Great."

"If you're actually serious about this, I have a secret I could tell you."

"A secret?"

"Mrs. Gareau told me. She didn't want you to know about it because of your opinions on magic… but Sundew didn't destroy your heart. At least, not all of it."

"What?" Row gripped his chest, not even feeling a weak pulse.

"It's not in there. It's back in Honey Walls. Rose's pen, she made it from the stem."

"B-but…" Row stammered. "It's magic. It can't be my heart."

Oxnard rolled his eyes. "Don't play stupid, you already knew that. You've known it for years. Your mother would never make a world like this. She helped you out. She babysat us when you tried to give up. She watched the stories when you ran away. You're the one that made everything. You're the Keeper of Cherrywood's Stories."

Row shook his head. "That's ridiculous. Magic isn't real."

"How can you still try and think that? You wanted it. When Rose—"

"Stop it." Row dropped his teacup. It shattered on the ground, splattering a balled up Oxnard in chamomile. Row's chest screamed with a painful, nostalgic burning. It pulsed through his blood, fuelling his return through the penthouse. Before he knew it, he was wrapped in his dad's coat and descending the elevator into the high tide.

The population of Cherrywood was packed with the books into the bookstore. It was a tight fit, but the store was the only part of town left untouched by Sundew's hair. Claire sat with one shoulder to Dan and the opposite to Azalea. All the while Dan was being fawned over and patched up. He rested his legs on two stacks of books, while Mrs. Waters doused them with hydrogen peroxide.

"Ah—" He jerked away and attempted not to swear.

"Hold still, I said it'd hurt." Mrs. Waters tutted and dabbed his legs. "What were you thinking? Wandering off into the woods." She shook her head.

"Mom, he was worried about me." Claire scowled and grabbed the bottle from Mrs. Waters. "You know this crap doesn't help, right?"

"Oh shush, people say that because it stings a little." Her mom snatched at the bottle. "And what were you doing out there, Missy?"

Claire cringed, not sure if she was worth responding to. Her mom was near indistinguishable from the typical women of Cherrywood with an awful perm ala Lilly the hairdresser. There were plenty of perms packed into the bookstore. "Quit torturing Dandy," Claire said, deciding not to start a fight.

"Torture?" Her mother gasped. "If he doesn't clean these up, they will get infected."

"You know what? How about we ask Dan what he wants since they are his legs?" She looked at Dan and so did her mother.

"I… uh…" He looked between the two. "It's a bit overwhelming. Could you give me a minute?"

"Sure," Claire said, blocking her mother from continued pestering.

Dan smiled, though it was likely due to nerves. He glanced at his legs, then up to the crowd. "So… uh… What's been going on since I left?"

"Exactly what it looks like," Azalea piped up. "Hair. Just hair everywhere. It grew out of the woods and now it's packed into every building but this one."

"And I'm guessing cutting it makes it worse?" Claire asked, remembering her previous feeble attempts to trim the hair.

Azalea nodded.

"Well, I guess the only solution is to go back to the source." Claire crossed her arms, looking back down the book tunnels.

"You'll do no such thing!" Mrs. Waters gripped her arm. "It's abundantly clear that that *woman* is some kind of monster."

"What?" Claire pulled her hand back. "She is not. We've spent the whole week together. She's just sad."

"Sad?" Mrs. Waters crinkled her brows. "Sad people cry, they don't flood the city with lunacy."

Claire rolled her eyes and squished her way to the door, past the walls of people and books. "Dandy, I'll be back. I'm going to—"

She bumped into Mr. Waters. He stood between her and the exit, blocking her path with a severe expression. "You're not leaving, Claire," he said, pushing up his glasses.

"What?" She looked from one side to the other, watching the concerned faces of the crowd. "Are you being serious? She's not dangerous. I'll talk to her and—"

"Not dangerous?" her mother interjected, motioning to Dan. "Do you know what's out there?"

"Wolves, Mom. Do you think Sundew controls wolves?"

"With what's going on, do you think I'd be surprised if she did?"

"Oh my god, Sundew does not control wolves. I'm going to go and talk to her about this and then we can all get over ourselves."

As she tried to move forward, she was stopped once again by Mr. Waters. "You're not," he said. "Your mother is right, it's dangerous out there. I'll deal with Sundew."

"*You* will?" Claire scowled. "You don't know anything about Sundew. What do you even plan to do?"

"Whatever works. I know plenty about the Gareaus and Sundew is no exception." He stood his ground between her and the door. "You stay here with everyone else where it's safe. I'll find out how to end this."

Row held his breath as he was dragged into the sea. The elevator didn't care about the high tide, it kept going down, and down, deeper and deeper. The lights flickered off, the edges of the elevator fading to shadow. It was like a bad dream, though Row felt like most of his life was (in general) a bad dream. This was a worse dream.

What sort of idiot are you? He shut his eyes, blocking out the ocean currents and dark water. The elevator was now nothing but an undertow, the water dragging him down. *Was it really worth this? Couldn't you have let him finish? You can't keep ignoring things.*

"Yes I can," Row said, and the water became air. He opened his eyes as the elevator dinged open. The ocean was gone, at least, as far as Row was concerned. If normal people could ignore it so could he, because Row was as normal as normal could be. He tightened his coat and powered through the lobby and out the glass doors.

He clutched the pocket of his PJ pants, making sure he still had his wallet, keys, and the remaining gifts from Zelda. He couldn't bring himself to go back and change into better clothes. He'd have to make do with his father's space PJs, at least they were a little subtle (though the fanciness of his father's coat made them look more ostentatious). Before long, it'd be all over, all he needed to do was find Sundew. Maybe then he could get rid of magic for good.

But what about Chrys?

He shook his head, beginning to search for transit, bus, subway, anything that wasn't a boat. He'd certainly return Chrys to the way she was before, but maybe it wouldn't be so bad to leave her with the socks. He could start a new life without her. It wasn't like he'd never done something so difficult before. It wasn't like he had to keep his heart if it ached.

His chest burned as the thoughts raced through his head. If he really wanted to continue living a normal life, running was probably the only option. If he wanted no one to catch up, he couldn't stop. There was a forward momentum in his life that needed to continue if he truly never wanted to look back.

Row hopped onto the first bus that he could.

Chapter Twenty-One

Reuniting With Old Friends
at the Worst Times

Row passed the night outside the bus terminal, in and out of sleep on a park bench until morning came. Any hope he had at returning to Cherrywood required him to wait until the wicket was open and new buses were running. He entered the building in the early morning, long before the sun came up, and went straight to the ticket booth. The lady behind the counter was helpful, managing to work out the complex series of transfers required to get close to the nothing town.

Once all was sorted out, he stopped at the nearest cafe and bought a ridiculously priced breakfast sandwich and hibiscus tea. With some time between breakfast and the bus, he sat down in the cafe. It was a lot like the one back near his house. He couldn't help wondering how Fox was doing… and Zelda. He could almost feel her pelting him with healing crystals.

"You rotten heartless boy!"

Zelda really was right about him. He finished his tiny sandwich in a few quick bites. It left him feeling empty inside, and there was not enough tea in the world to remedy it. He brushed the crumbs from his pants, taking his drink with him back onto the street. There was plenty of time to kill before the bus arrived.

Outside, the sun began to rise behind a clouded sky. The light which washed over the city was dismal, a depressed shade — or perhaps a benign emptiness. Row looked up just in time to notice a black bird above make her landing.

"I don't have anything else for you," he muttered.

"Did it not go well with you and your father?"

"It went fine." He glanced about the street. The early morning meant most of the street was empty, but he still didn't want to look anymore crazy than he already did.

"Oh, and where are the socks?"

"They've decided to stay with Oxnard and Aster."

"Oooh?" She cooed a little like a pigeon, then forced herself to caw. "So, you're abandoning everyone again?"

He stared at his shoes.

"I'd hardly say that I'm surprised, but I partly expected Oxnard to turn your bad behaviour around."

"What are we talking about?" Another bird fluttered forward. She was a white dove made of tissues and silver glitter.

Crow scooted to the side as the other bird bumped into her. "Oh, great. Another pigeon."

"Quit that, there's nothing wrong with pigeons — not that I am one." She cooed and fluffed her soft down. "I heard you talking about Oxnard. What a loveable little hedgehog!"

Row turned his back to the birds while they were distracted by one another.

"Not as far as Row's concerned," Crow cawed. "He's abandoning Oxnard right now."

"What?" Tissue Dove cooed as she fluttered down from the lamppost.

"Well, that's what he and I were talking about before you interrupted." Crow followed the dove, landing next to her atop Row's head. "Row is excellent at abandonment."

"Could you two leave?" He scowled up at them.

"See? Exactly like I was saying."

"Aw…" Dove sang. "Where are you going?"

"The bus."

"And where's the bus going?"

"Cherrywood."

"Really?" Crow spoke up. "What happened to the plan to find a star here?"

"It sounds like it's too much of a hassle," Row muttered. "And there's a part of my heart still out there. Hopefully that's all I need."

"A little heart can go a long way," Dove replied.

"I don't know about that, but I'm not being paid for advice."

Tissue Dove tsked. "You're so greedy, Ms. Crow."

"It's fine." Row reached into his pocket, securing his hand around his keys. He pulled them out and offered them to the crow. They were shiny, well-kept but minimal. Row didn't keep many keys aside from the ones to the house, his car, and two or three he didn't remember the uses of. "Take these, I won't need them anymore anyways."

The crow secured them in her beak with eager delight. "What sort of question do you have?"

"I don't know…" His shoulders slumped. "I— What am I supposed to do?"

"That's a very broad question."

"I know. And I know what I'm off to do." He sighed. "But what do I do when it's over… or if it's ever over? If I get my heart back, how will I possibly handle any of this? Oxnard hates me. Chrys probably hates me too. I don't know how I'll handle that if I get my heart back. If I can feel that even a sliver… I don't know."

The crow went silent as she thought.

"You know what? I don't need an answer. I want you to take those keys, then I won't even try to go back."

"Oh dear." Tissue Dove cooed. "Is this Chrys the one that you love?"

"He doesn't have a heart. You'd know that if you learned to listen, you glittery snot rag."

The dove ignored the insult. "That sounds like a lie."

"It isn't," Row said. "My sister ate my heart."

"Hm…" Tissue Dove fluttered down, landing in the palm of his hand. "Sir, pardon me for assuming circumstances, but even if it's true that someone can lose their heart, you don't strike me as the type. Maybe Ms. Crow has more insight on this?"

Crow shifted about on Row's head. "That could be an interpretation… I don't know all that much about hearts, though I suppose there are possible inconsistencies."

"Inconsistencies?" Row asked.

"I mean, yes. Minimal as it may be, there are moments where it almost looks like you're feeling something. Perhaps it's the residual reactions of someone who once had a heart, or maybe there's something still in there?"

"I doubt that," Row muttered.

"Why?" Dove asked.

"I just do." Row glanced up at the station, the large clock on its front nearing the arrival time of his bus. "I actually need to be off now, you two."

"Alright." Dove fluffed her feathers as she thought. "But I don't believe that anyone can go on an adventure without even the smallest speck of a heart. Adventures require courage. Courage is by its very definition a heart thing."

As Dove hopped off his palm, Crow dropped his key back into his hand.

"Huh?" Row looked up at her.

"I didn't answer anything. I don't want them." She leapt off his head, flying after her friend. "You need them anyways."

The solution was easy for Claire. She took Dan under her wing and slid between the aisles of books. Crammed behind the nonfiction section was the spiral staircase which led to their upstairs apartment. It was a similar situation amongst most of the Cherrywood population, to live above your work (or at the very least live next door to it). Claire and Dan hobbled up the steps. Dan knocked his head on the above spiral before ducking down for the rest of the way.

"You okay, Claire?" He held onto his head, nursing the sore.

"Yup." She curved around the final turn.

Their upstairs wasn't too different from the down. There were still piles of books, only slightly less packed to the walls. The books were their family's favourites, the ones they couldn't quite let go of. Claire shimmied past them down the hall before taking a sharp left turn into her bedroom. Dan stumbled along behind her, nearly smacked by the door as she slammed it shut.

Her room, much like Dan's, was an uncomfortable blend of the present and past. Obviously, there were overflowing bookshelves with both novels and picture books. They spilled over onto her single bed and its lumpy pink comforter. She'd had the same rotation of sheets since she was six, the occasional new quilt added to the rotation on her birthdays. She sat Dan on the bed next to her plush rabbits and dolls.

"So," Claire began. "You're going to stay up here far away from the ladies trying to drench you in outdated disinfectants. Meanwhile, I'm going to cut my dad at the pass and deal with Sundew."

"Claire, it's really dangerous out there."

"I know. Do you think I want my dad mauled by wolves?" Claire scowled. "And what the hell is he even planning to do about Sundew?"

"I don't know, what are you planning to do about her?"

Claire began toward her window. It'd been a long time since she'd escaped, but she was certain she could escape her own window better than the one at Honey Walls. After all, Claire had become an expert at escaping through it by the end of middle school. "I'm writing a story, Dandy."

"How's that going to help?"

"I'm going to write it with a magic pen."

"What?"

Claire turned back to face Dan. She crossed her arms and repeated, "I'm writing it with a magic pen."

"Yeah, I heard. But… what?"

Claire smirked at him. "Dandy, Dandy, Dandy, I think with all that's going on, a magic pen shouldn't be a difficult thing to believe in."

"Fine," he said. "And where is this magical pen?"

"Back in the writing closet. It's the fancy pen that she was trying to get you to write the story with." Claire replied. "I was considering writing a story before… but I chickened out."

"Why?"

She shrugged. "I don't know. Have you written up the obituary yet?"

He shook his head.

"Well, I'm feeling the exact same way. How will I ever be able to do her stories justice? Writing up some story for Sundew is one thing, but writing something new… changing the direction of things based on my choices?" She shook her head. "I shouldn't be as afraid of it as I am."

"It doesn't have to be perfect."

Claire nodded. "Same to you, dude."

Dan nodded back, bunched the sheets at his sides. "Why don't we finish both? Together."

"What do you mean?"

"That we go together and finish both of these stories." He pushed himself up on his feet. "We'll never do her justice, so let's try our best instead."

Her heart fluttered at the thought, leaving her dizzy and gripping the windowsill. "'Kay," she said softly. "I think we could do that."

By the final bus stop, Row was alone. The stop itself hadn't changed much since the night of November Nineteenth. There was a small shelter made of painted green planks and a faded black roof. On the nearest wall was a map and schedule printed on yellowed paper, protected by a pane of plexiglass. Row exited the bus and passed the shelter and its rickety old bench.

Down the empty road were barren trees. The bitter death of winter cold was inescapable, a black night overtaking the grey sky. Row started down the road. As he did so, things slowly became clear to him. On the horizon, Cherrywood was overwhelmed by dark boughs. They moved with the wind… but also spread forward. At a distance it was difficult to tell what was going on, but as minutes turned to hours, it became clear to him. The canopy of trees which led into Cherrywood was made of hair and vines. They continued to grow as he stared at them, knocking the remaining foliage to the dirt road.

"What is she doing…?" Row asked beneath his breath.

But the only answer was the howl of wolves cracking through the silence. Their eerie cries were not enough to turn him around. He braved the road, descended into the shadow beneath the canopy, a wall of deep darkness. His eyes adjusted slowly, and as they did, he grew wary of every rustle and crack. Though the air was still, the canopy was moving. While he expected to find his way to Main Street at some point, the path made its own decisions. He was guided forward by wherever the brush was less dense.

Needles on the vines scratched and snagged at him. The ground went from gravel to grass, and Main Street never came into view. However, he felt no more aimless than he had at sea. It was only a small comfort as the howls grew louder and he heard the rustles of footsteps. He braced himself to meet face to face with the wolves, presumably ones made of glass, the creatures that filled his nightmares when he was young. Instead… there was a man.

Mr. Waters was shivering in the dark. He pushed up his glasses, searching the woods from one end to the other. As he did so, his eyes met with Row's. "Who are you?" he asked, squinting through the shadow.

"Row," he replied. "How long has Sundew been up to this?"

Mr. Waters didn't answer immediately, allowing himself time to process. "Oh," he said as he remembered, then navigated himself back to Row's question. "It's been going on a little over a week… what brings you back, Rosie?"

His chest burned, the name stinging more than expected. After the ladies at the funeral and all the confused socks gendering him however they pleased, it was strange that there was any stirring inside at all. But there was.

"Rosie?"

"I… um… Sundew's causing me trouble too."

"Ah, I'm on my way to give her a talking to." Mr. Waters shook his head in dismay. "It's not so easy to find your way around this place. I'll manage, though."

"Right." Row glanced around at each dark corner, all the same, all aimless. "I got back from the city, met Aster… and stole his clothes."

Mr. Waters paled at the mention, the expression wiped clean of his face. "Did he have anything to say for himself?"

"He said he called and that you told him to stop."

"Told him to…" Mr. Waters shook his head. "It's complicated. We can talk about it later."

"You brought it up."

Mr. Waters sighed. "Rosie, your father didn't want to be there when your mother died. I told him to show his face and quit calling. That's the short of it, okay? I invited him to the funeral, he forgot about it. It's just the thing about Aster, he's a fair-weather friend. Now, let me deal with your sister and then maybe I'll give you the whole rant."

"Why not tell him when Mom got better?"

"I—" He froze before his sentence even started. "When your mom got better, I didn't come back. Dan had me thinking about the same thing. It really got me wondering for a bit. Do you think that she — you know what, never mind. When things clear up, we can talk about Aster."

"It's fine," Row said. "I don't think I care much about the answer."

"Rosie—"

"Please don't call me that," Row mumbled. "Aster got it right and he's — look, I don't care if Mrs. Fletcher doesn't care. But you've always been there when… um… never mind. You should head back where it's safe, I've got Sundew."

He stepped back on instinct. "Oh… alright."

Row sighed, shutting his eyes a moment before picking a direction.

"Row, wait." Mr. Waters stopped him. "This isn't about you. Okay? It's hard to let go of the past. You're the last real thing from back then. I can see why people are saying you look like Aster, but I can't help seeing Rose. I'm sorry. It shouldn't be your problem that I don't know how to say goodbye."

"It's fine," Row said. "But I'm nothing like her. She was there for everyone. I think I'm much more like my father."

"But you came back to fix things. Your father's still up in the clouds," Mr. Waters said. "That's enough to make her proud."

Row stiffened, unable to accept a thought so antithetical to all that he was. "Mom wasn't proud of me. There's nothing to be proud of."

"You were a good kid. Kept Claire out of trouble."

"Because Claire was always up to nonsense."

Mr. Waters glanced back the way he'd come from. "I could always trust you to do the right thing. Like right now. I'll head back to the bookstore. No matter how strange things get, I know you want to help your friends."

"I don't know about that," Row said. "But I'll see what I can do, Mr. Waters."

After climbing down Sundew's hair like a pair of handsome princes, Claire and Dan explored the forest. The night appeared endless, with no signs of stopping. They travelled the same similar passages as before, the nerves obvious in the way Dan managed to keep himself awake. He stiffened at the sounds of wolves, freezing in place and watching the shadows.

"Come on, Dandy." Claire tugged on his arm.

"Yeah, I'm coming." He followed along behind her.

The clearest pathway led up a steep slant. Walking up it caused Claire's ankle to bend uncomfortably. Dan occasionally knocked the raw parts of his legs against the dirt and rock. After a few long minutes of suffering and using Sundew's hair as a rope, they emerged atop the hill.

The sight was sudden and barren. The trees thinned out into the Cherrywood Cemetery, a sprawl of gravestones the hair and vines didn't dare grow near. Beyond the forest's edge, the dreary shadows were surprisingly lacking. The remnants of autumn still clung to the trees, painting the scene in subtle oranges. The greying and darkness wasn't enough to hide the splashes of colour.

Claire hesitated to move forward. She stood at the edge as if faced with a precipice. It'd been a while since they'd been at the burial. There would probably be a place holder at Rose's grave, her body awaiting a spring burial elsewhere. Claire felt tugged forward, unable to simply retreat back into the maze.

"We should pay our respects," Claire spoke up.

"Right now?"

"Yeah, for good luck." She smiled. "And to get her blessing, you know? It might help the writing."

"Alright." Dan began forward. "But we better make it quick, you want to reach Sundew before your dad, right?"

"Honestly, I have a feeling he's about as lost as we are."

Dan swayed his head from side to side, coming to an agreement after the deliberation. Claire tightened her hands around his elbow, biting back a fresh wave of nerves. They navigated the lot, along cobblestone paths and beneath the yellow light of old lamps. Rose's plot was a while past the Blackthorn mausoleum in a shady patch where all Gareaus were buried. Wildflowers grew unyielding over the older stones and statues. In the shade of a young magnolia bush, Rose and her mother's spots rested.

Had they taken the time to bury her? Claire wondered as she noticed a grave.

To her surprise, there was more than a placeholder. Covered in the wilted petals of the magnolias was a simple stone marking the spot. Claire bent down, brushing the dirt and petals with trembling fingers. Moss and grass grew atop the forgotten gravestone.

Across its worn surface it read:

Rose M. Gareau Sr.
1966-1997
"I'll be safe with the stars."

Chapter Twenty-Two

Wolves, Glass, and Truth
(As Well as Some Other Horrible Things)

Row's foot sank into the porous ground at the edge of the bog. He backed up before getting closer to the water. It was a black pool, almost indistinguishable from the rest of the dark forest. If memory served him correct, he was close to Honey Walls. The bog had often served as a landmark in his mother's stories, marking the first obstacle in a treacherous journey. He scanned the surroundings for the correct direction to pick.

A jingle like that of Zelda's crystal curtains chimed in the silence. Row turned his back to the bog, listening to the sound which came in a sporadic symphony. There was no defined source, the clinking and clattering came from all sides but the bog. From the shadows there emerged a silver paw. The reflective face of the glass wolf followed shortly. Its pack appeared from behind more of the trees.

The wolves were made of sections of shattered mirrors, mouths full of jagged glass teeth. As they stepped towards Row, their sections rattled against each other. They gnashed and growled. As they got closer, reflections became clear on their bodies. On the shattered forms was a distorted image of Sundew. She stared at Row, bathed in a similar darkness, segmented by the wolves' broken bodies.

"Sundew." Row watched the wolves warily. "We need to talk."

She said nothing in response. The wolves lunged forward, ravenous monsters unlike the many other creations. As their teeth neared Row's flesh, they yelped. He stumbled back, drenching his legs in bog water as he did so. Ahead of him the wolves were suspended by her hair. It entangled every last one of them, their limbs cracking under the pressure. Row remained motionless, watching them as they writhed and howled. But there was nothing he could do.

Ahead of him, the vines continued to move, parting to form a tunnel. The path, if it led him to her, really would be the only chance he'd get. He braced himself, taking a deep breath before stepping from the mud. He walked past the gnashing and gnawing wolves, entering the narrow cavern. The vines caressed him and tugged at his limbs. They fed into his forward momentum, guiding him through the remaining forest towards the ditch. He was pushed onto it and got a mouthful of dirt.

The threshold was overgrown with mushrooms. Row slipped along them as he climbed up through the ditch. Falling upward, he saw the ruin of Honey Walls. Sundew's hair was tangled in Rose's magnolias. The flowers wilted, grey, spotted with fading magenta. Everything was turned to grey. The paint on the house was peeling from the panels, the windows broken and littering the lawn with shattered glass.

"Monsieur! Be careful with your clumsy feet!"

"Oh!" Row moved back a step, spotting the tiny lace mouse. "Sorry, I got a bit distracted by the mess."

"Oh? It's all your fault, you know that?!" The lace mouse huffed. "I knew Sundew would do something like this, the minute Claire left, she lost her mind! Zut!"

"Looks it, but I'm going to stop her. Well, you could help, would you be able to get in there for me? I'm looking for a pen."

"Oh! No, no, no, no, no! Non, I am never going into that awful place."

"Alright, I guess I'll deal with her on my own." He glanced back at the mouse. "You go back to your home where it's safe. This may take a bit."

The lace mouse harrumphed her last and scurried on her way back to the apple tree.

Midnight cracked across the sky, wolves howled at a fragmented moon, and Row approached Honey Walls. The door opened with a long creak, waves of hair falling out. There was hair everywhere, piled on the floor, climbing the walls. Row waded through it, finding that the closer he got to the living room the thicker it grew. It stretched into Rose's office, tearing through her notes.

Row reached the closet and began searching the drawers top to bottom, looking over each pen. But nothing looked magical. He was uncertain he'd even know it if he saw it. "Great," he muttered. He'd have to speak with Sundew.

But there was no following her hair and finding a "source". She'd made a mess, just like when she was little, an unbrushable catastrophe. It lined the steps up to her room like a waterfall frozen in a moment. Even if it wasn't a direct path, it seemed like a good place to start. He crawled up the stairs, parting the hair and eventually navigating to the top. All the while, everything remained still. When he'd been in the forest there was constant movement, growth.

Now there was nothing.

Sundew's room was barren. There was a bed made of hoarded pillows and quilts, old blocks and puzzles sectioned away into a corner. At its very centre was a standing mirror. It was taller than Row with a thick black frame. And inside, there was nothing...

Row approached, looking to find his sister in his reflection. But she was no longer spying on him. All he could see was the room behind. He walked closer, heel cracking on broken chunks of window pane. An echo of footsteps followed him.

"You're back," said Sundew.

Row turned fast. In the doorway stood Sundew. She held onto either side of the frame, closing him in with her.

"You didn't like the story I wrote, did you?" She laughed slightly.

"I want the pen back, Sundew."

She smirked. "What? Did you figure out what it does? ...Or what it is?"

"It doesn't matter. It's mine, and I need it back."

"It isn't yours." Sundew glared. "You gave it to me. Twice."

"No, you stole it and then you tricked me."

"Stole it?" As she spoke, her hair curled around his ankles. "Tricked you?" His feet were pulled, his back pressing to the cold surface of the mirror. "I didn't choose for you to make me. I didn't choose to rip out your heart." From her pocket, she pulled out the thin branch. It was the stem of a rose, dried and de-thorned. She caressed its edge, raising her gaze slowly back to Row. "I know Claire will be disappointed in me, but as long as you're free, I will always live in the shadows. And as long as magic exists, you'll get free."

"What?" Row fought back as he was gripped tighter, pressed harder against the mirror.

"How much clearer do I have to be?" She tossed the tip of the pen aside. "I'm a monster."

The solid glass rippled, the reflection like water. A memory. He held his breath as it all came back. Every moment of his childhood where his sister had tried to shove him into the mirrors, the reflections of the pool. He gripped the edges of the frame as she continued to drag him inside. The pull was unrelenting. His fingers slid from the frame and fell into the glass. As he tried to reach back out, they were met by the wall of glass. Trapped inside.

Before he was forced through the mirror, Sundew tore his heart to pieces.

For the first time in her life, Sundew admired her reflection. She stood in front of the mirror and a woman stood inside it. Her eyes were green, her hair burgundy and enchanted like Sundew. As Sundew stepped forward, so did she. They met at the mirror's edge, and Sundew raised her hand. The reflection did this same.

Inside, it made Sundew feel a little sick. She touched her hand to the glass, like pressing against the woman's cold fingers. It reminded her of her own time spent inside the mirror, her lonely days trapped behind the glass. Her years being forced to act out Rosie's every whim. She glanced down at the torn up pieces of his heart. *Will he ever actually learn to feel my pain?*

Tears burned in her eyes. The mirror copied but she knew it felt nothing.

After years of trying to push her brother inside, she expected to feel more joyful. Or at least relieved. But her entire body was knotted up and her mind unsatisfied. The itch she'd felt was long gone, scratching it did nothing. Scratching it made her hurt.

"But it can't be undone now, can it?" She watched as the mirror mouthed her words. "Your magic is gone. My magic… unpredictable. Nothing good can come of it. Nothing good can come of me."

They both tightened their fists as more tears dripped.

"All I ever wanted was to be loved like you. I wanted a life. I wanted you to understand the monster that you made." She sniffled. "But I can't have that, can I? Claire's going to hate me. Cherrywood will rot away… and Mother's dead."

Their fingers trembled.

"Mother has always been dead."

She watched her reflection cry. Though she knew her brother was only doing as she did, it helped to imagine him in pain.

"Mother's been dead longer than I've been alive. You made me because you couldn't handle it. You made me because you wanted someone to take away all that pain!" The glass cracked. "But did you ever think what that did to me? Did you think I didn't care about my mother? No… I know you didn't, you're selfish. You didn't care."

Her hair tightened around the mirror, shattering the glass into fine pieces. The image distorted more and more.

"I never want to look at you again, Rosie." Sundew turned away. "You deserve to be forgotten too."

Cherrywood shook like an earthquake. Cracks cut through the graveyard, leaving black trenches shattered through the ground. Claire gripped onto Dan as the ground shook, crumbling apart into chunks. They stumbled back from the trenches, pressing themselves up against the gravestone.

The cracks in the ground were a foot wide each, spreading out endlessly in diverging paths. It was as if they stood on the surface of a shattered mirror. From the deep dark pits, more vines emerged with the same black tendrils of hair. They pushed on either end of the cracks, causing more shatters and shakes. As the tremors continued, Dan held Claire tighter.

"What is she doing?" he asked as they pressed closer to the gravestone. They tried to escape though there was no further they could go.

"You think I'm an expert on this stuff?" Claire threw her hands in the air. "Maybe she's having a tantrum? I don't know!"

"Sorry… I was just…"

"I know, Dandy." She huffed, no more forgiving of Sundew's outburst. "But whatever's going on, it doesn't change our plans. We've still got to get to Honey Walls. We've still got to talk to Sundew." She pushed herself to her feet, wobbling to stand on the shaking ground.

Dan looked away as Claire offered her hand. "I don't know if I can keep going, Claire."

"What?"

"It's just, my whole body is against me. My legs are hurting worse and worse... and I... I don't know if I can really help you with this."

"Dandelion Fletcher! I am not the kind of girl that abandons a friend." She glared at him and then threw her arms in the direction of the crack. "If I was, do you think I'd be on my way to talk to the witch having a tantrum? Of course not!"

"What?" Dan shook his head. "I don't think you're a bad friend if you want to go... or stay. With all that's going on, I think it might be safer if I stayed here. If you wanted to, we could both stay here. Maybe she'll calm down on her own."

Claire stopped herself from shouting the first response that came to her head. She wasn't having a yelling match with her mother, she had time to think things out. Beneath her, the ground had stilled without her notice. The throb of her ankle felt ancient... as if leaning on Dan had been long since needed. By all means, she could go without him. "I..." She shook her head. "Maybe we could wait it out," she muttered.

"There's no way you actually want to do that."

Claire slumped her shoulders. "Yeah, I don't."

"And you don't have to, I know you'll come back." He smiled at her. "Because you're right, Claire, we're friends. I want you to do whatever's best for you."

"I want to get to the bottom of this." Claire smirked back, stepping towards the crack and back towards the forest.

"Wait." Dan stopped her.

"What? You want to double back on what you said, Dandy?"

"No." He reached into his bag. Out of it he pulled his notebook and pen and handed them to Claire. "Just in case you can't make it to Honey Walls. Maybe writing a story in this will work. I can finish the memorial when you get back."

"Oh..." She hesitated before taking it. "Thanks... Baker Boy."

"No problem, Book Girl."

Chapter Twenty-Three

The Mirror

The house was dark and empty. She should have expected it to be that way. She should have known that with her in charge of the stories, everything would fall apart. At some point, Rosie and her had become two separate people, and the type of person Sundew was… well… reflections didn't get happy endings, they didn't. *Reflections,* as Rosie had thought, *are completely different people. They're liars and monsters, and not the real you.* Sundew began to cry.

"What are you crying about now?" A cat interrupted her tears. The lumpy grey cat was made of socks, one of Rosie's creations. However, the cat hadn't bothered Sundew for years. His name was Righty Grey Sock Cat, and he'd always been astute enough to see Sundew despite what she was.

"Go away," she grumbled. "I'm not talking to a sock."

"Why not? It looks like you want to talk to someone." He purred. "And I think I might be the puuurrrfect cat to lend an ear. I know what you did." He slid a shard of mirror across the coffee table. "I know what it's like to be one part of a pair."

"I'm not one of a pair, I'm a half of a whole." She glared at the sock. "I was never meant to be. Look at the mess I've caused."

"Look at you, as stubborn as your sister." Righty paced along the table, plodding his heavy feet. "You know, you can be mad, but you never noticed me either. There were always chances for friendship, but it took a few steps towards it."

Sundew pinched her brow, pushing the cat's prattling down before it hurt her head. "I really don't want to hear this."

"I know."

"I'm not a sock, I'm a reflection. We're not two separate people."

"I find that hard to believe." He yawned.

"Because we're different?" She scowled. "We're not cut from the same cloth, we're two different components of one thing."

Righty's tail swayed as he licked a paw. "It's like talking to a wall. A set of socks is a set of socks. Pairs are separates and wholes. Never mind, you'll understand when you want to."

Sundew glared at him as he hopped from the table. He left the shard where he'd placed it, beginning in the direction of Rose's writing closet. He held his tail up high as he made lazy steps through her hair. He ducked beneath the curls.

"Have you looked at your mother's last story yet?" he asked.

"What does it matter to you?"

"I don't know. It might lighten your mood a bit." He turned away from the cupboard. "I think she left a letter for you."

Sundew felt her body go cold. It passed over her like a wave. "Why didn't…"

"I tell you?" He caressed his tail against the writing closet. "It's hiding with the end of the story. I thought you and Claire would find it eventually… before you… well, Sundew, I don't know what in the world we're going to do about this."

Sundew grimaced, keeping her eyes on the cat as he sauntered away. He ducked beneath her hair once again, disappearing into the shadows along the edges of the room. Sundew wavered, her focus shifting back to the cupboard. If there really was an unopened letter, she knew it wasn't for her. Her mother wouldn't have taken the time to do something like that. At the very least she wouldn't take the time to do something for *her*. A reflection. She glared at the shard on the coffee table, cats always brought such awful presents.

Though, despite everything, she found herself standing up. She moved forward, her hair dragging and shaking the house. It gripped the edges, protesting her steps, begging her not to approach what her mother had written. But she continued forward all the same, the possibility of something different moving her. She entered her mother's hallowed space, becoming trapped between the narrow walls. She shifted through the papers and notes. But in the end, she found nothing remarkable.

Of course she didn't.

Once upon a time, there was a girl named Rosie Gareau. She was six years old, forty-four inches tall, and was the class expert on clock reading. Rosie spent a lot of time thinking about time, counting minutes and asking questions. She wanted to understand what adults meant when they said the phrase, "Your mom doesn't have much time left."

It made her imagine people as clocks, spinning on, and on, and on. Maybe her mom was dizzy, she did seem to have tummy aches a lot. But it also made her think about hourglasses too. She'd asked her mom about them before, when they'd showed up in her stories.

"What's an hourglass?" she asked, snuggling up in the hospital sheets.

"It's a little like the timer on the oven. It's a glass full of sand at the top, and it slowly drains out into the bottom. Once it's all in the bottom, the time is up." She stroked Rosie's hair. "Mr. Waters could show you one, there are some in the board games."

And Mr. Waters did. When they went home, he gave her one of the minute glasses, and for a minute it was very exciting. And then it stopped. The sand sat at the bottom of the glass, motionless. The time was up. Rosie shook her head and flipped the glass, starting the minute over again.

As the weeks passed, adults stopped using the phrase "time's running out". They all went quiet. In class the teacher would pat her back. When she went to the bakery, the Fletchers gave her free sweets. And when she was in class, even Claire would share her toys. She went home each day feeling strange in her tummy. One day, Mr. Waters stopped taking her to the hospital.

"Are we gonna see Mom tomorrow?" Rosie asked as Mr. Waters tucked her into bed.

"I don't know."

"Why not?"

Mr. Waters looked away, searching the piles of sock animals. "Where's

Oxnard?"

"I gave him to Mom, he's really brave and tough."

"And you'll be okay without him?"

Rosie nodded. "I've got Pillow Bear and her sock friends."

"Alright, you guys better be good company for Rosie."

"We're her best friends," Rosie said in a growly Pillow Bear voice. "We'll keep away all the monsters."

"Good." Mr. Waters smiled and gave Rosie a hug.

As he left the room, he turned out the light. Rosie's room wasn't entirely dark. Above her was the dim light of her glow-in-the-dark stars and spaceships. Her dad had pasted them before he left to the Sky World. Rosie assumed he was there looking for a real star. He'd return any day now, long before any hour glasses ran out. With a star in his hand, he'd make Rosie's mom feel better.

It comforted her for a little bit. Her eyes shut and she began to doze off. But nightmares started up in her head, hourglasses, clocks, her mother's coughs. Above her was a black and starless night. The sound of the telephone woke her up. It was ringing in the living room, over and over. When no one picked up, it started to ring again.

When they called back a third time, she heard Mr. Waters's grumpy steps. He shuffled down the hall, past Rosie's room and down the stairs. She heard the click of the phone and then his voice rasp, "Hello?"

There was quiet.

"Oh, yes, this is he… ah… that's what I thought." He grumbled to himself. "We'll see her in the morning, I'm sure Rosie's asleep. I wouldn't want to wake her up for this. We can tell her in the morning."

And then Mr. Waters hung up the phone.

But Rosie couldn't wait for morning. Her eyes kept open and she couldn't close them even if she wanted to. She stared at the plastic stars above her, making wishes that her mom was okay. Even plastic stars had to have some wishing power. She brought her hands together, clasping them as tight as she could.

"Please, stars, I need you to be real. Bring my mom back. It's not the same without her. I need your help I—"

She heard a loud wailing that she'd never heard before. It was a sound a little like a ghoul… or maybe a howling wolf. Rosie pulled her sheets over her head, and grabbed her dad's flashlight, her two best monsters defences. And since she didn't have Oxnard to help her, she took Chester the Ferret and Lefty Grey Sock Fox.

She crept out into the hall, spotting that the kitchen light was still on. The howling was coming from inside, and it sounded a little like the wolf had a cold. She climbed down the steps and across the dark living room. Then at last, she braved a look at the monster.

It was Mr. Waters.

He was sitting at the dining table, crying into his hands. It was the strangest sight she'd ever seen in all her life. His glasses were off his face and sitting next to a big bottle of juice. The noises he was making were so loud that he didn't even notice Rosie.

She walked up beside him and pulled out the chair. As she did so, she pushed Lefty into his face. In a Lefty voice, Rosie asked, "Are you okay, Mr. Waters?"

"Rosie?" He looked up. "You should be sleeping."

"Rosie is sleeping, she's just sleepwalking. I'm Lefty Grey Sock Fox, and I don't like when people cry."

Mr. Waters wiped his tears and looked at Rosie (who definitely wasn't sleepwalking). "That's sweet of you, Lefty. But I think you should be in bed too, it's really late."

Rosie watched as Mr. Waters drank his juice. "Mr. Waters, was that Mom on the phone?"

He froze mid-sip, more tears starting to well up in his eyes. "Actually, it was the doctors… your mom's not going to be calling anymore."

"Why not?" Rosie started to tear up.

"It's over, Rosie. She died."

Rosie froze in place, staring at Mr. Waters as he cried more.

"I'm sorry…" he managed through his tears. "Go to sleep, we'll go say goodbye in the morning."

"No," Rosie said, holding tight onto her friends. "Daddy's going to save her."

"Rosie, I told you she'd go away. No one can save her. We can't change it. All we can do is say goodbye." As Mr. Waters held back his tears, Rosie cried more. He stood up, searching through his things until he found an envelope. "She wrote you a letter to say goodbye."

In Mr. Waters hand was a pink envelope, the last words of Rose Gareau.

"No!" Rosie threw Lefty and Chester to the ground. Tears streamed down her cheeks. And Rosie ran. Rosie ran away as fast as she could. If Mr. Waters followed her, she didn't know, because she didn't look back. She went through the door, the flowers, and even past the mushroom ring. Her breath stung. Her heart ached. She tripped down the ditch, scratching up her elbows and knees.

She fell to the ground covered in dirt, looking up at the stars. Through blurred eyes she could hardly see herself reach. But she stretched up like the girl in her mother's storybook, stretched until it hurt. Her fingers stretched into the night, into space. She scratched the surface of sleeping stars.

They fell down onto her like confetti. They burned her. Every sharp inch of light absorbing into her skin, and collecting in her heart. More starlight and wishes than anyone was meant to hold cut through and merged with her heart. And while it already felt aching and sore, the magic made it hurt a million times more.

"Make it stop!" she cried. "I just want my mom!"

And while she didn't want to know it, the fallen star in her heart made the hourglass flip.

The wrong side of the mirror was cold. Row sat on the ground, watching the distant reality. Inside the mirror, dreams and reality blended and blurred. Everything shifted on a dime. One moment he was himself, and the next he was Sundew. His hair was long, spreading out into the endless shadow around him.

His chest ached with a furious and familiar pain. He wiped Sundew's dried tears from his eyes, clutching at his empty aching chest. He felt the heat of Sundew's words burn inside. *Mother's always been dead.* The memories he didn't want to think floated through his head. With wavering clarity, they surfaced and sank.

"It's just another story. It's not real." He shook his head more, unable to keep it back. He thought of his mother, the woman made of paper and fasteners. He tried to forget the first, the forgotten face made of flesh and bone. He wanted to stand up and run, but there was nowhere to go. No escape. He was alone. Just him and the silver wall.

"Why does everyone have to be like this?" He glared at the wall, wishing he could speak to his sister once more. "So I'm greedy, selfish, rotten, and heartless. I can't love anyone. I can't say sorry. I don't even remember what it's like to really smile. Does everyone think I wanted to be like this? Do you think I planned to rip out my heart?"

"Well… that is what you did, isn't it?" his mother's voice said from behind him, her fingers gliding through his hair, smoothing out the tangles with a soft brush.

Row's body locked, his mother continuing to stroke and smooth.

"You were the one that caught the star. You had the choice to create Sundew. Just like you had the choice to bring me back."

"I… I…" Row's fingers curled in, beginning to shake as he let the memory inside. "It hurt." He could nearly feel the starlight burning in his broken heart. "I wanted it to stop. I was a kid."

"I know." Rose said. "But it was still a choice you made, and a choice you keep making. You could have gotten your heart back at any moment. All you have to do is turn around and face what you've been running from… I can help you."

His body remained still, staring at the silver wall. If only there were another world he could go to, an exit anywhere. He hesitated. "How did you find me in a place like this?"

"I'm always with you, Row." Her hands rested down on his shoulders. They were weighted, and warm, and soft… and real. "As long as you need me, I've been with you."

"Because I've been holding on, right?"

She went quiet.

"That's what Chrys always says about ghosts, that us living people hold onto them." Row began to turn.

He met eyes with his mother's ghost. She wasn't the puppet, but not a living woman either. She glowed like moonlight, a summer dress swaying around in soft drapes of white and magnolia blush. She was far less frail than when she was sick, but he could still recognize her. A genuine smile began on her face.

She nodded, slowly taking his hands in hers. "You're right, Row, but us ghosts hold on just as hard." She guided his hand to his pocket where their fingers jingled against his keys. "I want to be able to take every pain I left away. But there's no way to do that, Row. Pain is a part of life."

As he pushed his hand into his pocket, he became himself again. The hair disintegrated like sand washed away by a wave. He faltered to look at his mother, awaiting her shock, but she already knew. She loved him no matter what.

"Are they in there?"

"Is what in where?" Row bunched his keys and wallet, nearly missing the tiny specks at the bottom of the lining.

"Zelda's gifts." She smiled wider.

"Um… some of them. I gave most of them away to Craft Feather Crow." He pulled out what he had left, and showed his mother the tiny rose seeds. "That's all I have."

"Good, because I have a secret for you." She pulled his hand closer, letting the seeds rest on his flat palm. "Hearts are not single beautiful roses that monsters can steal. They can be damaged, and hurt, and we can hide them away. But never, ever, can they be stolen. Because you see, Row, hearts are gardens."

In his hands he felt the seeds begin to stir, a golden glint in his palm.

"We can choose to neglect a garden. We can choose to let the weeds grow. But we can't kill the potential of a heart. Our gardens are as boundless as we want them to be. All they require is for us to tend to them."

Row flinched back, dropping the seeds as a pain flowed through him. It started deep inside, the familiar ache. But unlike usual, it kept getting worse, and worse, and worse. Until it was as if he were back in time seconds after he touched the star. A burning sensation surged through his body, causing him to fall forward. His hand pressed to his chest as the seeds grew against him, and he felt the first gentle pulse.

Golden thorns grew around him, spreading outward from where there were once tiny seeds. He trembled as the pulses rippled through him, and a heat began in his eyes that he hadn't felt in years. Tears spilled, dribbling down his cheeks and chin. Nothing could contain them. The more the vines grew, so did his pain. And as his pain grew, so did his need to cry.

Unfettered emotions rushed through him, sorrow, regret, anger. It was a river free flowing and flooding. He cried for his mother. For Chrys. For his father. He cried for every last mistake, each moment he'd tried to run away from the truth and let his heart wither. "I didn't want to hurt," he sputtered.

"I didn't want to feel this way."

"I know…" She kneeled down with him, wrapping him in her arms. "But we can't pick which emotions we want to feel. Joy and love require us to sometimes feel hurt and sad. We need to be able to grieve, remember, and appreciate what we lose and what we have."

He sniffled and wiped his eyes, unable to find the words to speak.

"I love you, Row, but it's time to say goodbye." She squeezed him tighter. "I know you're ready for things to change, I know you're ready for me to leave. If you weren't, you would have never allowed that puppet to die. You don't want to stay in this place. It's time."

Behind the film of fresh tears, Row looked into his mother's eyes. The aching was beginning to feel more manageable, cooled by a less erratic love spilling out from deep inside. "I… I'm sorry, Mom… I never want to forget you again."

Her smile returned, joined by her own tears. "I know you won't."

"There really aren't any more places to run to, and even if there was, I don't want to. I'm sorry." He wiped his eyes, feeling another wave of pain. "I'm sorry for everybody that I hurt. I'm sorry that I've dragged you along. I'm sorry that I abandoned my friends, Chrys, Oxnard. I'm sorry that I ignored your stories. That I tried to make them go away. I want to keep them going. I want to keep them alive… even if it hurts…"

The golden branches extended outward, growing into the endless dark. As they disappeared out into the dark, it became the glints of golden stars. Green leaves unfurled from the vines. Fragile blooms blossomed from the branches, unmasking more starlight on the surface of their red petals. They climbed the silver wall, rippling its surface, dispelling shadow and cracking through.

"Goodbye, Mom. I'll miss you."

"I'll miss you too, My Darling Little Row."

Chapter Twenty-Four

The Difficulties and Rewards
of Growing a Garden

The branches grew out into the silver wall, rattling it and causing waves to ripple across its surface. The solid wall became one of liquid. Row stepped forward, touching his hand to the wall first. Like the branches, his fingertips crossed over. And then Row followed. He stepped through and found himself back in Honey Walls. He was in the living room, stood above a small section of broken glass. Ahead of him was the writing closet, his sister curled up on its floor.

From the shard, the roses grew, overflowing the room with their golden light. They tangled with the lengths of hair. Their growth accelerated as they mingled with the shadow, cutting the strands and dispelling her magic. The grey haze melted away, the warmth of Honey Walls returning slowly. The branches swirled up Sundew's legs and cut her like she was made of the same shadows.

"Sundew, it's time that we returned things to the way they are supposed to be." Row met eyes with her. "I don't need you to stop my heart. I'm ready to take care of the stories. I'm ready to take Honey Walls."

"Of course you are." She practically hissed. "You're incapable of learning a lesson.

Go ahead, shove me back into the mirror. I'm worthless."

"I'm sorry…" He watched as the roses grew over her, pulling her back towards the shard. "I made you into a monster, but you aren't. You're just my reflection."

The tangle of dark hair dissolved, fading like smoke in the air. Sundew's vines withered to nothing. As every shadow faded away. The last which remained was Sundew. She stumbled forward on her hands and knees. The tips of her fingers turned clear, continuing up her arms.

"Row! What are you doing?!" someone shouted.

As Row turned to see who it was, a notebook nailed him in the face.

"Can't you two spend a second alone without trying to drown, kill or shove the other in a mirror?" Claire continued, no longer yelling but still speaking very loud.

"Claire?" Row groaned, stumbling back.

"Yes. Claire." She glared at him.

"You don't understand. I'm fixing things I—"

"Yeah, I heard. You want to put her into the mirror, which I know for a fact isn't going to help any of this." Claire scowled at both of them. "So stop it, talk about it. I get that you're both hurt. I get it. But whatever it is you're doing here isn't helping."

Row stiffened, looking to Sundew. The colour returned to her fingers alongside a redness to her cheeks.

"And you," Claire pointed at Sundew. "I said I'd be coming back. Not everything needs to become some sort of huge drama. Stop being stubborn and be honest, I'm not the only one willing to listen to you."

Sundew lowered her head, eyes becoming fixed on one of the blooms. "I don't think I'm meant to be my own person. You see what I did, someone like me isn't meant to exist."

"That's stupid," Claire said. "Instead of wasting your energy getting shoved into a mirror, why not fix things?"

Row interjected quietly, "She did turn my girlfriend into a mermaid and try to trap me."

"That doesn't mean you get to take revenge." Claire scowled. "And that goes for both of you. You need to build bridges here, eat apples and talk. You were practically the same person at one point, there has to be some sort of common ground."

They both nodded, and for a while they all remained quiet. Row and Sundew avoided one another's eyes as long as they could. Row felt words ruminate on his lips, but none escaped.

"You made me deal with all that pain alone," Sundew blurted.

Row nodded.

"You wanted to sweep that under the rug, huh?"

"What?" Row looked up. "No... I just... I didn't think to ask... I guess, I honestly still think of you as a monster. After everything you've done to me, even if I did make you take my heart, you spent our whole life trying to ruin everything. Whether you had a good reason or not, you still actively tried to hurt me."

"I guess so..."

"You guess so?" He scowled at her.

"Well... yeah, I don't know what I'm supposed to say?" She glanced at Claire.

"What about sorry?" he asked. "I'm sorry I killed your girlfriend, Row. I'm sorry I made you eat dirt, Row. I'm sorry I tried to trap you in a mirror, Row."

"Fine!" Tears dribbled down her cheeks. "I'm sorry I'm a monster! I'm sorry that I ruined everything. I know you didn't do it on purpose. I know you were a stupid little kid when you made me. I know you didn't plan for me to live in the shadows and be unlovable and forgotten. But who do I get to be mad at? Where's my magical fix?"

Row faltered without an answer.

"You're not unlovable." Claire knelt down beside her. "We can change the way things are. The two of you can be completely different people, and we can start our own stories. Right, Row?"

"I mean..." Row scratched his head. "I guess we could do that, but I'm taking Honey Walls."

"You are?" Claire perked up.

"Um... yeah... if I can pull off a bit of legal nonsense — you know what, never mind that. I promised Mom that I would." He glanced down at Sundew's averted eyes. "Maybe the two of you could take a trip out to the Sky World and figure out what you want to do. I met Aster, and um, I told him about you."

Sundew's eyes sparked with light.

"Look, I might not know everything about how it feels to be you, Sundew, but I do miss Mom. I'm sorry that you have to feel that too."

She jerked away, wiping the tears from her eyes.

"I'll keep my eyes on her." Claire smiled. "And if you decide to start trouble…" She raised up her notebook, causing Row to flinch. "But there is one thing, before you take Honey Walls, your mom said that I could have the last chapter in Oxnard's story. Would it be alright if a took that?"

"Um… sure… I actually have something really important I want to get to. You two can wait here and do what you need to." He gave Claire a slight smile. "But I'll be in touch, okay? With both of you."

"Actually?"

"Yeah, I'm not in the mood to abandon anyone, so there's a few people I need to catch up with first."

"All right, Writer Boy."

"Oh… no, I'm not going to be writing anything. I think I'll keep the stories alive in other ways…"

Claire pushed open the door to Rose's room. With the enchantments gone, it looked almost mundane. There was the bed Claire had sat by day after day, the dried vase of roses. Through the windows she could see the magnolias dying amongst the thriving red blooms. Claire felt weak in her legs. She neared the bed and fell down into the cushions. She pulled the quilts closer, wrapping herself in their warmth. And as she lay still for a moment, her eyes rested on the nightstand.

Rose's manuscript lay beneath a box of tissues. The papers were sectioned off into chapters and scenes by bull clips. Claire sat up, bracing herself against the pillows as she dragged the sections into the bed. She sorted through them one after the other. The story of *Oxnard and the Sky World* unfolded the same as before. She skipped ahead, searching for the final chapter. When all was set aside, Claire's hands quivered with the precious parchment in her hands. A pink sticky note was posted on the front with the words "For Claire" etched on it.

With shaking hands, Claire turned the page. But there was nothing. One after the other, Claire flipped the pages. They all were blank. There was no ending to the story, no shocking twist… it was up to Claire.

She leaned back, heart pounding and mouth gaping. As she glanced back toward the nightstand for another possible answer, she was met with a letter. However, it gave her no more instructions.

It was for Sundew.

Roses grew throughout Cherrywood. They sewed shut the cracks in the ground and washed away the shadows. The haze was lifted from the sky, allowing the full scope of morning light to shine down. Sundew stepped outside, looking up into the sky and feeling the cold air brush over her features. Above her hung the boughs of magnolias. Their petals fell from the branches, no longer grey but still wilting.

As Row left, the magic within the flowers diminished. The dusting of starlight dimmed and Sundew stepped forward. She waited on Claire as she busied herself with searching the stories. *Were they really going to the Sky World?* It felt impossible, awkward. It settled strange inside of her as an imperfect idea. She'd never been far from Honey Walls. Could she even exist outside of it?

Her thoughts were interrupted by rustling. From the trail, Dan hobbled forward. He stumbled over the ditch, locking eyes with Sundew. When he saw her, his mouth gaped for a bit. She couldn't discern why, seeing that he was the one looked like a wild man. "Is Claire okay?" he eventually asked.

"Yes, she's fine."

"Oh… okay…" He nodded to himself. "You look different."

"I do?" She glanced at herself, but found very little different. Her hair wasn't much shorter than before, she'd not even changed clothes since she'd last saw Dan.

"Hey Sundew!" Claire shouted, causing Sundew to jump. "Oh and hey Dan, glad you're okay."

He raised his hand and waved it in a so-so sort of wave. "I could be doing better."

"Really?" Claire smirked, her hands hidden behind her back. "Because I've actually got some news for you two."

Dan turned pale. "What kind of news?"

She threw her one hand forward, thrusting the notebook and pen into his arms. "I've got you a lead on this memorial. A real lead that'll help you finish it in no time flat."

"Who?"

"Aster Gareau," she continued to grin. "Sundew and I are going to be visiting for our own reasons. I know you wouldn't want to stay forever, but I thought us Musketeers could go to the city for once, just spend time there and figure it out."

"Right now?" Dan groaned.

"No, not right now." She scoffed. "You can crash for however long you're going to. I might see what's up around town eventually."

"Okay… but you didn't need the notebook then?"

Claire guided him inside, still keeping her hand hidden from Sundew. "No, I did. I've got my own now though."

"Ah, good." He yawned as he was directed to the couch. Just as before, he curled up, barely able to keep his eyes open as soon as he was sat down.

As the snores began, Claire turned on her heel. "What about you, Sundew? How are you doing?"

"Um… strange… are we actually going to see Aster?"

Claire shrugged. "I mean, I figure it might be a good place to start. Think of it all as the first page in a new story. You're not anyone but yourself. You get to choose whatever life you like."

Sundew tried to imagine something, but it was difficult to look past the shadowed world she'd created.

"Oh, and I have something for you, too."

As Sundew looked up, she was met with a pink envelope. On its face was her name in her mother's handwriting. She paused, looking around for the cat. "So it is real…" She reached out and touched the paper.

She slid her nail along the seam, searching for the words enclosed for her.

Dear Sundew Gareau,

We who are made of paper and string, reflections and glass, are as real as not what others say, but as much as we choose to be. Even if I never loved you a day, it couldn't stop you from being you, Sundew Gareau, a whole and wonderful person.

However, I do love you. I'm sorry I couldn't always see through the dark, and hope that one day you allow your heart to shine bright. Share your dreams and you'll find a world in which you are no longer alone.

Yours Truly and Forever,
Rose Gareau

The letter rested in her hands as she looked to Claire.

Memories live in the heart. As Row guided himself out into the nearly invisible ocean, he remembered a similar walk home. It was years ago, back when he'd finally settled back into life. He was walking home to his apartment in early spring, his arms full of books. His old apartment was always packed with books. Every other day he walked from the library and his house with new ones. He didn't always read them, mainly promised to, while spending his nights admiring the text.

But one day in the early spring, he was trying a shortcut through the park. While he'd considered taking the path for days, the conditions were never ideal. Too much snow, and then too much water, but that day he settled. He walked along the dirt path. Around it the green was porous, but the path was, for the most part, dry.

The trails converged at the centre of the park. There was a pond overgrown with cattails and reeds. The basin was formed by a manmade border of rock. A woman lay on one of the large slabs, eyes closed, hair resting in the current. Row was stopped in his tracks. Her feet were bare, curled around the grass. She didn't look like she was in any trouble, but Row approached.

"Are you alright?" he asked, hesitating on a step.

"Huh?" The woman blinked and pulled herself up. Her hair dribbled down her back, wetting her dress. "Yeah, are you okay?" She tilted her head.

Row tilted his to match her. He looked her over, enraptured by her oddity and beauty. "I'm fine," he said as his books slipped his grip.

"Careful!" She grinned, picking them up and offering them. "I'm Chrysocolla."

"Row." He snatched the books back in one quick movement. Their hands brushed against each other, and for a moment Row felt something inside which he brushed away. It was the moment he'd nearly forgotten, one which followed many more moments exactly the same, stronger and stronger.

When Row returned to the sock tunnels on The Island of Mismatched Socks, he didn't need any guidance. He pushed past the parades of shocked and bouncing ferrets. All that he needed was to follow his heart. And like a light in the dark, he found Chrys. Sat in the red wheelbarrow, smiling, giggling, being everything that Chrys was meant to be, they met eyes once again.

"Row?" She looked up at him, and for a moment her smile faded.

Inside his chest, Row felt his heart begin to race. He pushed past the gasping and chattering ferrets, wading through them until his hands met with hers. As he touched her, the ice in her blood thawed. He could feel the warmth spreading through her. As inescapable as pain and sadness had been, Row felt his love for her.

He smiled and then blushed at how ridiculous it felt to do so. *But who cares what's ridiculous?* he thought as he brought Chrys close. "Chrys, if normal means I never get to see you again, please never let me be normal. The only thing truly ridiculous was leaving you the way that I did. I'm so sorry."

"You are?" She looked up at him and was taken in by his smile, her own returning slowly.

"Chrys, I love you." He squeezed her hands tighter, feeling the warm continue to spread.

As he wrapped his arms around her, she pulled herself forward. Her arms circled his neck. Her lips warmed against his. And as they closed their eyes, disappearing into one another's touch, they felt light bathe their eyelids. And where the light of love filled, Sundew's shadow could no longer thrive. It washed away, leaving the Chrys he'd known and loved for years. Alive. She was untouched perfection, silly, beautiful, still no more quantifiable than on the day they'd first met... maybe even more so.

The Epilogue

by Claire Waters

It's perfectly acceptable to end a story with "Once upon a time" because endings aren't exactly real things. Little hedgehogs don't get happily ever afters, not because the world is big, sad, and scary, but because things are always changing. You see, once upon a time there was a house called Honey Walls. And inside this house there lived a little adventurer name Oxnard and his best friend Row. But after many wonderful memories, things changed.

After a long appeal process, Row is serving a ten year sentence for being a bad friend. Thankfully for him, I sent a lawyer to him from the Sky World (the place where all the best lawyers come from). Her name was Ms. Lefty Grey Sock Fox, and she brought excellent witnesses to the stand. This included Oxnard, Chester, and a lovely lady named Chrysocolla.

However, since Row is much larger than the Island of Lost Socks can handle, he was sent to live in a cozy little prison. It's a small little house in Cherrywood, situated in the middle of a mushroom ring and small ditch. While some could easily mistake it for the old honey house, its walls are teal, and roses and sunflowers surround it. On occasion, I visit, as does Oxnard, Aster, Sundew, and the people of Cherrywood. But mostly Row keeps to himself, drawing pictures and watching stars.

Acknowledgements

Writing a book is easy, finishing a book is hard. There are a whole bunch of people that I'd like to thank for helping me make Honey Walls into Done-y Walls.

Thank you to my writing group for beta reading this in all its states. A special thank you to Vanessa Ricci-Thode for not only beta reading it in its primordial state, but also editing my unique take on the english language. Also thank you for prompting the Great Elipsiscide of 2019.

Additionally, thank you to Jonathan Coventry for not only narrating the Honey Walls audiobook, but editing out additional typos. Your narration is stelar. Chester's voice is killing me. It's so good.

I would also like to thank all the illustrators in my life.

To my mom and dad for being incredibly talented, creative people. You inspired me to pursue art instead of engineering. This is your fault.

To Alex Dingley, thanks for making all of these wonderful illustrations. They are so amazing! All your hard work paid off. Good luck on your future comic!

To my wife, Ursula Gray, for reading this story five million times. You are the bee's knees.

Speaking of which…

Bees. Bees. Bees. Bees. Bees. Bees. Bees. Bees. Bees. Bees. Bees. Bees. Bees. Bees. Bees. Bees. Bees.
es. Bees. Bees. Bees. Bees. Bees. Bees. Bees. Bees. Bees. Bees. Bees. Bees. Bees. Bees. Bees. Bees.
es. Bees. Bees. Bees. Bees. Bees. Bees. Bees. Bees. Bees. Bees. Bees. Bees. Bees. Bees. Bees. Bees.
es. Bees. Bees. Bees. Bees. Bees. Bees. Bees. Bees. Bees. Bees. Bees. Bees. Bees. Bees. Bees. Bees.
es. Bees. Bees. Bees. Bees. Bees. Bees. Bees. Bees. Bees. Bees. Bees. Bees. Bees. Bees. Bees. Bees.
es. Bees. Bees. Bees. Bees. Bees. Bees. Bees. Bees. Bees. Bees. Bees. Bees. Bees. Bees. Bees. Bees.
es. Bees. Bees. Bees. Bees. Bees. Bees. Bees. Bees. Bees. Bees. Bees. Bees. Bees. Bees. Bees. Bees.
es. Bees. Bees. Bees. Bees. Bees. Bees. Bees. Bees. Bees. Bees. Bees. Bees. Bees. Bees. Bees. Bees.
es. Bees. Bees. Bees. Bees. Bees. Bees. Bees. Bees. Bees. Bees. Bees. Bees. Bees. Bees. Bees. Bees.
es. Bees. Bees. Bees. Bees. Bees. Bees. Bees. Bees. Bees. Bees. Bees. Bees. Bees. Bees. Bees. Bees.
es. Bees. Bees. Bees. Bees. Bees. Bees. Bees. Bees. Bees. Bees. Bees. Bees. Bees. Bees. Bees. Bees.
es. Bees. Bees. Bees. Bees. Bees. Bees. Bees. Bees. Bees. Bees. Bees. Bees. Bees. Bees. Bees. Bees.
es. Bees. Bees. Bees. Bees. Bees. Bees. Bees. Bees. Bees. Bees. *(I hope this is enough, Kris)* Bees. Bees
es. Bees. Bees. Bees. Bees. Bees. Bees. Bees. Bees. Bees. Bees. Bees. Bees. Bees. Bees. Bees. Bees
es. Bees. Bees. Bees. Bees. Bees. Bees. Bees. Bees. Bees. Bees. Bees. Bees. Bees. Bees. Bees. Bees
es. Bees. Bees. Bees. Bees. Bees. Bees. Bees. Bees. Bees. Bees. Bees. Bees. Bees. Bees. Bees. Bees

Kickstarter Backers

Thank you for making this possible.

PreciousKnightwalker
Seann Alexander
Shelby Miller
Mango Fritter
Carl Howarth
Laine Kenton
Anikó "PantherWolf" Juhász
BRO! Comics
Matthew Ann-Marie
Cinnmiel
Katheryn Cantu
Jennifer Neumann
Wendy Navarrete
Levi Dwyer
Cody Woodson
Briana Weiss
Peter Meneses
Megan Karasek
Amber Colyer
Fiona Nowling
Rebecca Pimentel

Further Reading
by Bones McKay

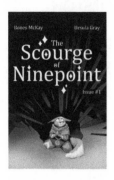

The Ninepoint Empire has suppressed the calicos for centuries. The kittezens rest in peace knowing that this "calico scourge" is disposed of. At least, that's what they thought.

Marble, a rare male calico, manages to escape his fate when he is adopted by a family of raccoons. As he grows he comes to learn about the world he escaped from. Meanwhile, the true scourge encroaches on the life of peace Ninepoint and beyond is accustom to.

There is no escape from Pinewood, this is the one thing Amanda knows. At least she thought she knew that, until Trixie, the new girl came to town. As the rules she once believed fall apart, Amanda soon faces the truth of her town. She isn't the only one that wants out. Amanda is left with a decision, to fight the town's monster or join it and finally be free.

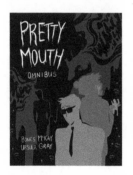

Evan is not a monster, he just has a few extra mouths. After what was supposed to be a one night stand with Rizo, a real monster, Evan finds things difficult to break off. Rizo just might be able to undo Evan's curse. With a monster in the woods, witches in the shadows, and laughing mouth without a body, Evan needs to decide if it's even worth putting aside prejudice.

Find Everything At:
linktr.ee/bones_mckay

9 781999 404482